HIS BLUESTOCKING BRIDE

HIS BLUESTOCKING BRIDE

A REGENCY ROMANCE, BRANCHES OF LOVE BOOK 3

SALLY BRITTON

Cover designed by Blue Water Books

This book is a work of fiction. Names, characters, places, and incidents either are products of the author's imagination or are used fictitiously. Any resemblance to actual persons, living or dead, events, or locales is entirely coincidental.

For inquiries, contact
sally@authorsallybritton.com

To Skye, because he said "I love you" first.

And to Bluestockings everywhere. Never be afraid to love.

CHAPTER 1

E llen flicked a black curl from her forehead, but the irksome spiral just bounced back. Her irritation mounted, and she wished her mother's maid had not thought to give the matron and her daughter the same curls.

"Ellen, try this." Teresa, the eldest sister in the Bringhurst family, pulled a hairpin from beneath her bonnet and held it across the tea things to Ellen. "And for heaven's sake, please tell Mrs. Rowlings to try something else with your hair. It isn't as thick as Mama's for all those curls to be practical."

What flattered her sixty-year-old mother did not do Ellen any favors.

Teresa resumed weaving tiny stitches into the little cap she held and turned back to the conversation with their mother. "What of Dorothea, Mama? Have you any news from her?"

"Not this past week." Mrs. Bringhurst leaned forward, prompting her two present daughters to do the same. "Though she hinted she would send for me soon."

Teresa tsked and shook her head. "The first confinement is dreadful. She will be glad of your company before the baby arrives."

"I miss Margaret today," Ellen said. "It is a shame she did not feel well." Margaret, born after Teresa and before Ellen, had announced her own impending increase and remained home from the weekly meeting of mother and daughters.

As the only sister unmarried and uninitiated in the ways of motherhood, Ellen had little else to say on the matter, for all she loved her nieces and nephews.

Although I likely know more than any woman without children ought to know about child rearing. Ellen bit the insides of her cheek to keep from smiling.

"The house will soon be full of grandchildren," Mama said, her eyes aglow.

Ellen nodded, thinking of her nieces and nephews playing in the gardens the previous summer. "And the miracle of children is that each one brings more love with them. We are a fortunate family." Sometimes when she thought such things, Ellen's stomach felt oddly hollow, as though she was missing something important.

"We shall keep you busy, traveling from one house to another to look after grandchildren. However will you manage, Mama?" Teresa asked, her manner teasing.

"Quite well, I should think. Ellen is here to look after the house and there is not much else to keep me occupied."

"There will be no trips to Bath this year," Ellen added, more cheer in her tone than necessary. If they had gone to Bath again, the distance from mother to expectant daughters would be the work of several days' journey. It had been the right decision, to stay at home.

And I have no desire to go and pretend a woman of nearly twenty-six years can compete in the marriage mart. Ellen kept that thought private but wondered if any of her family considered the same thing.

"Though I admit I will miss the society of a few friends, it will be much better to be nearby when you girls need me," her mother added.

"I do worry that Dorothea is farther away," said Teresa, her brows knitting in concern.

"Pashaw. She is five hours from here when I take the carriage, with the roads in good condition. That is but a morning's work of it." Mama adjusted the sewing in her lap, the white lace of a Christening gown trailing down her skirt. "And I will be with her for at least a week prior to her time."

"I think it's lovely we all managed to settle nearby." Teresa looked as unruffled as ever, her hair done up in an elegant twist beneath her bonnet and her gown the color of fresh peaches. Motherhood suited her. "We are ever as much in each other's company as we were before."

"Indeed. I have not had to give up any of you." Their mama looked happily between the sisters and both offered smiles in return. Ellen's felt strained, but she blamed her unease to fatigue from reading late the night before.

Ellen cut her thread and held up the handkerchief she'd been working on. "There. Finished."

"Lovely, dear," her mother said. "Your sister will like that gift very much."

Ellen relaxed under the praise and the conversation continued while she put her things away in the sewing box.

Looking to the window, Ellen took in the beautiful landscape, which remained familiar and soothing, wrapped in its golden shawl of autumn leaves.

But a tiny thought intruded upon her contentment. Though she loved the sight of the rolling hills framed by the oak trees of her father's property, sometimes she longed to view a different horizon, one that belonged just to her.

Ellen shook herself from those thoughts and set about tidying the tea tray.

The very first time she held her eldest nephew, Teresa's firstborn, she declared to the family that nothing in life was as precious as that little bundle. The proceeding infants were passed into her arms as well, and each she declared to be perfect and of infinite worth.

But she had always thought that someday there would be an infant of her own to hold and keep in her arms.

While twenty-six was not too old to wed and be a mother, she had given up on that hope. No man had ever caught her interest in that way. At least, no man she might actually have a chance with. The one man she had dreamed of, had dared to place in her imaginary world of husband and home, had never spent a single season in Bath.

Ellen swiftly closed the door on that thought.

The butler entered with a silver tray. "The afternoon post, madam."

"Lovely." Mama held her hand out to accept a letter. "Oh—it is in Dorothea's hand."

Teresa gasped and laid her things aside, attentive eyes on their mother. Ellen sat back on the sofa and folded her hands in her lap.

Mama read hastily, but silently.

Before they could ask what news the letter held, she stood and began waving the sheet of paper like a sailor's signal flag. "I've delightful news. Your sister has sent for me at last." Her excitement made her cheeks bright and she rushed from the room at a pace that was as near to a run as Ellen had ever seen her come.

Teresa grinned at Ellen, her joy for their youngest sister readily apparent.

"She must've gone to Father," Ellen said.

"Go with her, Ellen. There may be more to the letter." Teresa made a shooing motion with her hands. "And heaven knows I cannot run down the hall after her."

Ellen recovered from her surprise and followed their mother. Down the steps to the ground floor, she made it to the hall in time to see Mama burst into the study. Ellen tried to follow at a more sedate pace.

"Stephen," Mama said excitedly, her voice filling the room. "Dorothea has sent word. She has need of me. I must leave first thing in the morning." She handed Papa the letter, which he read with more deliberateness than his wife had. "We may only lack a few weeks until our new grandchild comes."

Reginald, the youngest of the family and the lone son, was sitting in a chair across from his father at the desk, watching with amusement. "Congratulations must be sent. What can I do to help you, Mama?" he asked solicitously.

Their father answered. "Send word to the stables. Your mother will want to leave early. Tell cook to prepare a hamper."

Reginald stood and bowed to his parents before leaving the room.

"Isn't this wonderful? My youngest daughter, a mother." Mama clapped her hands, beaming at Papa. "What a glorious thing."

"So it is, darling." Papa stood and came around his desk to embrace her. As they parted, sharing a familiar tender look, Ellen felt her heart constrict. She took a step back, recognizing their moment as one private between husband and wife.

Ellen quietly left the room but stopped at the staircase and sank down on the bottom step. The silence of the empty hall gave her room to collect herself.

Ellen had given up on a marriage and family of her own after five seasons. When she had her come out at last, she was already older than most *debutantes*. Her mother had wanted to wait until Margaret married, but at last gave in and allowed Ellen out in society as well. Then, partway into Ellen's season, the family was in raptures over Teresa's first babe and left Bath in a hurry to meet the newborn.

As the seasons came and went, her elder sisters married, had babies, and her younger sister was brought out. And Ellen remained the sole Miss Bringhurst.

She shook her head, trying to dispel the thought. It made her feel gray more often than not, and she knew she ought to put those feelings aside and be content. She did not need to be morose just because she was a spinster.

That dreaded word had never crossed her lips. But at twenty-six years old, without prospects, Ellen accepted the designation society would bestow on her for the rest of her life.

Plenty of families had a spinster or two lying about. Ellen knew this. Spinsters were useful sorts, called upon to help their family members as the need arose. She could assist in nursing the ill members of a household, serve as chaperone to her nieces one day in the future, or provide companionship for a sister, whatever they required, for the rest of her days.

Her mother emerged from the library and Ellen rose. "Can I do anything to help, Mama?"

"Not at present," her mother said cheerfully. "Teresa will be taking her leave soon. I must let her read the letter."

Ellen nodded, but did not follow her mother back up the stairs. Instead she retired to the library adjoining her father's study. This room was dearer to her than any other in the house, as it always felt warm and inviting. She liked the dark oak paneling and rich red curtains, finding they made her feel safe and warm, and she needed that comfort.

She returned to the volume of Sir Richard Harris's study of Roman Civic Improvements and settled in her favorite chair. The fire in the hearth kept away the chill November air.

Ellen had made her way through a single page of the volume when the door to her father's study opened. Her brother Reginald came striding out.

Reginald paused upon seeing her. "Ellen, what book is your nose stuck in today?" He spoke in a playful manner. "That tome is far too dangerous. It looks large enough to swallow you."

She raised her eyebrows and gave him a wide-eyed stare. "Perhaps it will, and then you shall have to search its pages to find me again."

"Not I," he insisted with a laugh, resuming his walk to the shelves. "Father sent me for a ledger. We are studying the effects of the weather on crop production."

"I was reading in an almanac that temperatures have been disturbingly cool of late." She rose from her seat to locate the book her brother needed, several shelves away from where he'd been looking. "It is disturbing, by all accounts."

Reginald made a sound of agreement, taking the thick ledger from her. "It cannot last forever."

"But I also read of a Russian explorer who found evidence of crops completely frozen and preserved in an ice field. I wonder if—"

He cut off her remark with a chuckle, shaking his head at her.

"Ellen, I've no use for Russian ice fields." He gave her a pitying smile and went back to the study.

"Of course not," she murmured as the door shut behind him. Never mind that *she* found the topic interesting. At nineteen, even Reginald knew his interests took precedence over hers.

Ellen picked up her book and left the library, deciding she would rather read in her room where she might be undisturbed.

She'd gone a few steps into the hall when the study door opened and her father stepped out.

"Ah, Ellen," he said, catching sight of her. "A letter for you. It was mixed in with my post. After the uproar your sister's note caused, I quite forgot about it."

Ellen blinked at him in momentary confusion, then a burst of delight filled her as she took the folded paper from him and kissed his cheek. "Thank you, Father."

She hurried to her room to read in private. She hardly ever received post, and this letter came from her favorite cousin's wife, a friend in her own right, Lady Marianne Falkham.

Dear Ellen,

Collin and I have been thinking a great deal about you of late. We have heard through the family that your home is busy with comings and goings as your sisters prepare to enlarge their nurseries. I cannot help but think it would do you a great deal of good to come visiting before winter sets in. Collin and I enjoy your company immensely and missed having you visit this summer. Please come visit for a fortnight?

Ellen read the rest of the note rapidly, her heart rising at this unexpected invitation. She left her room, looking for her mother and found her chambers. She was directing her maid in packing a trunk.

"Mama," Ellen said, loudly enough to gain her mother's attention. "I've had a letter."

"Yes, dear?" Mama looked over her shoulder, her manner distracted. "What is it?"

"It is a letter from Marianne."

"Lovely, darling." Her mother pulled a dress from the wardrobe and held it out to her maid. "Rowlings, I think this would be better than the blue. We aren't going to be hosting any dinner parties, after all."

"Yes, ma'am."

Ellen stood in the doorway a few moments more, but her mother did not turn around again.

She's preoccupied. Leaving tomorrow, of course she's going to be busy, Ellen told herself and went back downstairs.

She tapped gently on the door of Papa's study before letting herself in. Reginald was examining the ledgers on the desk, but her father looked up when she entered.

"Ah, Ellen." He held his hand out to her, inviting her in. "Has your post added to the happiness of the day?" He nodded to the letter in her grasp.

Ellen took her father's hand, allowing him to draw her near. Though estate business and training his heir took much of his time, Papa gave her attention and her opinion greater voice than anyone else in the family.

"I do have a little news." She held up the missive and he took it, raising his gray eyebrows. "Marianne invites me to stay with her and Collin in Hampshire."

"Indeed." Her father unfolded the letter and began to peruse it with narrowed eyes.

Ellen couldn't contain her question, her earlier desire to travel returning with force. "May I go? Mother will be with Dorothea. I don't think anyone here will miss my company."

Papa nodded, looking up from the letter at last. "Send your reply. You may be on your way after the coach returns from taking your mother to Dorothea."

Ellen gave her father a grateful hug. "Thank you, Papa. I will write at once." She fairly skipped out of the room. At last, something special, meant for her. Wasting no time, Ellen went to her room to decide what she would take with her.

Cousin Collin and Marianne were dear friends to her. Marianne and Ellen grew up playing at the Falkham home, though a gap of three years separated them in age. Marianne's family sent her there a few weeks every summer. Marianne, when she grew old enough, debuted in London and had set her cap for one man, her former playmate Collin.

Ellen had been happy for her friend when they married.

Marcus had come to the wedding too, looking more handsome than ever before.

Forbidding herself to dwell on that thought, Ellen pulled her traveling trunk from beneath her bed, noting its worn handles with a smile. She'd had the same piece of luggage since childhood and never thought on replacing it. It held too many lovely memories.

Being a girl meant Ellen was not always a desirable playmate for Collin, but she would do when he had no other children about. Most often his freckled, red-headed friend from school, Marcus Calvert, fulfilled the role as his companion.

Ellen came to regard them both with reverent awe, following them about and trying to take part in their games. When they were feeling generous, they would put her up into a tree or attic room and she could be a distressed Maid Marian or young Queen Elizabeth, needing a robber or a knight to save her. Thankfully, they let her take a book with her to pass the time until her rescue could be arranged.

Ellen went to her wardrobe. She looked from one side of the closet to the other, noting her prettiest dresses were from her last season in Bath, when her hopes of meeting a handsome man to wed finally faded to nothing.

None of the men she met matched the picture in her heart, where she carried an image of a gentleman with coppery curls and a charming grin.

But Marcus, the second son of an earl, spent every season in London. They never crossed paths socially. Only at the home of her cousin, for a month each summer, until the year she came out.

It would be good to see her cousin and his wife. Being among friends who cared for her would go a long way to lift the melancholy that had begun to creep into her heart.

CHAPTER 2

Marcus Calvert, second son to the late Earl of Annesbury, could not have received his invitation to stay at Falkham Hall at a more opportune moment. Fleeing London and his meddlesome mother before the start of the season felt much like he imagined escaping prison would.

Lord Collin Falkham had sent for him immediately after receiving Marcus's shocking news. Since the two had been friends for nearly two decades, Marcus answered the invitation at once.

Marcus had been ordered to marry by the dowager countess, his own mother, or forfeit his inheritance until her death. Given her good health and the fact that he loved her dearly, the edict did not come with any hope of a swift conclusion.

"You must marry," she had stated in their London town home, seated in her favorite chair. Her little dog yipped in her lap. "Until you do, I will not allow you to have Orchard Hill." Her dark red curls were twisted upward and tucked into a lace cap. He'd inherited both the curls and the hair-color from his mother and counted neither a blessing.

"But Mother," he had said with a laugh. "I'm not yet thirty.

There is no rush to marry, and I know you no longer wish to run the estate."

The estate they spoke of came with her into marriage and had always been intended for a second son, since the eldest would inherit the title and lands of his father. Marcus expected Orchard Hill to come to him when he reached his majority, but his mother withheld it, stating he had yet to mature enough to take over management of the property.

She sniffed and tilted her head up in a most determined manner. "I know precisely how old you are. Just as I know that your brother is *past* thirty."

"Lucas is the earl," he pointed out. "He already inherited his title and property. What has age and marriage to do with estate management?"

"Absolutely nothing," she admitted without blinking. "But if I could hold your brother's feet to the fire and make him wed I would. To my sorrow, I've no power over him."

"He's already married once."

Her tone softened. "I know. And his loss of Abigail was heartbreaking. But that was five years ago. He must move on and marry, he must find his happiness. I have spoken to him but he has yet to listen. Therefore, I have turned my attention to the son I am most able to manage. You cannot be alone forever, Marcus."

Had anyone other than his mother said such a thing, Marcus would have bristled up at once. As it was, he was merely annoyed. But she knew him and she knew what he had gone through. His loss may not have been as devastating as his brother's, but it was nearly as life-changing.

"What makes you think I will bow to your wishes, Mother?" He dropped into the chair across from her and slumped down in it, feeling a headache coming on. He resisted the urge to push his hands through his hair, trying not to show his frustration.

"You want Orchard Hill. You have always wanted it." She waved a hand dismissively before returning it to pet her dog. "You trained under your father. You have shown an admirable interest in being a good landowner. But you have not married to provide a progeny.

You have not looked for a lady to help you manage the estate. I will not let it pass into your hands until you have taken that important step. Until then you will live on nothing more than the allowance your father provided you in his will."

Marcus sat straighter and regarded her warily. "Father provided a mere pittance. He knew I would have Orchard Hill not long after he passed. That was two years ago."

She shrugged in a manner more suited to a Frenchwoman than an English countess. "Then you will live on that pittance until you marry, because my coffers are closed to you." Though her terms were harsh, her tone remained soft and gentle. "I love you dearly, Marcus. I have great hopes for you. But you have done nothing, absolutely nothing, to find happiness for yourself. Since before your father passed you have moved about society, had flirtations aplenty, but not taken the matter seriously." She put her dog on the floor and stood, brushing off her voluminous skirts.

"I wish for grandchildren. That is the selfish point of these stipulations. But I also wish for your joy, which I do not believe you can find alone. I would like you to marry before your thirtieth birthday. At which point, I will turn Orchard Hill over to you the moment the vows are said. If you do not marry, then we will revisit the situation."

Days later, comfortably situated in his brother's carriage as it neared the Falkham property, Marcus still did not understand her. The estate sat nearly stagnant, entirely dependent on his mother's old steward to make decisions on the management of the property. He knew she had not visited the estate since his father's death.

Why would she entertain an absurd notion of forcing him to wed instead of handing him the deed? The very idea was something out of one of those Gothic romances society debutantes liked to read.

He had no wish to put his heart at risk again, which would necessitate a marriage of convenience.

The carriage came to a stop, jolting him from his thoughts, and the door was swung open by a footman.

He released a long, slow breath to calm himself and left the carriage. The gloomy gray of the sky did little to brighten his mood. But when he saw Collin upon the steps of his home, and Marianne tucked into his side, he could not help but smile.

"Marcus, welcome." Collin did not bound down the steps to greet him as he did at the start of their boyhood summer visits. He waited, standing straight and tall, his arm around his wife. "Come in, before the sky bursts open and soaks us all."

Marcus took the steps quickly and clasped his friend's hand warmly. "Collin, it's good of you to have me." His friend, taller than he by a hand, looked unchanged since their last meeting. He still had straight, black hair worn longer than considered fashionable, and his clothes were more suitable to riding about the countryside than sitting at home and hearth.

Collin's expression twisted into mock-disgust. "I? Invite you? Never did such a thing. Marianne insisted you come, otherwise I would not have had you here. My wife seems oddly fond of you. Can't say that I see why."

Marianne laughed and stepped forward with her hand raised for Marcus to bow over it. "Don't listen to him, Marcus. We are both very glad you've come." Her fair coloring was a contrast to his friend's looks in the most complimentary of ways.

"Especially after we received your letter," Collin added, expression more serious. "Come in and clean up. We have refreshment for you, when you are ready."

Marcus thanked them both and went to his room without further delay. After his valet, Cray, saw to it that his person and clothing were made respectable, he took himself off to the parlor where his hosts waited with a tea tray and sandwiches.

After all three had partaken of the light repast, Collin settled back on the couch, arm around his wife, and dove into the thing most plaguing Marcus's mind. "So, you must find a wife."

Marcus finished the last of his tea and returned the cup to the table at his side. "According to my mother, I must find a wife *or else*."

A frown appeared on Marianne's face, her bright eyes studying him intently. "Does this distress you, Marcus?"

Of course it did, but he was trying to keep that from showing. He offered her a confident grin. "Not entirely. A man usually gets to determine when and how he takes a bride, but I have been left with the ability to choose whom. The other factors are predetermined. I must marry before my thirtieth birthday. The sooner the better, actually. How I do it seems to matter little as long as it is quickly."

"You poor dear." Marianne looked up at her husband. "Although the problem presented is straightforward enough."

"What do you intend to do?" Collin asked, studying Marcus curiously. "There are any number of ladies who would be willing to be your bride. Many a young miss in London has flirted with you and with the notion of taking you to the altar. You make the rounds of every ballroom every season."

Marcus's smile turned bitter at that and he looked down. "Flirting is all they do, Collin. I am a second son, with a small allowance, and an estate that no one knows about except that it is of no great consequence. My future bride will not host grand balls as my brother's might, nor will she maneuver in the highest order of society. The matchmaking matrons know this, if their daughters do not, and set their caps at loftier heads than mine."

"Surely not," Marianne protested while Collin chuckled. "You are dreadfully handsome and amusing. I think a girl would fall in love with you quite easily."

"I hardly want a girl who must settle for me." Marcus shook his head and refocused his attention on the lady of the house, ignoring her comment on love. He did not want love. "In fact, I don't want a girl at all. My estate is not large and will require careful management if I am to improve it. I would prefer to have a woman of sense running my household, not a child whose only training has been to ensnare a husband. My birthday is in six months. The London season begins in one month."

"What has that to do with anything?" Collin asked, his brows pinching together in confusion.

"I have five months to find a woman on the marriage mart, court her, and arrange a marriage. In the whirl of society, that gives me little time to fulfill the expectations of a *girl* in the midst of a London season."

Collin made a humming sound. "Not to mention the gossip would make the rounds. Your desperation could easily become common knowledge. In that atmosphere such matches take a great deal of time."

"Marry before the season." Marianne smirked at his start of surprise. "Oh, come now. If you marry before January, when no one is yet in town, you avoid the gossips and the lengthened courtship time. Expectations are not high for courtships that take place outside of London."

Marcus argued against that insane notion at once. "Did you forget that the season begins in *one* month? Where am I to find a woman to marry at such short notice? They hardly advertise such things in the *Times*. I would need to have the banns read this Sunday." Marcus said adamantly. "No. That will never work. Unless you are hiding a flock of marriageable young ladies somewhere about the country."

"Advertisements in the *Times* and now flocks." Collin shook his head, lips pursed in amusement. "You truly know nothing about obtaining a bride."

"Obviously not, as I am now several years behind you in doing so," Marcus grumbled, not at all amused.

Marianne glanced from one man to the other, her eyebrows pulled down. "Marcus, we have discussed your situation at length and hit upon a scheme you may find reasonable. If Collin will be serious for a moment, I might explain it to you."

"If it is a scheme of Collin's there will be nothing reasonable about it." Marcus scoffed but Collin cast his wife a long-suffering look. "Marianne, please share your thoughts on the matter. It will be a pleasure to hear what a lady of such fine taste, with the exception of her taste in husband, has to contribute to my sorry cause."

Marianne leaned forward, her eyes glittering with mischief. "We know the perfect woman to aid you. She is practical and intelligent, which are both qualities you seem to want in a wife."

"Is she an antidote, too?" He raised his eyebrows in question.

"Of course not. I would say she's lovely," Marianne protested.

"Does it really matter, given your time constraints?" Collin asked with a chuckle. "You are already being dreadfully specific about her abilities, but now you want beauty, too?"

Marcus glared at him. "I would prefer to avoid absolute beauty actually, but a wife with a pleasant countenance and all of her teeth in good repair is not too much to ask. There are the future children to consider." Beautiful women could rarely be trusted, present company excluded. His heart had to pay for that lesson in life.

Marianne huffed with impatience and stood, necessitating both men to leap up as well. "Marcus, you are being far too flippant and I am of a mind to let you find your own way out of your mess." She stormed to the window and snapped over her shoulder, "Oh, sit down, both of you."

The men exchanged looks, her husband one of chagrin and Marcus of surprise.

"Are you certain you want to marry?" Collin winked at him and darted a look at his wife's rigid back.

"Quiet, Collin. We mustn't upset her further." Marcus gestured to the chairs and they sat again. "I apologize, Marianne. Please forgive me, but my irritation with my circumstances has grown extreme." He sighed and pushed a hand through his hair, remembering he must get it cut soon before his unwanted curls appeared. "Please, tell me more about this lovely and intelligent woman."

Marcus hoped this woman wasn't one of the ladies he had considered. The *ton* was full of social-climbing sycophants, women with little else in their minds but advancement and large sums of pin money. Orchard Hill would not provide for anyone of that ilk in what they would consider a satisfactory manner.

The few women he knew without such ambitions were in search of love matches, which was something he would not give them.

Marianne glanced over her shoulder at him and made a dismissive gesture. "There isn't much for me to tell you except that you already know her."

"I have been wondering who of my acquaintance might be willing, but I confess I found none particularly appealing. Who do you have in mind?"

The lady looked to her husband, that dangerous twinkle in her eye again. "Someone I doubt you even considered."

"Because you do not run in the same circles," Collin amended. "Not because she is an antidote. She is dark haired, with brown eyes, the usual sort of figure for a woman of six and twenty. Very intelligent. Well read."

Marcus looked from his friend sitting at ease on the sofa, to his hostess standing at the window. His mind searched out who of his acquaintance, familiar to the Falkhams, could fit such a description.

When he hit upon the memory of a young woman with black curls and starry eyes, he grew still. "You cannot mean—" He stopped himself and shook his head. "But she's your cousin, Collin. Surely you wish better for her." A weak laugh escaped him.

Collin and his wife exchanged a look, communicating in that silent way of married couples, but Marcus knew enough of them both to see their concern. They were treading carefully, he realized, and had a plan.

"Wish better for Ellen?" Collin leaned back, as though completely unconcerned with the matter. "Who better for her than my closest friend? I know you well, Marcus. I know you are able to care for a wife once you have your inheritance. You will provide for her. Keep her in comfort. Treat her with respect and honor."

"I'm the second son of an earl, with a small estate inherited through my mother." He raised his hands in a confused gesture. "Why would you want *that* for her?"

Marianne came forward and laid her hand on his arm, looking up at him with an earnest expression. "You may not realize what you have to offer a wife, Marcus. Especially someone as kind and sweet as Ellen. Besides that, she has grown up with all of us. She knows you. You know her. Could you at least give her a chance and see if she would suit?"

Marcus sighed and closed his eyes. "What am I to do? Show up at her door, before the season begins, and ask for an audience? The only place I have ever seen her is at this house during childhood, and at your wedding two years ago." Though he had seen her that recently, he had trouble recalling exactly what she looked like as an adult. He kept attempting to conjure an image of the woman she had become and could only remember a young girl with freckles across her nose and that nose glued to a book.

"That could be considered strange," Collin acknowledged, holding a hand out to his wife. She took it and joined him again on the plush furniture. "Which is why we have invited her to stay with us while you are here."

Marcus's eyes widened. "You did what? Ellen's *here?*"

"She is arriving today, actually. You both have excellent timing when it comes to accepting invitations," Marianne said demurely. "I expect her before dinner."

CHAPTER 3

Ellen stepped down from her father's carriage. The sky grew dark, the shorter days of December meaning lamps must be lit sooner each evening. She did not mind the nip in the air when greeted with the bright windows of her cousin's home. Collin and his wife stood at the top of the steps, doubtless alerted to her arrival by a servant keeping watch, looking as happy together as when she'd seen them the summer before.

Wasting no time, Ellen took the steps quickly and walked into Marianne's embrace. "It is so good of you to have me," she said sincerely. "I have missed you both, and your home is one of the dearest places on earth to me."

Marianne laughed and returned the hug whole-heartedly. "I am glad your family could spare you. It is always wonderful to have you with us."

"As long as you are behaving like a lady instead of a hoyden," Collin interrupted, extending his hand to her.

"When have I ever been anything other than perfectly behaved?" she asked, feigning an indignant tone. "All of my memories revolve around you creating mischief while I was told to play elsewhere or else had to become the damsel in distress."

He laughed outright and gestured to the door. "Come, if we are going to reminisce we ought to do it in a warmer environment."

"And I'm sure you wish to freshen up after that carriage ride." Marianne brought her attention to a maid waiting inside the door. "This is Sarah. She will attend you while you are with us."

"My own maid," Ellen said with a bright smile for the young girl, who could be no older than fifteen. "I am certain we will get along splendidly as I already feel very spoiled to have you, Sarah."

"Thank you, miss." The girl dipped a curtsy and took hat, bonnet, and gloves with a nervous smile on her lips.

"Sarah is a gem and hopes to be a proper lady's maid one day." Marianne turned her attention back to her guest, still smiling brightly. "Please take your time settling in. We won't expect you down until dinner."

"That's very kind of you."

"Show her to her room, Sarah." The maid bobbed once and led the way to the stairs. Ellen followed, her step light.

A spacious and well-appointed guest room waited for her, a fire already lit against the cool night air. Her trunk arrived when she did, carried by a footman. Sarah bustled about, putting things to rights and finding evening clothes. Ellen took a seat at the dressing table and began to unpin her hair.

"Have you worked here long, Sarah?" she asked. She felt it important to acknowledge servants as people too, with hopes and dreams. Ignoring the person waiting hand and foot on her had never been possible.

"Two years." The girl's cheeks, rosy more with pleasure than exertion, were full and round when she smiled. "This is my first time serving a guest, miss. I hope you'll tell me if there's anything I can do for you. A special way to do your hair or your favorite sorts of hot house flowers for your table."

Ellen began to brush her hair, releasing the tension caused by travel. Her hair might be black, but it wasn't drab. It fell in soft waves around her shoulders, shining like silk. If only society allowed women of her age to wear their hair down more often.

"Would you lay out my blue gown, please?"

"Yes, miss. Lady Falkham said I ought to suggest you wear your best gown tonight, if you thought of saving it for another occasion." The maid approached her from behind, biting her lip, just visible in the mirror over the dressing table.

Ellen's eyebrows raised. "Did she say why?"

Sarah shook her head, eyebrows furrowed. "No, miss. But I imagine it's something to do with our other guest."

Turning fully to look up at the maid, Ellen hoped her expression did not entirely give away her curiosity. "Oh? Who else is visiting? Another member of the family?"

"No, miss." The girl's smile returned, along with the pink in her cheeks. "It's a handsome gentleman, one of His Lordship's old school chums. Mr. Calvert is his name. Might you know him?"

Know him? Ellen could feel the blush rising in her cheeks the moment his name passed Sarah's lips.

"Yes. He often visited during the summer as I did. When we were children." She turned back to her toilette, her eyes not knowing where to settle. "But please, lay out the blue dress anyway. It will do well enough for Mr. Calvert." Though she felt tempted to request the pale pink evening gown she knew set off her complexion, she would not allow herself to change plans for *him* when he likely gave no thought at all to her. No more than any man would give to a spinster.

Finally feeling more composed, Ellen affixed a smile to her face and looked back up at Sarah. "How are your skills with hair? I would like something simple this evening, I think. But appropriate."

Sarah instantly began to describe all her favorite ways to style hair and seemed more than well practiced, having grown up with several sisters both older and younger, all in service as maids throughout the county. Ellen let her talk, offering comment when necessary, trying not to think overly long on the other guest lurking somewhere about the estate.

But the effort was wasted. Marcus Calvert was in the house with her, the same as he had been during her childhood. She had never slipped through a London ballroom to dance with him, never seen him across a drawing room at a morning visit, nor would she ever do such a thing. Though they shared many childhood memories, she had never known the man he had become beyond what rumor brought her.

Doubtless he came to see Collin before the start of the season, to discuss the society and politics they shared, before going to town. She would do well to remember this and stay close to Marianne, enjoying the company of a woman who was not one of her expectant sisters.

Ellen squared her shoulders as her blue gown was settled about her by Sarah, who turned out to be a genius with hair, and told herself to enjoy her time away from home. It would not be long until her services were required there and her days of freedom were at an end.

~

AT FIRST TORN between exasperation and surprise, Marcus had not been certain whether to thank his meddling friends or flee the premises. His trust in Collin and Marianne at last convinced him to stay.

Entering the parlor ahead of dinner, Marcus realized he did not arrive first. Pacing before the fire, expression one of distraction, and figure finer than he remembered, was Ellen Bringhurst. She wore a gown the color of sapphires, a darker color than most debutantes favored during the season. Her hair glowed in the firelight, turning parts of the deep black to a midnight blue. He stood in the doorway for several long moments, taking her in.

The last time he had seen her, at her cousin's wedding, she'd not made this much of an impression on him. Of course, he had been distracted by his heartache at the time, not wishing to notice any woman beyond paying the idle compliment. He ought to have taken more time to renew their relationship instead of wallowing in misery.

Ellen paused in her march before the hearth and turned her head, noticing him at last. She stood frozen for a heartbeat, but her expression warmed and a smile curved her lips. She dipped a curtsy, remembering formalities before he could take two steps forward. "Mr. Calvert. Good evening."

Marcus quickly returned her smile and bowed. "Miss Ellen. It is a pleasure to see you again."

Her smile faltered. "I'm afraid it's Miss Bringhurst now. All my elder and younger sisters are married, leaving the surname to me to bear."

He came further into the room and slipped into the role of charming gentleman with ease. "That is a shame. Your Christian name is lovely. Might we dispense with formalities, given that we have nearly always known one another? You may call me Marcus."

Her head tilted to one side and her expression relaxed. Her dark eyes, a shade of brown as rich as chocolate, took him in with open frankness. "I suppose we can allow for that, at least in Collin's home. You have held me hostage in towers too often to be formal."

He laughed outright, memories flooding his mind of a disgusted girl sitting with arms folded, demanding to know when she might be rescued so she could go about her own business. "You put up with a great deal from us during our school years."

"Indeed." And while her expression stayed pleasant, and her eyes honest, he realized how different she was from the other women he had flirted with over the years. Nothing about her person, her smile, her stance, suggested she was flirting with him. "I imagine you did the same with a girl following you about all summer long."

He gestured to the couch but she sat instead in one of the chairs near it, adjusting her skirts with practiced ease.

She folded her hands in her lap and looked up at him, not at all reticent. "It was a surprise to learn you are visiting Collin and Marianne. I hope it is for pleasant reasons."

Marcus took the seat she ignored, his eyes taking her in again. "Being here in this house has always been a pleasure. I am more at home here than anywhere else in the world, I think. It is to my great advantage, however, that I am visiting at the same time as you. Though we cannot play at our past games, remembering them together should prove amusing."

Her smile grew for an instant before she shook her head. "That will grow dull indeed, speaking of the antics of children. I would much rather know how you have been of late. What things have you seen? Where have you visited? I am often confined to my corner of the county and I must know more about the world beyond that place."

"I am afraid one county is much like the other," he answered dismissively. He hardly wanted to speak of current events or gossip when he had before him a likely candidate for marriage. "I will tell you of myself, however, if you will tell me more of your corner and your doings in it."

Though her lips remained upturned he thought he detected some of the light leaving her eyes. "I am not sure you will like that bargain in the end."

"Why ever not?" He leaned forward in his seat, eyes meeting hers squarely. "It is never a hard task to learn more about a beautiful lady."

Instead of blushing or demurring modestly, as most young women were wont to do, she surprised him by laughing. The sound did not come out as a polite giggle either, but a full laugh. She covered her mouth, her eyes remaining bright with amusement.

"Did I say something amusing?" he asked, truly surprised.

"Oh, Marcus." His name was nearly a sigh but one of amusement instead of adoration. How utterly flummoxing. "You can save your flattery for London. I am not at all fooled by your flirtations. *That* much of London behavior I am well aware of."

"Flirtation?" He pretended to be offended. "My dear lady, I spoke with utmost sincerity."

"You called me a beautiful lady. We both know I am not that." She scoffed, her eyes shifting away from his. "Passably pretty, but not beautiful."

Although bewildered by her protest, he could not give in to her declaration. "Modesty."

"Not at all. But we were speaking of a trade of information. I will tell you about my doings if you tell me of yours. As I am a lady, I will go first." She folded her hands primly in her lap and sat straighter. "I am afraid I have spent a great deal of time in the company of my two elder sisters and mother, discussing nothing but nursery matters. As those can be of little interest to you, I feel no need to share the details."

"Ah, but you're wrong. Nursery matters fascinate me. You see, I have missed being in a nursery for many years. It seems there were many more opportunities for fun in that time." He sighed, drawing his eyebrows down in a dark frown. "And more biscuits."

She laughed again, as brightly as before. "I'm afraid my discussions with them were less about biscuits and more about Christening bonnets."

"Ah. Those I've no use for. My turn, then." He tapped his chin with one finger, glancing away from her and affecting a thoughtful frown. "I have been in London visiting my mother. She stays there year-round. Prefers it to the country. She is in good health, should you wonder."

Ellen smirked at him. "I always liked your mother. She is a very determined sort of person."

He let out a huff of air and shook his head, his mind going back to his purpose in sitting with Miss Ellen Bringhurst. "You have no idea how right you are." He made a gesture toward her. "Now it is your turn again. Besides discussing bonnets, what else have you done?"

"Very little. Except read. I have read a great deal this summer. Usually out of doors and without a bonnet, of Christening size or otherwise. My mother despairs of me and my freckles." She held a gloved finger up to point at her nose and he took the opportunity to lean in close, searching for the dots.

She didn't draw back, nor did she blush, but she raised her eyebrows and crossed her eyes as if to look at the tip of her nose herself. "There, you can see a smattering of them."

He bit back a laugh at her ridiculous expression and looked at the offending marks. "Not at all. A sprinkling, but not a smattering." He sat back on the edge of the settee. "What were you reading in the sun without your bonnet?"

"Whatever came into my hands," she confessed with a shrug. "Periodicals. News sheets. My father obtained a pocket Encyclopedia recently and I spent more time than any lady should indulging in its pages."

"Dear me. A lady reading more than Mrs. Radcliffe's novels. This is hardly an acceptable past time." He attempted to fix her with a stern look but she appeared as though she might laugh again so he changed tactics. "At least as concerns society. But what do we care for society?"

"Hopefully," a voice chimed in from the doorway, "you care for *our* society. Or else we should not have invited you." Collin stepped into the room with Marianne on his arm. "I must say you both have deplorable manners, arriving ahead of your hosts like this."

"It is shameful." Marianne shook her head slowly. "You ought to be in your rooms making us wait on you. That is how proper guests behave."

Having risen to his feet at the sight of Marianne, Marcus now bowed to them both. "My humblest apologies. If you wish it, Ellen and I could withdraw and enter the room after you have both settled."

"No, it's all spoilt now." Marianne sighed dramatically. "We had better sit and hope the servants have enough manners to keep us waiting a few moments for dinner."

The butler entered at that moment and spoke with solemnity. "The meal is ready, my lady."

Marcus felt sorry for the man when all four of them burst out laughing. He offered his arm to Ellen, who took it in a perfunctory manner. The woman did not seem affected by him at all. She did not blush under his gaze or his compliments, did not demure in their conversation, and took his arm as a matter of course instead of fluttering her eyelashes or preening the way others had done.

He saw this as evidence of her practicality. Ellen must be a woman with a good deal of sense and lovely to look upon. A man could do much, much worse in a wife. Perhaps, with more time, he might put the question to her.

Perhaps.

CHAPTER 4

S itting at her dressing table while Sarah brushed out her hair, Ellen relaxed beneath the maid's ministrations and allowed her mind to wander.

Seeing Marcus again, being alone with him before dinner, created all manner of conflict inside her heart and head. For years she held him up as an ideal companion, but never dared hope he would pay her attention. Yet he called her by her Christian name almost at once. Such familiarity made her feel heady. Excited. But she could not allow that.

Such an intimacy could be one of his methods of flirtation. Though they knew each other as children, most would put away that familiarity upon entering adulthood.

As far as society was concerned, she barely existed. She was not important. Apart from their meeting here in her cousin's house, she would likely never see Marcus again.

That thought did nothing to lift her spirits.

A light rap on the door startled her. She exchanged a glance with Sarah, who hurried to answer it. The girl opened it a crack, then stepped back to allow the person outside entry.

Marianne entered wearing her wrap, her hair in a long blonde braid. "I am glad you are not abed yet. I wished to speak to you before you retire. We did not get the chance for a private word today."

"Shall I go, miss?" Sarah asked, hovering near the door.

"Yes, of course. Good night, Sarah." The girl bobbed a curtsy and disappeared, closing the door behind her. Ellen began to braid her hair, watching Marianne in the mirror.

"Is the room to your liking?" Marianne walked about, straightening a cushion on the chair near the fire.

"Yes, very much." Tying off the braid with a ribbon, Ellen turned fully in her chair to face her friend. "I am glad to be here."

Marianne glanced up with raised eyebrows. "But?"

Shaking her head, Ellen confessed her thoughts. "Why am I here at the same time as Mr. Calvert? Is he to be Collin's guest and I yours?"

"No." Marianne shook her head. "If anything, I have sincere hopes you will spend your time here keeping each other company."

Ellen frowned, uncertain she heard correctly. "Keeping each other—? Marianne, what are you saying exactly?" She stood, gripping the back of her chair tightly. "You are not playing matchmaker."

Marianne's face remained serious. "I certainly am."

Ellen took one breath and then another, her thoughts flying quickly through her mind. How could her friend and her cousin do this to her? Why would they set her up for such a dismal failure? Especially when Marianne knew, and had for a number of years, that Ellen admired Marcus? In a moment of youthful folly many years past, she told Marianne that marrying Marcus would be dreadfully romantic.

Marianne must know that Ellen left that dream behind her long ago. "Five seasons, Marianne," she said at last, loosening her grip on the chair. Her knuckles had turned white. "I've had five seasons in Bath. I am firmly on the shelf. I accept that. Please. Do not make Mar—Mr. Calvert's time here difficult by throwing me at him." She met her friend's gaze, pleadingly.

Marianne came across the room, reaching out to embrace Ellen. Ellen hoped this meant her friend accepted her request.

But Marianne's next words dashed that idea. "You are perfect for him, Ellen. Marcus just doesn't know it yet."

Ellen stepped away, wrapping her arms about herself. "No. I'm not. He is the son of an earl, he goes to London every season, he can have his choice of women."

"But what if his choice is you?" Marianne asked with a wide gesture of her arms. "You are both here. No distractions. No meddlesome family. Just the two of you. Why not give it a chance?"

"Because it would be terrible. Can you imagine me trying to flirt with him? Win him over?"

A snort escaped the proper Lady Falkham. "He sees enough of that behavior in London. I want you to be yourself." Her look became earnest. "I want you to talk to him and be honest."

"Honest?" Ellen moved to sit on the edge of her bed, shaking her head. "I dare not be honest. You know, Marianne. You *know* how I have always felt about him. I think that would terrify him to know a bookish little nobody fancied herself in love."

Marianne winced. "Maybe not that honest. I meant that you should behave as you would with Collin and me. Not the way your mother wishes, or society expects. The way you wish to be. I think he will find it endearing."

A suspicion formed in Ellen's mind and she gasped. "He knows! He knows that's why he's here, doesn't he?" She felt her cheeks burn. "Marianne, tell me he doesn't know."

Marianne began to blush as well. "That isn't precisely—" She swallowed. "I suppose I'd better tell you the whole of it. Marcus does know what Collin and I hope. But he didn't flee when we spoke to him of our thoughts on the matter. That must count in your favor."

"Likely he is amused by the very notion of me as anyone's bride," Ellen said, closing her eyes and rubbing at her temples. "Oh, how could you? Don't you realize—"

Marianne spoke impatiently. "He needs a wife, Ellen."

Ellen opened her eyes to see Marianne looking sheepish.

"I shouldn't have said that," the baroness muttered, looking away and reaching up to play with the ends of her braid. "Oh dear. Collin will be disappointed."

"Why does Mar—Mr. Calvert need a wife? And why wouldn't he choose one from the throngs of women in London?" Ellen realized she was clutching the blankets beneath her in a manner which would make her hands sore in a moment. She hastily let go and tucked them in her lap. "Tell me, Marianne. Or I will order a carriage and leave at first light."

Marianne approached the bed and sat down daintily. "Collin will not like that I told you. I must ask you to not say a word to him about this." Her face had paled and she looked stricken enough that Ellen sighed and offered her a nod of agreement. "Very well. Marcus's mother has told him if he does not marry soon, she will not allow him to inherit Orchard Hill as long as she is living."

Ellen's jaw dropped. "That doesn't sound like Lady Annesbury at all. It sounds most unfair, actually."

Marianne waved that comment away. "She wants him settled and with grandchildren for her to spoil. She doesn't believe he is ready to manage an estate without a woman to manage the house."

Ellen stood, walking across the room. She took several deep breaths before facing her friend again. "Even if this is true, if he must take a wife, why would he choose me with the ballrooms of London as a hunting ground? I have heard how he flirts. It's said that a young woman cannot consider herself truly out until she has made her curtsy to the Queen and been winked at by Marcus Calvert."

"His reputation has run wild." Marianne attempted a laugh but stopped when Ellen raised a hand to cover her eyes. "Ellen, reputation aside, Marcus would still be a wonderful husband. He is thoughtful, attentive, and moves about society with ease."

"If Marcus is truly such a wonderful catch, why would he bother wasting even a second with *me?*" Ellen gestured to her body and threw her arms out in exasperation. "I am not important, not a diamond of the first waters, not an heiress, not titled, I have no connections, and I would be on my seventh season if my family had not decided against the wasted time."

When Marianne gaped at her, Ellen realized she said more than she meant to say.

"They will not send you to Bath this year? But why?"

"I told you. I will remain unmarried." Ellen crossed her arms, holding in all she wished to say on that matter. What good would it do to rail against her fate? No one would have her. No one she wanted. She was too old, too intelligent, and too poor to tempt a man to marry her.

"I cannot believe that. When you finally have a year that would be all your own." Marianne huffed, her expression indignant. "Year after year, you had a sister either expecting, marrying, or coming out and getting engaged. You have never had a season to yourself."

"That is the way of it in large families." Ellen began pacing again. "What did Marcus say when you suggested me as a wife? What were his actual words?"

Marianne frowned and looked down. "He actually said that we should not want *you* to marry *him*. Because of his lack of position."

Struck by the absurdity of the situation, Ellen stood in silence for several moments before she felt her lips slip upward into a smile.

"If positions in society were rungs on a ladder, I would be several steps below him. The poor fellow wanted to be civil in his refusal of the idea." Ellen relaxed and came back to the bed, sadder but immensely relieved. "He will humor you and Collin, then go back to London."

Marianne opened her mouth to speak but closed it again. She stared at Ellen for a long moment. "If that is what you wish to think, I will not dissuade you. Please, Ellen, do be polite to him while you are both guests here."

"Of course. He is a friend and he cannot help the horrid situation you put him in. Attempting to play matchmaker." Ellen pulled her braid over her shoulder on the pretense of tightening the ribbon at the end. "Do you have any other interesting news to share?"

When Marianne remained silent, Ellen looked up to see a different sort of smile on her friend's face.

"There is one other thing of interest. Collin and I are to be parents. In the spring." Her cheeks pinked, and her eyes took on a starry quality Ellen had seen before in her sisters.

Ignoring a small twinge of envy, Ellen leaned forward and embraced her friend. "Congratulations, this is wonderful news."

The conversation remained on the impending need to set up a nursery and all the other details important to an expectant mother. Ellen listened attentively, happy for her friend, but longing for such a joy to come to her.

Whatever Marianne believed, Ellen's chances of marrying were slim. She accepted her place in her family and in society.

At least she tried to.

By the time Marianne left to seek her rest, Ellen knew it would take time for her to settle into sleep. Though their talk ended on a pleasant note, her mind kept turning back to the idea of marrying Marcus.

What would it be like to belong to him? How would her life change?

She slipped beneath the coverlet and snuggled into the plush feather pillows, then toyed with the end of her braid in the semi-darkness. The biggest change for someone like her, she knew, would be running her own household instead of being at the behest of her mother or sisters. She would be free to do things her way as the mistress of an estate. It would fall to her to make certain the servants knew their jobs and fulfilled them well. She would set all the menus. Direct the gardener. Meet with the housekeeper and butler.

If they had tenants, she would go out to meet all of them. Come to know their children. Take them Christmas and Easter baskets of gifts and foodstuffs. Her duty to the community would be important. Ladies' societies, teas, visits, charity groups, all would become part of her life.

That would be the day-to-day changes. But there would also be the possibility, the expectation and hope, of children.

Ellen allowed her thoughts to linger there, trying to picture a little boy with her dark eyes and Marcus's curls. She found the image came to her too easily. She waved her hand in the air above her as she attempted to wipe the picture from her mind. Pulling the blanket over her head, she whispered to herself.

"Stop. It will never be."

Her practical mind failed her and Ellen shed a tear over her fate.

CHAPTER 5

Miss Bringhurst has already breakfasted," the butler informed Marcus when he asked after her the next morning.

"I see." Marcus looked at the empty table.

"She went directly to the gardens," the butler added, nodding to the door which led outside.

Marcus looked at the spread on the side table with momentary longing, but he thought it best to begin his course with Ellen sooner rather than later. He took a slice of toast and made his way to the hall to obtain his great coat. He could not imagine what would take a lady out into a garden when it could not possibly have anything in bloom.

He found her easily, walking through the hedgerows, her eyes unfocused as though she looked inwards more than outwards.

"Good morning, Ellen," he greeted as he drew closer. As he suspected, she looked startled and completely unaware of her surroundings until her eyes met his. At least her pleasant expression came readily, her eyes brightening.

"Good morning, Marcus." She looked up at the clouded sky and then back at him. "I thought I was the only one foolish enough to enjoy a walk in this weather."

"You are," he said without hesitation. "But I'm foolish enough to think you ought to have company." He shivered theatrically. "I'd much prefer to be on horseback on a day like today. Staying warm with some exercise." He stood before her and offered his arm.

Marcus continued down the path she had been walking, matching his stride to hers. Though shorter than normal for a woman, she did not take mincing steps. He admired her confident stride.

"Why do you enjoy walking in weather like this?" he asked.

"The cool air helps me clear my mind of cobwebs."

"Have you many such sticky things in your brain box?" He paused and made a show of peering at her forehead. "I cannot imagine that to be pleasant."

She shook her head and spoke with a trace of humor. "I think anyone with a thought worth having also has several that are *not* worth having. Clearing away the dust and cobwebs leaves room for better thoughts. Greater focus."

"And you have much to think on this morning?" He kept the inquiry polite but could not keep his grin from growing larger. "What weighty matters has such an enchanting lady to consider?"

"The matters common to a spinster and therefore of no interest to you, Marcus Calvert." She smirked at him and took another step, which made him continue in order to keep her arm.

No matter how he tried to flirt, she turned his words and compliments back on him, seemingly unaffected. He decided to try a different tact. Perhaps seriousness would beget seriousness.

"I find it difficult to consider you a spinster. Every time I look at you, I can still see the girl from the schoolroom glaring at me across the library. Do you remember the time I caught you reading that book by the revolutionary, Benjamin Franklin? I told you it couldn't be suited to a young lady's taste."

"And I told you that you were correct, but it was suited to *mine.*" He felt her relax and saw the look in her eye change, softening the amusement. "It was a good book. I convinced Father to order a copy for our library."

The girl had always kept a book about her person. He imagined the woman before him did the same. "You still read a great deal?"

"I try to, yes. Father contributes to our village lending library, so we often receive the books and periodicals first." Ellen bit her bottom lip before continuing, hesitation in her voice. "I know I should not admit to it, but I enjoy reading about all sorts of things. If a book in our circulation is especially good, Father trusts my judgment and buys a copy to add to our personal library. I think having wise words and knowledge close at hand is important to a family."

He nodded and regarded her from the corner of his eye as they walked, turning a corner around another hedge. "What are you reading presently?"

At last he had the pleasure of seeing her blush, but not from his pointed attempts to cause such a reaction. When her cheeks turned pink, her freckles stood out more. She could not have above thirty of them, but they were scattered from one cheek to the other, bridging her pert nose.

"I am reading nothing of consequence."

"Is it scandalous?" he asked, lowering his voice conspiratorially.

She didn't look shocked by his question. "Only a little silly to admit. I am reading a children's book. I find it interesting to see what sorts of things are written for children. It is a collection of Shakespeare's plays. They are told in a narrative style instead of a script for the stage. There are beautiful illustrations."

He could not resist a teasing grin. "The child who read Franklin's autobiography reads children's books as a woman grown. Your tastes are varied and not limited by your age or sex, I see."

"They are not." She smiled, her blush gone. "Although you've hit upon the reason that my mother despairs of me most. I am something of a bluestocking." A note of apology hung on that word. Bluestockings, in his mind, were not pretty ladies who read interesting books, or conversed with such ease.

"I think that term need not be negative when applied correctly."

He gave her gloved hand a pat with his own, his tone only half-serious. "You are not planning on writing a stack of religious tracts and socially demanding poetry, are you?"

Ellen smirked. "Not at the moment, no. I have no desire to lead the life of Hannah More, nor the social standing to do so. I am content to read and learn, and share what I learn with those willing to hear it. I do not presume to know how to tell others to go about their lives."

"Nor do you go about in a mob cap or black skirts, with spectacles perched on your nose, telling us all how superior your knowledge is. That is my idea of a bluestocking of the severest form."

"Marcus," she said slowly, "you have given me a wonderful idea. I think I shall share your picture of an enlightened woman with my mother. If she knew I had not sunk to that level she might be more at ease with me as I am now."

"If you like, I could send her the description myself, and illustrate it as well," he offered, grinning.

"Do you still draw?"

He faltered in his step and they both halted because of it. "Draw?"

"Yes. I remember you used to have a sketchbook you brought places with you. There was that picnic for all the children." Her eyebrows drew together in thought. "You were with the older set, but you sat in a tree with a sketchbook instead of pretending to flirt with the girls your age."

"They didn't want to flirt with me," he murmured, looking at her with interest. Ellen's attention to detail impressed him. He could have sworn no one ever saw him with that book in hand. "They wanted to flirt with Lucas, the future earl. Whenever he was in company, I could never hold any attention."

"I doubt that. I recall you being sought after frequently. But you didn't answer my question." She fixed her dark eyes on him, determined. "Do you still draw?"

He cleared his throat. "On rare occasions, when there is nothing better to do."

"Oh." She looked away, with an air of disappointment.

"It's hardly a masculine pursuit," he said, needing to explain himself. "When ladies speak of accomplishments, they always mention drawing. Men talk of sport."

He looked up at the sky and at their surroundings. "Have we cleared enough cobwebs? Shall we turn back?"

"Yes, I think so." She turned and he took her arm again as they retraced their steps to the open air of the gardens nearer the house. They moved through the hedgerows in silence and he tried to remember the qualities he thought important in a wife.

Practical. Sensible. Not given to romantic notions. Intelligent. Respectable. Willing to marry him and be a credit to his family.

He realized the list, which he thought impossible to fulfill, now felt entirely too short in requirements. The woman on his arm, from what little he knew, fulfilled each of them perfectly. Except the last. He did not know if she would be willing to marry. Ellen's thoughts on herself put her squarely on the shelf. Perhaps she liked it there.

As the house came into view again, Ellen stopped walking. "There is something I feel I must tell you, Marcus. Though it causes me some embarrassment to discuss it." Her eyes lowered to the ground as she spoke and the blush returned. Her freckles made her seem much younger than she was.

"If you feel you must then you must. I can promise you I'll be a complete gentleman and listen attentively." His attempt at levity was met with a quick glance from her.

"Thank you. I appreciate your word on that." Her eyes darted away again before she took a deep breath, fortifying herself. "Yesterday evening, Marianne came to speak with me. She revealed her purpose in inviting the two of us to visit."

Her blush darkened but she pressed on. "I'm incredibly sorry that my cousin and his wife put you up to—to paying your addresses to me, or even entertaining such a thought. I know this is a difficult situation and I wanted to release you from whatever promises you made to them."

Marcus stared at her through her speech, his amusement doused as though he'd fallen through a frozen pond. He felt the heat creeping up his neck and knew his ears must be blazing red. She knew. She knew what he had been about. When she halted in her speech, she met his gaze, and he saw something he did not expect.

Though Ellen Bringhurst put on a brave face, her eyes were sad.

Marcus reached out and took both her hands in his. "Ellen. There is nothing awkward about this. Please put your mind at ease, or your face will burn up completely."

She pulled her hands away. "I'm sorry. But it's humiliating to know that my dearest friend and my cousin would try such an underhanded scheme. Thinking if they threw us together something would come of it." She looked toward the house. "They acted out of concern for my well-being and for your inheritance. They worry for us both."

"You know about my mother's stipulations?" he asked, studying her profile. The red was receding and Ellen began to look more stoic. She nodded to answer his question. "Yet you think that I am out here, walking about in this abysmal cold, because my friend and his wife put me up to it?"

Ellen shrugged and adjusted her cloak, pulling it more tightly around her. "Yes. I think you made them a promise and you are now fulfilling it."

Marcus reached for her hand, which she relinquished to him with a curious expression. He pulled her to a low retaining wall with naught but fallow earth inside it and gestured for her to sit. Once she did so, her eyes still on him, he ran a hand through his hair and looked up to the sky, hoping for some guidance.

"I promised Collin and Marianne nothing. They asked nothing. They presented the idea to me, informed me of their thoughts on the matter, and left it at that. I had no reservations about considering you as a bride, except that you might want better than such as I am." He tried to make light of those words and even managed a grin after he said them. "I have been told in clear terms that the second son of an earl, with one small country estate, is not the best catch."

A snort surprised him, coming from her slight frame. "If the requirements for a good marriage were that a man must have a title and vast tracts of land, where would any of us be? I fail to see how your wealth or title matter so much as whether or not you can support a family and will treat those under your care with fairness."

She spoke with sincerity, her tone almost wistful.

"Those are the things that matter to you in a husband? Fairness? Basic provision?"

"Oh." She smiled in a self-depreciating way. "I suppose I made my list as any schoolgirl does. But I know what matters most. Safety and relative comfort. Kindness. Intelligence is something I must add, as it would be dreadful to be stuck with a lack wit."

His heart thrummed hopefully in his chest. He could give a wife those things. After all, she hadn't mentioned love.

Marcus stepped forward, hopeful for the first time in weeks. "Then you would consider it?"

She blinked up at him, confusion written across her features. "Consider what?"

He wanted to kick himself. He had not actually asked her, and Ellen was under the impression he never would. "Consider marrying me. I find that you are precisely the sort of wife I would seek."

Ellen gaped at him, all the color leaving her cheeks. He rushed to say more before she could say no. "Unless you have your hopes set on being a spinster, as you said before. I can give you those things. Safety and security. I will be a kind and honorable husband. I will make certain you have all that you need. And I am somewhat intelligent, even if I have done a terrible job of proposing to you. You cannot really blame me for that." He attempted to use his charm again, to tease a smile from her. "You brought up the topic, so my speech is not prepared at present. But I could say a few pretty things later if you like."

She stared at him with such shock he couldn't guess what else was in her thoughts. Before he attempted another word, she lowered her hands to grip the side of the wall and looked down at the stone walkway.

"The pretty things are not necessary. In fact, I would prefer if we left *pretty* out of this discussion entirely and focus on the plain words. You would marry me to get your inheritance?"

"I must marry," he stated firmly. "And I would prefer my wife to be a woman of my choosing. A woman who will be a good partner in marriage and the running of an estate. Orchard Hill is not much at present, but it has a great deal of potential. If I have someone sensible running my home, I can focus on the land and income. I can make something greater of our holdings, to benefit future generations."

Her chest rose and fell as she gulped in air, looking stricken. Pained, almost.

"Have I said something to upset you?" he asked, dropping to one knee before her in an attempt to better see her face. "Ellen? Are you unwell? I must've shocked you."

"Something like that, yes," she murmured, not meeting his gaze. "This is very sudden. I thought you would laugh about Collin and Marianne's idea and we would part as friends. Your proposal—it is a great deal to take in. May I have time to think on it?"

He had startled her. He approached the whole matter like a complete fool. But she did not turn him down immediately. If she was as sensible as he believed, she would seriously consider the offer and accept him. Why not? He fulfilled all her stated requirements.

Hope rose within him and he had to repress a smile. "Yes. Take all the time you need, Ellen. I will not press you for an answer now. I am grateful Marianne and Collin brought us together. Meddlesome as they are."

The corners of her lips turned up briefly. "They will never let us hear the end of this." Though it sounded suspiciously like an agreement to his proposal, he did not press her. "Would you please go in and act as though nothing has happened? I don't wish to discuss this with our hosts at present. I need to compose my thoughts."

"Clearing cobwebs of my making this time." He lifted her hand from the wall, surprised by the grip she had on the stone. He bowed over it. "Good morning, Ellen."

"Good morning, Marcus." She nodded but otherwise did not

move. He released her and went into the house, his step light. Even if she did not accept his suit, at least the moment of uncertainty was over. He had not known how to approach the subject with her, but Ellen took the matter in hand. He blessed Marianne's inability to keep a secret.

If Ellen said no, he would have reason to fret again. But for now, he would find some calmness of spirit in hope.

His last marriage proposal hadn't gone well. It had nearly destroyed who he was, and certainly unmade the world and his place in it. But this was different. There was no risk here. He hadn't given his heart away. He had been wise, practical, and as near to indifferent as one could be when proposing.

Though it had not been his intention to lay the matter before Ellen so soon, it relieved him to have it over with. He had to wait for her answer.

CHAPTER 6

A blue sky was a rare sight in December, but Ellen did not take it as a good omen. She looked up at the light color, a shade for which she had no name, from the window seat in Marianne's morning room. True to his word, Marcus hadn't told their hosts of his unexpected proposal, and neither of them spoke in private for the rest of the day.

Marianne and Collin shared several knowing glances across the dinner table the previous evening. Ellen had tried to ignore them. The couple was as invested in the matchmaking scheme as ever.

Marianne's topic of conversation the next morning left no doubt of that.

"What if he fell in love with you after you married?" Marianne sat with an embroidery hoop, working on handkerchiefs to give out at Christmas. "It has happened, where affection grows with time and constancy. A man who flirts as outrageously as he does is bound to have a little romance tucked away somewhere."

"I suppose there is a chance of that." Ellen gave her friend a weak smile and moved away from the window to perch on the edge of the plush pink sofa. "I like how you've set up this room."

Marianne sighed in exasperation. "Do not change the topic under discussion."

The room was like Marianne. All lightness in color and feel, in hues of pink and green, the delicate furnishings scattered about in a whimsical manner, and the wall adornments were pastoral scenes of peaceful milkmaids and rolling fields. It suited the woman of the house.

If such a room belonged to Ellen, how would she decorate the walls to put her mark of ownership upon it? She'd never bothered to think on it since her third season on the marriage mart, when she began to understand no house might ever be given to her.

"I am not really trying to change the topic." She picked up her project, a pair of mittens for her oldest nephew, and went back to knitting a thumb. "Since you brought up the possibility of marrying, I have been trying to think what it would mean for me."

"Oh?" Marianne's hand stopped moving, her eyebrows shot up. "Besides a life no longer dedicated to the whims of your family?"

Ellen could not help but make a tsking sound. "That is harsh, Marianne. My family hasn't been making demands of me."

"Not yet. I have seen what family members do to the unwed sister. I have an Aunt Polly. That is all anyone ever calls her. Not even her proper name anymore. But she is shuffled about from one of my cousins to another, back to her brother's house, and then does the whole round again. Wherever there is sickness, Aunt Polly is called, with no regard for the fact that she is sixty years old and should have respite. If there is a death, birth, or sudden attack of nerves, Aunt Polly. She has no proper home. She is forever a guest, but one expected to earn her keep."

Marianne looked down at her embroidery and thrust the needle through the fabric with more force than necessary. "I mean to have her come here. She need never leave again. I will give her pin money and a personal servant."

Ellen could think of nothing to say. Finally she murmured, "Your aunt will be glad, I'm certain."

"Indeed. But we were talking of you and how being a wife would change your future." Marianne sniffed daintily. "I want to see you happy, Ellen. It will distress me greatly if you remain a spinster when you could be happily married."

Ellen nodded, her eyes falling to the work in her hands. Although she had no great talent for knitting, the mittens she made were always passable. Her hands knew the work well enough for her to speak as they moved.

"I am glad to have you as a champion." She glanced up, trying to keep her tone light as she spoke. "Being a mistress of my own home would be a vast improvement to my situation." She looked around the room again, taking comfort in its peaceful colors and decor. "If I married, I could have a room like this to myself. I could redo the cushions any number of times. Rearrange paintings. Order new drapes. I could make it to suit myself."

"What of Marcus? You're talking about furnishings when I would much rather hear how you would manage a husband." Marianne's eyes danced and her crooked smile turned devious.

Ellen shook her head and huffed with playful impatience. "Marcus likely will not mind how I furnish rooms so long as I stay within a budget. I understand that is the way of things with husbands."

Marianne dropped her embroidery hoop in her lap with undisguised frustration. "Ellen, you have always had tender feelings for him. Dream a little. What would it be like, how would it feel, to be his bride?"

Although the warmth of a blush crept up her neck, Ellen swiftly swatted down any romantic notions forming in her mind. "As Marcus has no idea of what my feelings for him are, and it would be nothing more than a means to an end for him, I imagine I would do my best not to let my feelings run away with me. If we could begin as friends we would do well together. Many marriages of such a nature have been made with both people content in their choice."

Delicate, lovely, proper Marianne gaped at Ellen with an open mouth, her eyes wide as saucers. "That is the most unromantic thing I have ever heard."

Lifting one shoulder in a shrug, Ellen kept at her work. "It's practical."

"Nonsense."

"Perfectly sensible."

Before Marianne could counter again, they both became aware of a sound from the front of the house. The door knocker.

"Who could that be?" Marianne muttered, putting her embroidery aside.

Ellen could not resist teasing. "Are you certain it is not another bachelor you've invited in an attempt to find me a husband?" She put her knitting back in her basket and pushed it beneath the sofa.

"I only invited the one," Marianne answered saucily. "And I'm not at home to visitors today."

The butler appeared at the doorway. "My lady, your cousins Miss Wright and Miss Verity Wright."

Ellen suppressed a groan and could tell from the look Marianne sent her way that her friend did the same. It had not been charitable of them, but in the past they referred to the cousins as Miss Right and Miss Very Right. The two ladies, though younger than Marianne, had always been in possession of a superior manner in their mind, if not in truth.

"Send them in, Russell."

Marianne stood with Ellen, neither saying a word.

"Oh, look," Miss Verity, the younger of the two, said without preamble. "Cousin Marianne has redone the room."

"My, my. Cousin Marianne, it is lovely, if not entirely fashionable. You know the new style is heavily inspired by the Greeks, I believe." Miss Wright, aged twenty, took her seat in a chair with all the dignity of a dowager duchess.

"Yes. Our neighbor, Sir Norvall, has brought in a great deal of furniture with the Greek influence apparent. The chair legs are like Grecian columns. They are very smart." Miss Verity took the empty space next to Ellen and smiled demurely. "He is ever so good as to share his copy of the *Repository* with us. It has all the latest in *décor*."

"A kind neighbor indeed," Marianne said with an indulgent smile before she rang for tea. "It is good to see you both. I hope you will take some refreshment with us. You remember Miss Bringhurst, of course?"

"Yes, of course." Miss Wright nodded as graciously as a queen might to a lesser subject. "It is always a pleasure to see you. Will you be staying long?"

Marianne answered before Ellen could say a word. "I do hope so, as Miss Bringhurst has been my particular friend since childhood."

Miss Verity nodded. "Yes. You two have always been close."

Ellen believed she owed her good friendship to these two. If they had not lived nearby, and always been insufferable, Marianne might never have sought companionship with the cousin visiting the Falkhams.

"We have had word that Miss Bringhurst is not your only guest." Miss Wright's announcement was accompanied by a calculating look.

"News travels swiftly," Marianne murmured, exchanging an amused look with Ellen. "But you are right. Lord Falkham has invited Mr. Calvert to stay with us for a time. I think my husband misses male companionship on occasion. Tell me, how is your mother?"

"Healthy as always," Miss Verity answered, undeterred. "How is Mr. Calvert enjoying his stay?"

"As he has been with us three days, I hope he has no cause for complaint." Marianne rose as a maid entered with the tea tray and took charge of arranging things on a table out of the way.

As Marcus had put his proposal of marriage to Ellen, she doubted he had yet to find anything in his visit to dismay him.

Miss Wright looked about slowly, her eyes taking in the room further as she spoke. "I do hope Lord Falkham does not intend to keep Mr. Calvert cloistered up with him. The neighborhood would benefit a great deal from a new face."

Quietly and aside to Ellen, Miss Verity whispered, "Especially such a handsome face." She giggled behind her hand and Ellen could not help smiling in return.

Marianne answered with a disinterested tone. "I am certain Mr. Calvert would be happy to receive invitations from other gentlemen. I know Uncle Wright enjoys shooting."

"Do you still read a great deal?" Miss Verity asked Ellen when the conversation hit a lull.

In her younger days Ellen would likely have prattled on about what she had finished reading, but she knew better now. Aside from her confession to Marcus about her habits, she tried not to let people outside her immediate family know how often a book was her companion.

"A little less. Is there a book you have enjoyed of late?"

"I enjoyed Mrs. Edgeworth's novels. Papa recently borrowed *The Absentee* for us. It was thrilling. You ought to read it." Miss Verity very nearly bounced as she spoke. "It's all about true love and how a gentleman must escape the schemes of his parents and diabolical women in Ireland. I wish it hadn't been set so much in Ireland." She pouted and shrugged. "It all ends happily. There is a secret inheritance."

Having read the novel herself a few years past, Ellen could not help feeling amused that Miss Verity only saw the love story. In truth that particular book was more about the relationship between a landed gentleman and his tenants, the gentry taking responsibility and ownership of their properties, and treating people of the working class with greater respect. Mrs. Edgeworth's point was not that love conquered all.

"I appreciate your recommendation," Ellen said politely. She read one novel for every ten works outside of fiction. Poetry, histories, Encyclopedias, newspapers, and botanical guides were more often found in her hands than a Gothic romance.

"It is good to hear you do not read so much as you used to," Miss Wright said with a sage smile. "Mother says if your nose is always in a book, it will damage your appearance. Men prefer *young* ladies who focus more on the presentable arts. Painting, drawing, music, dancing." Her emphasis on the importance of youth in snaring a husband was not lost on anyone in the room.

"Of course," Ellen agreed with a slight nod.

Marianne appeared to be biting the insides of her cheek in irritation but Ellen doubted the cousins noticed.

The clock on the mantel chimed the hour. "Ah. It is two o'clock.

I asked Cook to have a light luncheon prepared for us. My dear cousins, won't you stay and partake with us?" Marianne's ability to remain the perfect hostess truly impressed Ellen.

The sisters agreed immediately and Marianne led everyone to the dining room. The less formal dishes and cutlery were used for the afternoon meal, with the drapes fully open to allow natural light to fill the room. The meal consisted of cuts of cold meat, bread, fruit tarts, and a dish of olives.

"It is a very simple repast," Marianne said, motioning them to the sideboard. "I did not expect we would have more company or I would have made changes to the menu."

"It's almost like a picnic," Miss Verity said, picking up a plate and helping herself to the dishes. She had always moved about the world with an almost child-like perception, but followed her elder sister's example otherwise.

Marianne stood near her and leaned close to whisper near Ellen's ear. "The gentlemen will arrive shortly. Poor Marcus."

Ellen bit her lip to keep from laughing and took her usual chair. No sooner did she seat herself than another door opened from the main hall, and gentlemen's voices drifted in ahead of their owners. Both men sounded to be in good spirits.

Collin entered first, a wide grin on his face, until he saw the company gathered. He sobered immediately, cleared his throat, and bowed. "Ladies. My apologies for our late arrival. I did not know we had guests." He moved to his wife's side and bent to kiss her cheek, which was apparently too demonstrative for the sisters as they both blushed and looked away.

Ellen didn't understand the strictures society placed on married people. A husband could not dance with his wife at a ball, they could not be seen to be affectionate in public, and did not even use each other's Christian names before people outside of the family.

It struck her as sad, especially in instances like Collin and Marianne's where the couple truly cared for one another. The whole idea of living one's life to please other people was most unjust.

Marcus did not appear ruffled by the presence of guests and made his bows with a welcoming smile. "A pleasant surprise to see you both again, Miss Wright and Miss Verity." He took his seat amid their polite greetings and delicate waves.

He appeared as handsome as ever and when he glanced in her direction, Ellen struggled to stay calm. It would not do to blush from no more significant a thing than eye contact. She maintained her pleasant expression and turned her attention back to her plate as swiftly as was polite.

"Mr. Calvert, it is simply divine to see you again," Miss Wright said hastily. "It has been an age since the last time, at the Havershams' ball in London."

"Has it been so long?" he asked with feigned surprise. "Indeed, but you ladies look as fresh and lovely as you did on that evening."

Ellen raised her eyes and did her best not to react to his obvious flattery. Did every young woman succumb to his words?

Miss Verity giggled prettily behind her slice of cold ham. "When we learned you were in the neighborhood, Mr. Calvert, we knew we simply had to renew the acquaintance."

Miss Wright blushed but before she could say a word Marcus turned his warm smile to her. "I must admit, I thought of you both when I accepted Falkham's invitation. This near the season, one is never sure who is in town and who lingers in the country."

Ellen caught the slight twinkle in his eye and had to cover her mouth with a napkin to avoid letting out a chuckle. Though the younger women were pleased by his words, Ellen did not think Marcus meant them in a complimentary way.

"Oh, we're always here until Christmas," Miss Verity said, tossing her curls. "We leave after Boxing Day, no matter when Parliament opens."

Talk of London continued between the Miss Wrights and Marcus with Marianne occasionally chiming in. Ellen remained quiet, watching the interaction with interest. Marcus complimented the young ladies in nearly every word he said to them and offered them each his most charming smile when they spoke. The unmarried ladies, for their part, blushed prettily and fluttered their eyelashes at him.

Ellen believed what people said of his ability to flirt. An odd sensation in her stomach discomforted her, and she found herself holding her utensils too tightly. Although she discouraged Marcus's flirting with her, it occurred to Ellen that he could well continue the practice where other ladies were concerned.

Perhaps Marianne realized the same thing, as she looked from Ellen to Marcus with greater frequency before trying to draw Ellen into the conversation. "Miss Bringhurst, I believe you have a sister residing near London."

Miss Wright took the bait before Ellen could say a word. "Oh, yes! Dear Miss Dorothea—whom we must now speak of as Mrs. Dalton. What a lovely name. Dorothea Dalton. We came out around the same time, of course, but I believe all the Bringhurst sisters have had their seasons in Bath?" Her single arched eyebrow communicated a vast deal of meaning in that question.

"Indeed, we have," Ellen agreed with a pleasant smile. "Though it may not be as fashionable as London, nor as large, we have always enjoyed our time there. All three of my sisters married relatively quickly, two settling near my family's home, so my mother has always been pleased with the town." To allude strongly to the marriage market in mixed company might be generally frowned upon, but Ellen did not enjoy being slighted for her family's lack of clout.

Marcus spoke next, his expression as polite and charming as it had been throughout the discussion. "The Bringhursts ought to be pleased. Their daughters are accomplished and lovely. It is no great surprise to me that they did as well in Bath as anywhere. It is likely they could have stolen the hearts of many a London gentleman had they gone there."

Meeting his gaze, Ellen wondered if his compliment extended towards her and could not decide one way or the other. "That is very kind of you to say, Mr. Calvert."

He appeared amused with her unaffected response. "It is the truth, Miss Bringhurst."

Marcus held her with his eyes longer than necessary, causing her heart to flutter. He spoke with more sincerity than she'd heard from him since the Wrights' arrival. But she tucked that thought away swiftly.

"All this talk of London," Collin interjected suddenly, "does not sit well with me. We are to travel there soon enough, and then it will be all business and too many social engagements." He shuddered. "If I could remain here in the country forever, I would. I find it much more pleasant."

Miss Wright hid a giggle behind her hand. "That is because you are married, dear Lord Falkham. We *young*, unmarried people must look forward to the spectacle and enjoyment. London is exciting and presents many opportunities to renew acquaintances, attend glorious balls, and possibly—" she glanced towards Marcus, "— partake in romance."

"I completely agree with you, sister." Miss Verity turned her attention to Marcus as well. "Do you look forward to your time in London, Mr. Calvert? Your family hosts the most wonderful balls and concerts."

Marcus's smile remained, but the light in his eyes dimmed. Ellen saw the change immediately. Could the mention of his family be an irritant because of his mother's stipulations? Or was something else causing him to lose his cheer?

"My mother enjoys entertaining a great deal, though possibly she does too much on occasion." They were the first words he uttered without adding a compliment on the end of them. Ellen glanced about but saw that no one else noticed the change in his demeanor.

Miss Verity sighed and fluttered her long, dark eyelashes in Marcus's direction. "I am certain she longs for the day when a daughter-in-law might take over the role of hostess."

Ellen saw the knuckles of his right hand go white as Marcus's hold on his fork tightened, though that perfectly amicable smile remained. "You are likely right. Of course, we all hope my brother finds it in his heart to take another bride, though we yet mourn Lady Abigail in our hearts." His tone had dropped several degrees in warmth.

The two young ladies looked confused and the conversations faltered for a moment.

Ellen took it upon herself to bring levity back to the table. "Miss Verity, tell me more of that novel you mentioned. It sounds very entertaining and I would enjoy hearing about it in detail."

The young woman smiled gratefully and launched into an animated description of the novel, the horrid villains, true love, and Ireland as a less than ideal setting for such a *romantic* tale. Only when she had warmed considerably to her topic did Ellen chance a glance at Marcus again.

His attention appeared to be focused on the vibrant Miss Verity. But she could see his jaw working in a manner which suggested that he mulled quite a different subject in his mind. He caught her looking and his lips twitched. Marcus winked at her.

Ellen looked away, determined not to be flirted with.

The meal ended with Marianne proclaiming her fatigue and wish for a nap, the Wrights took their leave with an invitation for Marcus to visit soon. They added Ellen to the invitation belatedly, as she was a guest in the neighborhood as well. Ellen thanked them and excused herself while claiming fatigue as Marianne had.

Being in a room with either of the Wrights much longer would test her patience past politeness.

CHAPTER 7

Ellen did not go to her room, though Marianne certainly disappeared and her husband with her, but she went to the library. When Collin's father had been alive, he made it a point to tell Ellen she could treat the books as her very own when she visited. She adored her uncle for that and spent many hours of her childhood curled up in a chair beside a window, learning of distant lands and reading of things no one would ever speak to a child about.

She walked along one row of shelves, her finger sliding beneath the titles of books she knew as old friends, and paused when she came to a translation of an old Italian anatomy book. Her lips twitched as she recalled blushing through that one, turning pages and learning more about the human muscular structure than any lady ought to know.

When she went home that summer, she worked up the nerve to ask her father to take her to one of the surgical theaters in London. Anyone could observe surgeries, autopsies, and the like, whether they intended to become a doctor or not. While her father pretended to consider it, her mother flew into a tirade on proper behavior and threatened to end Ellen's ability to visit the Falkham family if that was the sort of thing encouraged in their home.

"That is a faraway sort of smile," a deep voice said from the doorway.

"Marcus," she greeted him, her voice quieter than necessary, still wrapped warmly in her childhood memories. She didn't turn around immediately, trying to compose herself. Keeping her feelings in order would be difficult if he kept surprising her with his presence.

"I was thinking of Uncle Falkham. Missing him." Ellen turned towards him and clasped her hands before her. "Have you not disappeared to take an afternoon nap?"

"If I did nap, I would then be up half the night. Napping is a terrible practice for anyone not of a delicate constitution." Marcus fully entered the room, leaving the door open behind him, and came to stand near her. Looking at the bookshelves behind her, he appeared amused. "Ah, the medical section. Will you be concocting healing salves for the lot of us?"

"I'm not terribly knowledgeable about such things. Why?" She attempted to smile, though his sudden nearness made her feel a trifle unsteady. "Have you need of a remedy?"

Marcus appeared thoughtful for a moment and shook his head. "I suppose not. But you never know when one might be useful."

Ellen studied him openly, unabashedly, noting the slight curl of his hair. He kept it trimmed shorter than fashion dictated and she suspected it was because of that curl. His hair had been redder in their childhood, but now it was darker, more coppery, like a shiny new ha'penny. His eyes were brown, but a lighter shade than her own. And while he teased her about freckles, she could spot several on his Roman nose and high cheekbones. But they served to make his smiles more charming, lending a bit of boyish mischief to his handsome features.

She did not know how she could avoid falling more deeply in love with him. Would a match between them mean disaster for her? Loving someone who may never love her in return? She could not be sure. But being the wife of a kind, handsome, intelligent man such as Marcus would be a better life for her than any other option she imagined.

"You stare at me in such an intense manner," he said, his tone soft. Marcus tilted his head to the side and studied her back. "Dare I ask what you make of me?"

She shook her head. "I have known you since my childhood, Marcus Calvert. I think I may know you better than you realize. I have been puzzling over our luncheon conversation with the Misses Wright. I think I know what upset you."

He looked away, his smile fading. "I wasn't upset."

"But you were." Ellen did not move, though her hand nearly lifted to touch his arm, to draw him back to her. She quelled that urge swiftly. "I think you did not wish to talk of your brother to young ladies whose minds are on marriage. What I cannot decide is if it is out of some duty to protect him or a measure of envy."

As she spoke he grew tense, and after she waited in silence for a response he sighed and looked back at her. "Maybe it is a measure of both."

Ellen gestured to the wide sofa before the fireplace. "Would you care to sit down, Marcus?"

"If you will join me." He waited for her to take a seat before sitting on the opposite end of the furniture, a plush sofa with enough space for two people to sit comfortably.

He spoke in the same serious tone he'd used in the garden the day before.

"While my brother may be without a wife at present, I believe he will remarry one day and carry on the family line. He will see it as his duty." Marcus folded his arms across his chest, his eyes on the ground before them. "I would not wish to be in his position. Sometimes, people assume as the second born I would prefer to have all that he has. But my brother and I are friends. I want him to be happy and I know he does a credit to his position."

"You do not envy him," she murmured, eyes watching his profile as his brows drew together and a frown appeared where there was normally a smile.

"As I have asked you to share my life and join my family, it is best I explain a few things about myself to you in order to inform your choice." Marcus tilted his head to the side enough to look at her, wearing a smile that did not reach his eyes.

"You need say nothing. I will not press you." Ellen folded her hands in her lap and studied the carpet.

"There will be no secrets between us, should we marry," he said, his voice firm. "I have seen marriages torn asunder under the secrets people keep." He gave her one of his most charming smiles, though it appeared tired.

Ellen's heart rose into her throat.

"I have always been second to my brother in birth, society, and romance. I learned long ago to be a likable person if I wanted people to pay attention to me. The truth is that people prefer the heir. They want an earl on their guest list and an earl paying court to their daughters. I have had young women introduced to me since the first time I stepped into a ballroom, usually with the sole purpose of gaining access to my brother."

"That must be a difficult way to live. Not knowing who cares for you and who cares for your connections. But is that not all society is? Connections?"

"Indeed." His smile returned briefly and he gently squeezed her hand, causing a strange tingling sensation to rush up her arm and into her chest. "It is a game that influences the lives of everyone from the Regent down to the street urchins of London. Who we know, the people we can claim as friends, changes the way we are treated and perceived by others."

It took a great deal of effort to remain breathing calmly, to appear as though sitting near him, speaking in such an intimate manner, did not make her mind spin and the bottom drop from her stomach. Especially knowing, as she already did, how the conversation would end.

"After my brother married Abigail, I noticed a decline in my invitations. Certain young women no longer smiled at me across crowded rooms. I did not entirely care, but I paid attention to who still counted me a friend."

"That would be a difficult thing to experience," she said, watching his expression as he nodded.

"Then Lucas lost Abigail, and the whole family went into mourning. Lucas never looked so broken as he did in the weeks and months after her death. In many ways, he's still broken. I'm protective of him. After a year passed, my invitations increased once more. Mothers smiled again. Young ladies flapped their fans and batted their eyelashes at me. I thought I saw through each and every one of them. I knew their plans. Their hopes."

"Then why encourage them?" she asked, remembering his flirtatious manner at the table that very day. "Why compliment and converse with such familiarity?"

He turned to study her again, his eyes more amused. "Because everyone in society performs and my role is to please others by saying what they most want to hear." He shrugged and sat straighter, at the same time moving closer to her. "I never lie. I flatter. I am amiable and courteous. Besides, I have noted that saying a kind thing to a young woman, especially one used to propping up the walls of a ballroom, can never go amiss. Every lady deserves to feel lovely at a ball."

She narrowed her eyes at him, uncomfortable with his explanation but unable to articulate why, she let it go. "You said you *thought* you saw through those people."

"Your attention to detail does you credit. Yes." He cleared his throat and glanced away again.

She could not allow him to guess at her emotions, not when his own were so far from being deciphered. This man wore a mask and acted a part to please people around him.

He didn't need to worry. Ellen already knew she would accept his offer.

"I mistook the motives of one woman. Lady Selene Garrington. She is the daughter of another earl. A woman I knew of but never had spoken to. She went to finishing school on the continent and traveled widely after that. The first time I met her, she didn't seem to know my family name. She is a beautiful, sophisticated woman and I became ensnared quickly." He abruptly came to his feet and began to pace before the couch. "I fell in love with her."

Ellen swallowed away the lump which formed in her throat and tightly folded her hands up again, determined to keep hold over her feelings. "I heard rumors, gossip really, about you forming a serious attachment."

He went to the window and stood, arms folded before him, staring out at the blue sky. "I allowed her into my family's circle. After a season of courtship, I went to her home with the express intention of requesting her hand in marriage."

Though it was hard to hear, Ellen focused on Marcus's expression, on each word he spoke, deciphering as much meaning as she could from all he said. She could read pain in his expression and regret in his tone. Did he still love Lady Selene?

"I learned on that day that my *sweetheart* never entertained any idea of marriage to me. She laughed when I proposed." Marcus's voice grew taut with grief.

How could his offer of love be laughed at? Her heart ached for him.

He turned away from her again, not seeing her reaction and hiding his expression from her. From the hard lines of his posture, Ellen could imagine the discomfort he felt at revealing these details of his life.

She wanted to stop him, to avoid hearing how a woman so unworthy had won his heart, but he continued before Ellen could say a word.

"Lady Selene informed me that I was unworthy. She spent time with me because I amused her, and there was always the chance my brother might take notice and want her for himself." He took in a deep breath and expelled it slowly.

"This is why ladies like the Wrights upset me with casual mentions of my brother. I know they see me as a way to get to him. To women of substance and breeding, I will never be the first choice for a husband."

But he could ask someone as insignificant as Ellen for her hand and have at least a hope that she would accept.

While that thought smarted, Ellen couldn't deny it made sense. She neither had ambitions for the things society valued or any other prospects for marriage.

If a woman of *real substance and breeding* didn't wish to marry him, then she must be neither of those things. For she wished to marry him, despite knowing all she did about his thoughts on the subject.

Ellen studied her hands in her lap, uncertain of what to say. She could not tell him how she felt. His next words solidified her resolve in that matter.

Marcus spoke into the silence, his voice softer. "I have no intention of entering into a romantic relationship again. I have risked my heart and lost it. I will not promise you more than a fair partnership, working together to build a life which serves a purpose. Building an estate we can leave our children. Assisting our tenants to do the same for their children." He turned to face her, expression earnest.

"You will never want for safety, protection, or companionship. I will be an honorable husband and one day a good father to any children we have. I ask that you honor our vows in the same manner. We've grown up together. We can be friends. But that is all I can give you."

Ellen's heart cracked with each word. To be loved, the thing she most desired, would remain outside of her reach.

She took in a breath and closed her eyes. "I understand."

Ellen rose and ran her hand down her skirts to straighten them and smooth out the ripples from sitting. It took her a moment to build the courage to look up again, meeting Marcus's light brown eyes.

"I have pondered your proposal and I appreciate your forthrightness on the subject. If you are certain you could be content with me as your wife, I'd like to accept your offer and give you my hand in marriage."

The serious look he wore changed to an expression of shock, then melted into relief.

Marcus crossed the room to take up her hands. "Thank you,

Ellen. You are a wonderful woman. I will do all in my power to make you happy." He lifted one hand and kissed it, his lips brushing the bare skin of her knuckles.

Ellen's heart shuddered but she ignored it, pushed her feelings aside, and gently retrieved her hand from him. "Though I am past the age of majority, I would ask that you speak to my father for his blessing."

"I will go and obtain it at once." He walked to the door, giving his words surprising immediacy.

Ellen's heart stuttered. Anxiety struck her. "At once?"

Marcus paused at the doorway and turned back to her, his customary smile in place. "Why delay? If I speak to him now, we can read the banns this Sunday and be married after Christmas."

She balked at his words, her heart racing. "After Christmas? But that's four weeks away!" She shut her mouth abruptly when his eyebrows drew together. The smile remained but he looked confused with her hesitation. "It is not a great deal of time, is all," she stammered. "What of your mother? Your brother? I should like our families to attend."

He came back into the room a few steps. "I think it should do, barring a bad turn in the weather. Ellen, what need have we to wait? If we marry before January we can go to London for the season as husband and wife. It will mean less gossip on the part of society. And you will have a London season at last."

Ellen forced a smile. His reasoning made sense for an arrangement such as theirs. "I suppose the very idea of marriage has taken me by surprise. Are you really leaving now?"

"As quickly as my valet can pack a bag for me. I'll send to the stables to have them ready my horse. I will be there and back again in next to no time." He half-bowed and whirled on his heel to make for the door but stopped at the threshold. "I suppose I should also dash off a note to Mother. She will want to speak to you and make arrangements."

Ellen nodded and raised both hands, making a shooing motion. "Go on, then. You might make it halfway to Oak Lodge before nightfall." Although she wished to say something cleverer, something to make Marcus smile, she bit her lip and watched him leave, this time making it out the door and away from her sight. She waited a few moments longer, to be sure he would not return, before collapsing onto the sofa, all energy drained from her.

While she ought to have been happier than she had ever been, though she should have been rejoicing in obtaining what had been a dream, Ellen experienced a heavy sensation upon her fragile heart, a weight of disappointment instead of the elation she always thought marriage would bring.

It should have been flattering how quickly he wished to gain her father's blessing and have the banns read. But Marcus wanted his inheritance secured. He wanted the wedding behind them when they went to London, to avoid gossip and save them both the bother of a society-sanctioned wedding.

It would not be the marriage she dreamed of for herself in the years before accepting spinsterhood. There would be no spring flowers to decorate a church vestibule. No specially made gown.

Instead, she would pick her favorite dress, add lace where she could, perhaps borrow her mother's pearls, and invite those who would be near enough to attend. Dorothea would not come with a young babe at home. But the others would be there.

Ellen didn't know how long she sat in the library, thinking through her wedding plans and mentally composing a letter to her family. It could not have been long, because Marcus came back into the room with as much haste as he'd left, dressed in travelling clothes with a large coat draped over one arm.

Though her posture had slumped in the time she sat there, she didn't straighten upon his reappearance and stared at him, allowing herself to take in his handsome face and the dimple in his left cheek when he grinned at her.

"Haven't moved, have you?" he asked cheerfully. "I have informed Collin of my departure and its reasons. I think Marianne will likely swoop down upon you if you remain out in the open. Have you any message to send your family? Anything I can tell them?" His eyebrows raised and he leaned forward slightly, antici-pating her words.

Ellen knew she ought to send word of her happiness or give them her love, but she shook her head. "I will not burden you with extra words. Your presence will be confusing enough. You are welcome to tell them I accepted your proposal with no reservations. That ought to help, I think."

His eyebrows drew together, his lips pursed slightly. "Confusing?"

"I think my family planned to keep me to themselves for the foreseeable future." She straightened at last and came to her feet. She saw his cravat looked rumpled. Almost she stepped forward to fix it, but instead she dropped her hands. Fixing a damaged cravat did not sound like something a wife of convenience ought to do. He would muss it while riding, at any rate.

"I will bid you a safe journey, Mr. Calvert." She kept her words light, but she could not entirely bring herself to call him by his Christian name.

"Thank you." His confusion cleared, he bowed once more. "I take my leave of you, Miss Bringhurst." He grinned as he said her name, as though it was a joke between them. Marcus disappeared from the room in another instant and she heard the echo of his boots in the entryway before the large front door of the estate slammed shut.

The house remained silent for several moments and Ellen wondered what she would tell Marianne or anyone else of how her engagement had transpired.

CHAPTER 8

R iding through the night was not an option, but Marcus made it more than halfway to his destination without having to strain his horse. The coaching inn where he found a room was comfortable enough, but he was up before the sun and on the road again.

The sooner he procured permission for Ellen's hand, the better. If he could have the banns read in each of their respective parishes by the coming Sunday, they could marry on December twenty-ninth, before the year was out.

The long ride gave him time to think. While he rushed through his last conversation with Ellen, it did not escape his notice she appeared less than enthusiastic when accepting his proposal. When he went over in his mind all they said, each detail he shared, he understood why.

Collin and Marianne told him how practical Ellen was, and he remembered her being an exceptionally level-headed girl, but at one point she must have had dreams of how her wedding would be, what sort of man she would marry.

Reality had a way of putting aside dreams as easily as an adult putting away a child's playthings.

He arrived at Oak Lodge shortly after the household had taken breakfast. The butler informed him, with nary a smile, that only the Bringhurst gentlemen were at home. This suited Marcus perfectly.

He was shown into a comfortable study, where a fire burned high and warm, and father and son worked bent over a table. They straightened as he was announced and returned his bow.

Never, Marcus thought, had two men looked so confused.

"I am sorry to arrive unannounced, Mr. Bringhurst." Marcus came closer to the table, trying not to smile when the two continued to stare at him. "I know it's been many years since we've met. I believe Master Reginald was still a boy, no more than ten, at the time."

Reginald Bringhurst collected himself, recognition dawning in his eyes. "Ah, yes! Cousin Collin's friend. We met when I went to Aunt Falkham's with Dorothea and Ellen one summer." He held his hand out and Marcus shook it firmly. "Father, this is Mr. Calvert, the brother of Lord Calvert, Earl of Annesbury. He and Lord Falkham have been friends for years."

Even when coming to ask for a lady's hand, he was known first and foremost as the younger brother of an earl. Though it irked him, Marcus kept smiling.

"Ah, yes. The years have seen you grow into a fine man, Mr. Calvert. I did not know you at all. Still more of a boy when last we met." The father now extended his hand and shook Marcus's heartily. "Any friend of our family is most welcome. Are you in the neighborhood for a time?"

Marcus, amused by his welcome, tried to anticipate the confusion Ellen said he would stir with his errand. "No, I plan to leave again after my horse is rested. I have come from the Falkhams' home, actually."

The older man nodded. "Please, Mr. Calvert, sit. Tell us what brings you here."

Marcus waited until his host was sitting behind the desk to take a chair across from him. Reginald leaned against the table and folded his arms, frowning. Though the youth had no part in this conversation, Marcus saw no reason to dismiss him from the room.

Marcus sat on the edge of his seat, leaning forward slightly. "I have come with a very particular mission, Mr. Bringhurst. One which involves your daughter, Miss Bringhurst. Though you may not know it, we often spent time together as children. She joined Collin and I in our games."

"What has any of that to do with your visit today?" The father scratched his chin and sat back more comfortably in his chair. "Has she sent us a message through you? Is she in good health?"

"Miss Bringhurst is in excellent health," Marcus assured him, repressing his smile as best he could. "I have come to ask your blessing on a marriage between Miss Bringhurst and myself."

Reginald took in a sharp breath. His father stared, eyes wide. The man opened his mouth and closed it no less than three times, preparing to speak, only to stop himself. He did not wear a smile and while the look of confusion was brief, it was not replaced with anything more pleasant.

"I am sorry," Marcus said, looking from father to son. "I have given you a shock. I did not expect that." Indeed, he had expected a moment of surprise, then either a line of severe questioning or else happy congratulations.

"You have asked Ellen?" Reginald said when it became clear his father must gather his thoughts. "She accepted you."

"Yes." Marcus directed the answer to the lad, who did smile. At least someone was happy for Ellen.

"Ellen accepted?" Mr. Bringhurst repeated quietly, drawing Marcus's attention back to him. "I'm surprised. I thought she had no wish to marry."

"You did?" Marcus's eyebrows raised. "I'm certain she liked the idea once it was presented." What sort of father would expect his daughter would not wish to have a husband and home of her own?

Sighing heavily, the older gentleman looked to his son. "This is unexpected. Do you know anything of Ellen's wishes?" He turned back to Marcus before the young man could answer. "And how long have you been courting her without my knowledge?"

Ah, a protective father was someone Marcus understood. "It is unexpected for everyone involved, but I hope it is pleasant news. I am in need of a wife. Miss Bringhurst and I happened to be present at the Falkhams' home at the same time, we renewed our acquaintance, and I put the question to her. I find your daughter to be an intelligent, practical sort who meets my requirements for my wife perfectly. I offered her my name and protection, she accepted, on the condition we receive your permission and blessing." He shrugged. "I have written a note to the steward of the estate I will inherit after marriage. He will be sending an accounting of all that I hold by courier, so you may look over things and be assured that your daughter will be well provided for as my wife."

"Being related to an earl will help her in society, too, Father." Reginald came forward to stand behind his father's chair, a half-smile on his face. "Think what this will mean for Ellen. A home of her own, a family. She need not be uncertain of her future."

"Uncertain?" The man blustered, looking up at his offspring and back to Marcus, his eyes wide. "How could she be uncertain? Many families have an unmarried miss who is welcome in every home. She would reside here, throughout the life of her parents. Then possibly go to one of her sisters, should you and your future wife not require her."

Marcus listened in shock. While his suit had not been denied, it certainly wasn't being accepted.

"Mr. Bringhurst, have you objections to my engagement to your daughter? If so, I would like to know. You are keeping me in some suspense." He tapped the arm of the chair, impatient with the man and his strange vision for Ellen's future.

The father stood and paced to the window and back, shaking his head all the while. "I cannot think of a good reason to deny you. I should like to talk to Ellen in person, to be certain of her mind. I give my blessing, contingent on hearing from her this is what she wishes. Reginald, go back with Mr. Calvert as my envoy. Send word on what you find your sister's state of mind to be. If she is well, then we will proceed."

Marcus stood. "Then we must go at once. Have you fresh horses? I would like mine to rest."

Reginald looked surprised. "But you just arrived."

"I know. I would like the banns to be read as soon as possible, in both our parishes as custom dictates. I wish to marry before Parliament convenes."

"A man who knows his own mind. I suppose that is something." Mr. Bringhurst nodded. "Yes, yes. Take our horses. I will dispatch a letter to Ellen's mother to apprise her of the situation. Please, take some refreshment while Reginald prepares for the journey. Quick, boy. Mustn't keep a prospective groom waiting." He sighed deeply and shook his head again. "Very strange business, but nothing should surprise me anymore. Four daughters, married. That will be a feather in Mrs. Bringhurst's cap."

"Indeed." Marcus settled back into his seat. Mr. Bringhurst said little else.

Marcus's body might not thank him for the long hours on horseback, but he would happily travel twice the distance to ensure his future with Ellen and Orchard Hill.

CHAPTER 9

T he week following Marcus's return with Reginald in tow
kept couriers and the postal coach busy traveling between
Ellen and her family. Her mother wrote to her, a short
missive.

*Your sister's time has not arrived yet, and I do not think it will for a
fortnight. If such is the case, I may not be able to attend your wedding. I do
not understand Mr. Calvert's haste, but he must have his reasons. You will do
well as his wife and will be a credit to the family. I give you my blessing. Be
happy, Ellen.*

Ellen's heart fell as she read it, though she recognized her mother's difficult position. A wedding could be gotten through without
much anxiety but the same could not be said for childbirth.

Her father would give her away. And Reginald, and her elder
sisters, would be present.

They had yet to leave for Oak Lodge, though Marcus had deliv-
ered Reginald and left the next day to see to the business of their
marriage. He would make certain the banns were posted and read,
begin work on the legal documents, and see to it Orchard Hill
would be ready for him to take possession.

Ellen would have left for home and her own preparations, but Marcus's mother had announced her intention to call upon Ellen at the Falkham home. Which made sense. Her father was not able to entertain nobility in their house without his wife present, but Collin and Marianne had room and were delighted to host a dowager countess.

Marcus took the time to inform Ellen of that visit before he left to see his steward and solicitor to draw up contracts, the bridal agreement, and check into his affairs to arrange matters before they appeared before the vicar.

Ellen felt more upside-down than anything. Her only comfort was being with Marianne and Reginald as one letter after another arrived and preparations were made for her future mother-in-law to arrive. Marcus's brother sent his congratulations and accepted her invitation to attend the wedding.

Lady Calvert, of course, knew full well why Marcus and Ellen rushed to be wed. She had tightened the purse strings and threatened him into matrimony. The woman might, however, take one look at Ellen and retract the conditions or change them if she found Marcus's choice undesirable.

Ellen didn't think Lady Calvert to be especially cruel or underhanded, as all her memories of the woman were pleasant. But the irrational idea that she would be rejected at once took hold. It took Reginald's cheery disposition and Marianne's kind words to keep her from pacing from morning to night.

The carriage bearing the Earl of Annesbury's crest arrived on December the tenth, two days after the banns had been read. Alerted by the staff, Ellen, Marianne, Collin, and Reginald all waited on the steps for the stately dowager countess to descend from her vehicle and pass judgment upon the prospective bride.

Marianne subtly squeezed Ellen's hand as they stood, watching the Countess emerge wearing a dark purple traveling suit, complete with a hat festooned in black feathers. The woman descended regally and looked up at them with a surprisingly pleasant countenance.

Collin bowed deeply, with Reginald following suit while the

women curtsied. "Welcome, Lady Calvert," he said formally. "Please, allow me—"

"Oh, enough, Collin," she interrupted, making a shooing motion with her hand. "Let us all get inside before we catch our death. I declare, it is much colder here than ever it was in London. Inside we can have a proper discussion." She swept past all of them.

The welcoming party hurried inside to find the dowager countess divested of her coat and gloves.

"It is not sensible to stay out on the stoop in December. Young people of good health never understand such things. Now. Let me look at you, Miss Bringhurst." She folded her hands before her and lifted her chin, not to be put off for even a moment.

Ellen stepped forward, her nerves making her hands shake. She dropped a curtsy and murmured her greeting softly. "I hope your journey was pleasant, Lady Calvert."

"Of course, dear. Good weather made it acceptable." Her ladyship tilted her head to one side, looking Ellen over head to toe. "I must say, you have blossomed into a lovely young woman. Lady Falkham, Miss Bringhurst and I have the need of your parlor."

Marianne looked startled but nodded. "Of course. Shall I have tea sent in?"

"That will be satisfactory," the matron said with a smart nod. "Come, Miss Bringhurst, if you will." She gestured for Ellen to walk beside her, which Ellen hastily moved to do. Though she tried to stop trembling, her anxiety must have been evident, as the dowager reached out to touch her arm as they moved down the hallway. "Do not worry so, dear. I am merely curious, and anxious, to know who my son chose for his bride. I am not willing to go through another hour or more of niceties when you and I could be well on our way to coming to know one another."

Ellen looked askance at the woman. "I suppose that is practical."

"Yes, isn't it?" Lady Calvert looked amused and gestured for Ellen to sit near her on the sofa in the morning room. "Ah, look at this. Marianne has excellent taste."

"I have always liked Marianne's decorating," Ellen acknowledged with a smile, her heart beating rapidly.

"I am interested to see what you will do to Orchard Hill," the dowager said, folding her hands primly in her lap. "It is not so large as this house, but I always found it lovely and comfortable."

Ellen tipped her head to one side, regarding the woman carefully. Did this mean the lady accepted her son's choice? "I am afraid Mr. Calvert has not taken the time to tell me much about Orchard Hill yet."

"Do you call him Mr. Calvert to his face?" the woman asked, eyebrows drawing together, making Ellen's pulse jump. Would the inquisition begin in earnest?

"He has asked me to call him Marcus," she answered truthfully.

The woman nodded and continued. "I remember the girl you were, your hair in a braid and your parasol perpetually lost." She sighed and shook her head, a gentle look in her eyes. "You spent many summers here."

"Most of them," Ellen agreed.

"Your aunt was one of my dearest friends. I don't recall ever meeting your mother. I take it she is not present now?"

Ellen shook her head.

Lady Calvert looked carefully at her. "From what I know of your family, the Falkhams included, you are a good, dependable, honorable group. Would you say that is accurate?"

"Yes, Lady Calvert." Ellen could attest to that much.

"And I remember you are a quiet and clever sort of person. Tell me, will you let my son run roughshod over you or will you stand firm on your decisions and convictions? Do you know your own mind?"

Ellen answered firmly. "I know my own mind, Lady Calvert, and your son has given me his word to show respect for my opinions."

"Good." She relaxed visibly. "I had worried he would run off and marry the first ninny who would have him. But I am pleased by his choice. I think you will do the family credit."

Ellen stared, hardly believing what she heard. "If that was such a great concern, Lady Calvert, why make him choose a bride at all?"

As soon as the words left her mouth, she worried she ought not to have spoken so freely, but the woman's frank manner was both disarming and refreshing.

The dowager countess began laughing, but she softened the sound by reaching out and squeezing Ellen's hand. "Dear child, you will be perfect for him. I suspect my son did act hastily, but he has sound judgment. In time, he will realize what a treasure you are."

She released Ellen with a pat on her fingers. "I will answer your question, as you have been so good to answer mine. Marcus is a good boy, but in the years since his father passed, he has been adrift. From season to season, he flirts from one end of a ballroom to the other. Then he shuts himself away the rest of the year. I have worried for him. I believe he needs to be spurred into action and obligation. He needs a reason to truly thrive. A wife has a way of keeping a gentleman aware of his responsibilities."

If Marcus wanted to shut himself away, that should be his right. Forcing him to marry hardly seemed the appropriate response to his problems. But Ellen bit her tongue rather than voice her thoughts.

"You are not convinced." The shrewd woman reached out and patted Ellen's hands. "You will see. I feel certain of it."

A maid entered with a tea tray.

"Now, Miss Bringhurst, what plans have you for your wedding?"

CHAPTER 10

Marcus arrived at the home of Henry and Margaret Ashby, brother-in-law and sister to Ellen, not long before Lucas's coach came into the yard. The Ashbys were hosting the brothers the night before the wedding. Shortly before dinner, Mr. and Mrs. Ashby politely withdrew to see to their children, giving Marcus and Lucas time to themselves.

"I'm glad you came," Marcus told his elder brother. He leaned against the mantle with one elbow. "Having you present will put me at ease." He hadn't seen Ellen since delivering her brother to her weeks ago, and though letters had been exchanged from Orchard Hill, London, and Oak Lodge, none had been directly from her hand.

What if she'd changed her mind?

Lucas sat in an overstuffed chair, his hands dangling over the armrests. "I cannot imagine why. I believe it is tradition for brothers to be a trial to one another on occasions such as this." He winked, though no smile accompanied the jest. "I should be saying awful things to you about marriage. But as you are forced into the arrangement, I have decided against being unnecessarily cruel."

Marcus's lips twitched at that and he straightened. "That does not sound at all amusing for you. I should tell you, Ellen is a very pragmatic woman. She is intelligent and enters this agreement knowing the whole of my reasons for it. I think we will be content in one another's company."

"Perhaps that is the best way to begin," Lucas said, closing his eyes. "Keep the heart out of it."

"I do believe so. There are no expectations, save what I have explained to Ellen already. Therefore, there can be no let-downs."

"True enough." Lucas cracked one blue-gray eye open. Lucas took after their father in appearance. Marcus inherited his mother's brown eyes while Lucas's were the stormy blue of their father's. "How do you think she will get on in society?"

"I am not overly concerned. She has been raised a gentleman's daughter, took part in Bath society, and carries herself with confidence and grace. Ellen will enter London society with a blank canvas."

"A daunting task for those of us without artistic inclinations," Lucas muttered, closing his eye and settling deeper into his chair. "Has she seen your sketches?"

Marcus drew himself up straighter and cast his gaze into the crackling fire. "No. I don't make it a habit of showing them to people. Especially since I've given it up."

"Then you are not entirely honest with her." Lucas popped both eyes open and sat up. "Are you?"

Marcus shook his head. "They were the scribblings of a bored man. I have no time for them any longer."

"If you are certain." Lucas shrugged and stood, stretching. He took a few steps toward his younger brother and put his hand on Marcus's shoulder, meeting his eyes. "Be careful, Marcus. Guard your heart but know you must be protector of hers. You are responsible for her happiness. Loving one's wife is a good thing."

"But you advise against it?" Marcus asked, taking in his brother's stern face. He hardly smiled since Abigail's death. Lucas had loved his wife from childhood and losing Abigail not long after their marriage had sunk Lucas into a hole he struggled to crawl out of again.

"Love is sweet while it lasts. But when it is taken away, there is nothing more painful than its absence. I will not advise you one way or the other, except to tell you to be kind to your wife."

Marcus nodded and his brother squeezed his shoulder once more before letting go and moving to look out the window.

"You will go to Orchard Hill?"

"Immediately following the wedding breakfast." Marcus came to stand next to his brother. "It is past time for things to be taken in hand. I have already visited. While I cannot say Orchard Hill has been neglected, I also cannot say that it thrives."

"How long will you be there?"

"A few weeks. Long enough to get things settled. Then I must come to London and allow my wife to enjoy a season while we support you in Parliament. But I would much prefer to stay in the country."

"You would disappear into the hills forever if we let you. I think that must be one of the reasons Mother wanted you wed."

Marcus rolled his eyes. "One among many. It is incredible how she believes taking a wife will cure me of all my ills."

Lucas clicked his tongue against the roof of his mouth. "Mother is always right, Marc."

Marcus laughed for both of them. "Then I suggest you make haste to leave as soon as possible after the wedding, lest she decide you need the same treatment as I."

Lucas remained sober in his expression, but his eyes glittered for a moment. "She has no power over me, I'm afraid. If I marry again, it will be because I wish to. The idea of another in Abigail's place—" He stopped speaking and cleared his throat, looking away.

"I know." Marcus would have said more, but their hosts returned with the announcement that dinner awaited them.

Marcus sensed Lucas didn't entirely approve of his decision to wed without love. But what would Lucas have him do? Love simply hurt too much.

CHAPTER 11

T he day of the wedding dawned bright. Ellen woke in her bed chambers at Oak Lodge for the last time. It had been decided that Marcus and Lucas would stay at Margaret's home, Lady Annesbury would stay at Oak Lodge, and the Falkhams were with Teresa. Guest rooms were in short supply, but not many other family members would make the journey for a small church wedding. They would wait for a more spectacular event in London, which Marcus's mother promised would be the talk of the season.

Ellen did not spend a moment lolling about but rang for a maid at once. The wedding would be held immediately following morning services and the final reading of the banns.

One of the upstairs maids appeared with a small tray of chocolate and muffins. The wedding breakfast would be a grand affair, but Ellen didn't think it wise to wait to eat. She needed her wits about her. Besides, the memory of her sister Dorothea fainting from hunger and nerves the morning of *her* wedding had made a strong impression upon Ellen.

Marcus wanted to marry her because of her practicality. Practical brides ate something before their wedding.

After eating, Ellen allowed the maid to do her hair up in

ringlets, piled elegantly atop her head. She liked the effect, though she well knew her wedding bonnet would cover most of the efforts. She stepped into her best gown, made over with some silver ribbons, and the maid helped her tie and tuck everything into place. A deep blue cape went over the ensemble. Her light blue slippers were the last thing she put on, tying the ribbons about her ankles.

Her mother's last missive returned to her thoughts. Dorothea had yet to deliver.

Write down everything about this day and keep your thoughts close. A woman's wedding is a precious treasure to hold onto for the rest of her life.

Though nothing of great consequence had occurred yet, Ellen went to her writing desk and found her commonplace book. Normally, she recorded philosophical thoughts or notes on her studies. Today, it would have to do as a sort of diary, too.

Upon opening the small book, where she recorded the words of philosophers and ideas from men of science, her gaze fell upon a quote recorded but two months previous, from Shakespeare.

She will die if you love her not, And she will die ere she might make her love known...

When first she read the words, she thought them beautiful and worthy of remembrance, a clever witticism on the state of one in love. Circumstances had changed since then. The words delved into her heart and soul, removing her ability to form a sentence of her own.

Ellen closed the book and put it back into the writing desk. "See to it this is placed in the carriage to go with me to Orchard Hill," she directed the maid, laying her hand flat on the wood.

She took one last look at herself in the glass and went out the door, determined not to be nervous. Servants moved about, between their staircase and the room for Lady Calvert. She found her brother in the entryway, seated on a covered bench, reading.

He glanced up when he saw her and stood, a wide smile on his face. "Happy wedding day, Ellen. I did not think you would be ready early. Isn't a bride supposed to take a great deal of time before a mirror?"

Ellen hesitated before answering, still shaken by the words she read. "Do you think I ought to do something more to my appearance?" She bit her lip and looked down to adjust the fingers of her gloves. "I thought I looked well."

"Ellen," Reginald said softly, reaching out to still her hands. "Ellie."

Her gaze darted up to see him smiling at her, his eyebrows furrowed. "You have not called me that since you were a boy," she murmured, looking into his deep brown eyes.

He lifted one shoulder in a shrug and dropped his chin. "I may not call you that again, either, now that you join the ranks of esteemed married ladies."

She laughed and squeezed his hands. "Call me whatever you wish, Reggie. For I will not hesitate to use any number of pet names before your wife someday."

He chuckled and stepped back, taking her in. "Back to your question. I believe you look beautiful and I am surprised it did not take you long to achieve it. You have always been pretty."

"You are a sweet brother," she answered. "But you and father are the only men who have ever bothered to pay such a compliment."

"Which I have never understood." Reginald sat down and gave the bench a pat so she would join him. "I hope you hear such things every day from now on. Marcus must think you good looking to go through all the trouble of marrying you." Though he said it lightly, a sparkle in his eye, Ellen wondered how he could tease about such a thing. Perhaps it was a moment of youthful dreaming on his part.

She gave his hand a pat and then leaned back against the wall, careful of her bonnet.

He looked up the staircase. "How much longer do you think our esteemed guest will be?"

"I haven't the slightest idea. But our carriage should be at the door soon. Where is Father?"

"Here," said a voice as their father appeared from around the corner, coming from his study. "I have been looking through the library and wondering which books I ought to send to Orchard

Hill. Most of the new additions have come from your recommendations. It hardly seems fair that you are leaving those behind."

He came and stood before her, looking her up and down, then nodded smartly. "You make a charming bride, Ellen." He held his arms out and she stood to enter his embrace. "My girl. You know, I thought I would keep you here to read to me in my old age and debate the finer points of politics and poetry." He released her slowly and looked down with a stern expression, though Ellen thought his eyes looked suspiciously bright. "Calvert should be grateful to have you, and if he is not, you remind him of your estimable qualities."

Ellen could laugh at that, feeling her eyes moisten. "Which qualities are those, Papa?"

"Your kindness, consideration, intelligence, and gentility all lend themselves well to whatever you put your mind to." He punctuated his statement with a kiss on her cheek.

A rustle on the stairs brought their attention to Lady Annesbury, descending with grace. "Gracious, I hope I have not kept you," she said. "I did not know everyone would be ready this early."

"Not at all, Lady Annesbury," her father said with a brief bow. "Have you sent for your carriage?"

"Yes, it ought to be ready."

A footman appeared at that moment, confirming both carriages were outside the front door.

"Then we had better be off," Lady Annesbury announced, pulling her cloak around her. "Ellen, I must say, your wedding attire is perfectly suited to you." She reached out and squeezed Ellen's arm gently, nothing artificial in her smile. "I think Marcus will be pleased. You look lovely."

"Thank you." Ellen took in a deep breath and gave her father her arm. "It's time."

Her father led them out the front door to the waiting carriages. Normally, even in cooler weather, they walked the short distance to church to save the trouble of keeping the horses standing during services. But her father would not countenance such a thing on her wedding day. They arrived in good time, with hardly a moment to speak on more than the weather. They went in to the family pew and Ellen looked around for her bridegroom.

Marcus stood along the opposite wall of the church, engaged in conversation with her sister Margaret. The moment she saw him, his hair shining copper in the morning light, his posture sure and his charming grin in place, her heart picked up speed. He looked up and saw her, his eyes sweeping her form briefly before he sent her a gentle smile. Margaret touched his arm, pulling his attention back to whatever she was saying.

The vicar entered, signaling the start of services. Marcus looked toward her again and offered an apologetic smile, shrugging his shoulders. Ellen returned the gesture and then faced forward, determined to remain calm and collected, while her heart raced inside her chest.

Even if she did not marry for love, and Marcus had no intention of allowing such feelings into their arrangement, Ellen could find contentment in their partnership.

The vicar's sermon felt like it went on much longer than usual. Yet the priest said, at the last, "And now, for the most choice of sermons, we have the blessing of witnessing the marriage vows between the Honorable Mr. Marcus Calvert and our own Miss Ellen Bringhurst. The wedding couple invites all who wish to attend to stay and bear witness."

Ellen rose on the arm of her father and noted that no one took the opportunity to leave. The members of their community looked on with warmth and smiles. She saw the Falkhams seated in a pew behind her, and her sisters sat in their customary places next to their husbands. She wished her mother and Dorothea might have come.

Marcus joined her at the front of the church, gently accepting her arm from her father. Then he took the last step with her to stand before the vicar.

Ellen tried to pay attention to each and every word as the vicar recited from the Book of Common Prayers. But she kept glancing at Marcus, standing straight and firm beside her. He looked every inch the perfect groom, from his freshly-cropped hair to his polished black shoes. He wore a suit of deepest blue with a gold vest. His snow-white cravat was tied in an elegant, cascading fashion with a sapphire stickpin holding it in place.

At last came the vows and Ellen's heart stuttered.

"Wilt thou love her, comfort her, honor, and keep her, in sickness and in health; and, forsaking all others, keep thee only unto her, so long as ye both shall live?"

"I will." Marcus said those two words evenly, without reservation, promising something he told her he could never give.

Ellen had not thought of the vows until that moment.

She wanted to wilt where she stood. Draw back, declare it could not be so. Instead, she murmured her own promise. "I will." But it must have been loud enough to satisfy the vicar. He did not even pause in his recitation.

Ellen would keep her vows. She already loved Marcus, after all.

Marcus took her hand and repeated after the minister, looking her directly in the eye as he spoke. "I, Marcus James Calvert, take thee, Ellen Bringhurst, to be my wedded wife, to have and to hold from this day forward, for better or worse, for richer or poorer, in sickness and in health, to love and to cherish, till death us do part, according to God's holy ordinance; and thereto I plight thee my troth."

Ellen's knees went weak and her mouth dry. Could she really give herself to him, hearing such beautiful vows and knowing they were not true? How could he cherish her without love?

She said her part without thinking on it. She repeated as she was bade, held out her hand to receive her ring, knelt and bowed her head as the minister prayed over them, giving his blessing and God's on their union.

The wedding ceremony went on and on, with Ellen doing her best to keep her eyes trained straight ahead. Could she fulfill her vows without love?

Marcus must've sensed her wandering thoughts—he gave her arm a gentle squeeze, bringing her back enough that she glanced at him. His lips twitched slightly and his eyes met hers, amusement twinkling in them.

How could he be amused at this, the most serious moment of her life?

Ellen's spine stiffened and her eyes darted back to the vicar, her whole body attuned to his every word. Here she had stood, taking the situation most seriously, losing herself in thought of how to accomplish all she promised, and he looked as though he were enjoying the whole thing as some sort of show.

The vicar finished at last and put his final blessing upon them and presented them to the congregants as husband and wife. The music began, the people assembled raising their voices in a final hymn.

Ellen and Marcus followed the vicar into the rectory where they signed the church register. Ellen realized it would be her last time to sign her maiden name, Ellen Bringhurst, on any document. From now on, she would be Ellen Calvert.

Her head threatened to set the world to spinning, but Ellen tamped down on the odd sensation.

"I thought we lost you in the middle of the sermon," Marcus said as they stepped back into the chapel. "Your eyes looked far beyond the church. What were you thinking about?"

Ellen eyed him for a moment before adjusting her bonnet. "I was thinking that we were both making a great deal of promises and that I must be sure to remember them all." She pulled her cape closer about her and looked out the church doors where she could see her family and neighbors gathered, a small arbor held up by her brothers-in-law for them to walk beneath. "We should hurry. All those poor people in the cold are waiting on us."

He leaned forward, trying to catch her eye, but she ignored him and put her hand on his arm. "My sisters shouldn't stand in the weather overlong."

He made a sound of agreement and escorted her outside. Cheers erupted around them, ladies waved handkerchiefs, the arbor was hoisted upward. Ellen glanced up at Marcus to see him offering a large grin to the crowd, waving his free hand at everyone, whether he knew them or not. As though he was incredibly happy.

Gaining his inheritance must mean a great deal to him.

She forced her smile but kept her head ducked as they climbed into the carriage. Marcus settled in beside her, tucking a carpet around their legs after the door swung shut. "One more ordeal before we can go home," he said cheerfully, sharing his smile with her.

Was that all it had been to him? An ordeal? Of course. It was a necessary step to gain what he most wanted. His inheritance. "The breakfast. Yes. We need not stay long, if you wish."

"These are your neighbors," he said, sitting back in his seat. "I think you ought to determine the time spent with them."

She waved a hand dismissively, turning her attention to the window of the carriage. "It need only be enough for us to eat a little. I would like to get our journey underway as soon as possible." The trip to Orchard Hill would take a total of twelve hours on the road, should the weather stay fine, which already necessitated a stop at a roadside inn.

As the carriage turned onto the lane to her father's house, Marcus leaned far enough forward to catch her eye, pulling her attention to him. She looked up into his light brown eyes, surprised by the gentle expression in them. His lips turned upward but his smile felt sincerer and less teasing.

"I must admit, I was nervous this morning. I wondered for a time if you might not come."

Ellen's lips parted in surprise and she knew not what to say.

"You certainly could find a better husband than me, you know," he added, tilting his head to one side as he studied her. "Though I doubt I could find a prettier bride willing to put up with me."

His attempt to set her at ease, his silly compliment, self-effacing as it was, gave her pause.

"Marcus, I promised I would marry you. I always keep my promises," she said, thinking on that twinkling look in his eye before.

"It's over, at any rate. Now we enjoy a meal and go on our way, home to Orchard Hill." He spoke the name of his estate with relish. Ellen smiled in return, a small hope rekindled in her heart.

CHAPTER 12

The journey to Orchard Hill gave Ellen time to reflect on the matters of her heart. They stayed at an inn overnight, in separate rooms joined by a small sitting area. Ellen felt no awkwardness over this, having known the plan ahead of time. Knowing that her husband did not, in fact, think of her in any way other than a friend, also gave her no expectations of consummating their marriage any time soon. Still, it was hard to sleep in a strange bed.

Thoughts of her wedding vows, and Marcus's, kept her wondering if this had been the right thing to do. He did not love her. He professed his intention to never give his heart to another after Lady Selene's ill treatment.

Would Ellen's love be enough to sustain their marriage? Enough for her happiness?

The following morning dawned without any answers.

They rode in relative comfort and enjoyed easy conversations. He told her about the tenants he met, the state of their homes, and the apple orchard from which Orchard Hill took its name. She asked question after question, enjoying his eagerness on the subject.

Just shy of three o'clock in the afternoon, he leaned toward the window and gestured for her to look. She had to lean across him to do so, but Marcus helped to hold her still amid the bumps of the carriage, his arm wrapped around her shoulder.

It was the most he had touched her since she accepted his betrothal, excepting when politeness required he take her arm.

She tried to ignore the way his proximity made her feel. As a married woman, she could not let herself be undone by polite touches such as these.

Looking through the window, she saw a long lane, lined with sleeping apple trees. At the end of the lane, settled on a grassy knoll, was a red brick house. It stood three stories tall, with wide windows and a beautiful four-column porch, larger and grander than Ellen expected.

She held her breath when Marcus helped her from the carriage, directing her eyes upward to the dark slats of the roof and deep green shutters at every window. The driveway was covered in small white stones and the steps leading up to the house were made of brick.

Standing before the house, in a short line of starched aprons and somber colored suit coats, was the household staff. Butler, two footmen, gardener, and under gardener stood on one side. Then there was the housekeeper, two maids, the cook, the cook's assistant, and one familiar face among them, standing barely behind the housekeeper.

Ellen felt her heart lift at the sight of Sarah, the maid from Marianne's home, smiling shyly at her.

Marcus leaned closer to her. "I thought you would be pleased. She was eager to come and be of service to you."

Ellen could not speak her thanks but cast him what she hoped was a grateful smile. He led her to the housekeeper.

"Mrs. Calvert, I would like to introduce you to Mrs. Burk, a fine housekeeper if ever there was one."

It was the first time she heard her new name. At last she'd no longer be the last Miss Bringhurst. She was forever linked to

Marcus, as his wife. She had little time to dwell on the pleasant thought.

Mrs. Burk dipped a respectful curtsy. She had graying hair pulled back into a soft bun and wore a deep blue gown suitable to an upper-level servant. There were lines around her eyes and when she smiled Ellen could see the beginnings of wrinkles at her mouth.

"It is an honor to meet you, ma'am," she said in a sweetly maternal voice.

Ellen's confidence lifted. This woman, she hoped, would be a good partner in managing the household.

"Thank you, Mrs. Burk. I look forward to working with you. Will you please introduce the rest of the staff?"

Each person respectfully welcomed Ellen to her new home, and she did her best to remember their names and faces.

"After you are settled, we will send refreshment to your rooms," Mrs. Burk informed Ellen after the final maid curtsied. "If that is satisfactory."

"Yes, I think that will do." Ellen glanced at Marcus to see him in conversation with the butler. "For now, I think we all ought to get in out of the cold."

"A wise idea, Mrs. Calvert." The housekeeper had a warm manner Ellen immediately liked. She allowed Ellen to lead the way back into the house, after Marcus rejoined her and gave her his arm.

Ellen imagined that entering a fairy ring could feel no less magical than the first time she stepped over the threshold into her home. Orchard Hill *belonged* to her in a way no other place ever had. Here, she was mistress.

The floors were dark, well-polished gray stones. The entry hall stretched all the way to the back of the house, where a wide window would allow the early morning sun to light the open space. The walls were covered in soft-yellow paper with a green leaf pattern. A few objects hung upon them, paintings of landscapes. A set of stairs grew upward, slightly curving as they went, hiding the first-floor landing from view. They were bright, polished wood with a green carpet running across the middle of each step.

A table stood a short way from the door, and upon it several small portraits of people she knew must be family. She recognized a drawing of Marcus, due to the red-colored curls on the boy's head and the brown eyes. A mirror hung over the table, giving her the opportunity to inspect her appearance. The rosy color of her cheeks surprised her, but she gave her reflection a pleasant nod. Was the delight in her eyes really so apparent?

"Come, Ellen." Her husband extended his hand to her and Ellen turned to meet his curious stare. He guided her to the stairs. "I hope to give you a tour this evening. But what do you think so far?"

She let her hand trail along the railing as they ascended, her eyes taking in every detail around her. "I think it's beautiful," she said.

He nodded, but his expression didn't change.

Ellen halted when they came to the landing and he stopped as well. "Marcus, truly. It's such a lovely house. I am looking forward to coming to know every inch of it and making it my own, but I already feel such peace here."

His uncertain eyes searched hers, the lines around them softening. "I'm glad. If you found it lacking, I would feel like the very worst sort of man. It isn't as grand as my family's other holdings."

She shook her head and allowed some of her excitement to show, turning her widest smile up at him. "It is perfect for me, Marcus. I wouldn't know what to do with a *grand* holding. But I think I will come to love this new home with all my heart."

Marcus's gaze never left hers and as she spoke, a light sparked within his eyes. He picked up her hand in both of his and brought it to his lips, kissing the back of it in a gesture so full of tenderness and gratitude that Ellen's whole body felt the impact of his lips against her skin.

It took all her willpower not to yank her hand away, or worse, lean into him.

How could he? she wondered, trying to ignore the way her insides felt, as if she'd swallowed feathers that tormented her with a tickling sensation she could not escape. Ellen didn't want him to act affectionate when they both knew, as he had taken pains to tell her, that this could not be a relationship based on emotions.

He lowered her hand and cast her another odd look. The light in his eyes dimmed and he cleared his throat, gesturing down the hallway on their right. "That way are the upstairs family rooms." Then he pointed down the hallway to the left. "Those are the family and guest chambers. Would you like me to show you to your room?"

Ellen nodded. "Yes, please."

Marcus went down the hall, not taking her arm or hand again, and she followed a step behind. They passed several doors before he stopped and laid his hand against one. He stared at the wood as he spoke.

"I didn't give the staff much notice, and I wanted you to feel you could change whatever you like about the room—the whole house. But I did offer some suggestions here that I hoped would make you comfortable."

The admission from him sounded vulnerable, but Ellen didn't have time to puzzle that out before he'd turned the handle and pushed the door open, gesturing with one hand for her to step inside.

Ellen barely made it two steps inside before she froze, looking around her with delight. Her windows faced east, so the light coming in through the curtains was not overly bright in the waning afternoon light.

The walls were papered in soft blue, the mantel made of white stone. A vase of hothouse roses was on the mantel. But all of that, while lovely, did not capture her attention the way the bookshelves on either side of the hearth did. And before the fire, ready and waiting for her, was an armchair covered in yellow fabric with bursts of white roses. The bookshelves were half-filled, with volumes bright and new, and beautiful baubles. She approached to make a closer inspection.

She opened a small box of polished wood and found a delicate pair of lace gloves inside. A tiny clock sat on one shelf, an empty basket on another, and a tiny elephant on a taller shelf. Her fingers touched the spines of the books as she read the titles, some known to her and others new. She turned to where Marcus stood in the doorway, leaning against its frame with his arms crossed.

"It's beautiful. Bookshelves, in my bedroom?"

"You are welcome to move them if you wish. We have a small library. But I thought you might want to keep your favorites, or your current studies, nearby." Marcus lifted one shoulder in a shrug.

"Thank you, Marcus."

She saw her trunk already on the floor, as the footmen had brought it up directly after their welcome by the front doors.

"I have a gift for you, too. Though it feels silly and small now." She hurried to kneel by her trunk, unlatching it.

"That isn't necessary. You being here has given me Orchard Hill."

Ellen lifted her writing desk out of the way. "What kind of a bride would I be if I didn't give my bridegroom a wedding gift?" she asked. She found what she searched for and lifted out a large leather portfolio and a small wooden box, then stood and approached him, keeping her eyes down.

"I couldn't think what you might wish for, but this reminded me of you. I know you said you don't sketch anymore, but I thought you might wish to take up the practice again." Ellen held the sketchbook and pencil box out to him. She darted a look up to see what he made of the gesture, her heart very nearly in her throat.

Marcus's expression confused her. His eyebrows were drawn together, but he wore a crooked smile. As he accepted the gifts, his fingers brushed hers, reminding her of the kiss on her hand.

"This is very thoughtful, Ellen," he said, his voice betraying neither pleasure nor annoyance. "Thank you."

Ellen's heart fell and she released her hold on the book. He would not use it, she knew, and Ellen could not decide if she was more disappointed in her inability to please him or his refusal to use what she knew must be a very real talent.

"I remember your sketches," she said, lowering her eyes to his cravat. "They were beautiful, when we were children."

"Thank you." He tucked the book beneath his arm and kept the pencil case in his hands. "I'm going to freshen up. My room is next to yours, that way." He nodded down the hall. "If you need anything, there is a bell-pull next to the bed and Sarah should be waiting in your dressing room."

"Dressing room?"

He pointed over her shoulder to a door near one of the bookshelves. She hadn't noticed it before.

"Oh. Thank you."

Marcus nodded again and pulled the door shut as he left.

Ellen stepped forward and leaned against the door, taking in her perfect bedroom again.

"Stop trying, Ellen," she whispered to herself. "Be the woman he wants you to be. Useful. Sensible."

It was hardly sensible for a newlywed woman to cry. Ellen forced herself to square her shoulders and went in search of Sarah to restore her appearance.

This home is mine, Ellen reminded herself, taking in the room with one sweeping glance. *And I will be happy here.*

～

MARCUS WAITED for Ellen in the upstairs drawing room, thinking over their recent interactions. Their wedding vows still weighed on his heart. Why had he never paid attention to that list of promises made before God and man? He had attended several weddings, but since the words were never said by him he had not given them enough notice.

Wilt thou love her.

When had that been written? What did it mean? Romantic love had been a chance thing until the last few decades. His parents had been part of an arranged marriage, and they got on well enough. Had they made the same promises of love when they barely knew each other?

Then there was Ellen's declaration after the service. *I always keep my promises.*

Did she mean their wedding promises?

Marcus shook away the thoughts as best he could, pacing

from the irritating crackle of the logs in the fire to the window and back again. Their promises hadn't bothered him until he arrived at the house with her. That was when it struck him, holding her hand to help her down from the carriage, that their vows sealed them together for good or ill for the rest of their lives.

He looked at Orchard Hill with new eyes. Was it enough to present to a bride? It was not even so large as the home she had been brought up in. Oak Lodge was statelier than his inherited home.

As brother to an earl, it would be his duty to remain part of society without ever holding title or rank, to reflect well on Lucas and the family. But he would have none of their wealth or importance.

He could not even give his wife love, though he'd promised it in the church the day before.

Then he watched Ellen's reaction when she saw their home.

Ellen's lovely face had born an expression that nearly took his breath away. Her eyes shone with a joy that returned his pride to him. The house did not disappoint her. She retained that look of near-awe when they walked inside, an energy radiating from her that nearly put his fears to rest.

The house pleased her, he thought with a measure of comfort.

His addition to her room, the bookcases, delighted her.

And suddenly, without warning, Marcus wondered if *he* pleased her. Yes, she made the choice to wed him, but would she ever look at him with such unabashed joy as she did at so simple a thing as shelving?

That isn't what I want. Theirs was a practical arrangement. *Nothing more.*

A soft knock preceded her entrance. Marcus turned to face the door as Ellen stepped in, no longer in her travelling clothes, but wearing a dress of deep blue. Her bonnet was gone, replaced with a bandeau to tame her black hair. When his stare met hers, Ellen's cheeks pinked and she wasn't smiling.

Possibly she was upset by his reaction to her gift. He'd put the sketchbook in the study's desk, with no intention of using it, though touched by her thoughtful gesture.

"It is nearly dinner time," she said, not stepping fully inside.

Marcus beckoned her forward. "Then we should begin our tour here. It will not take long, I'm afraid."

"It might," she said, coming three steps inside. "I may wish to take in every detail, you know, as I am to be mistress." She sniffed and raised her nose in the air, giving him a narrow-eyed look that surprised a laugh out of him.

Relieved, he responded with honesty. "You *are* mistress here, Ellen. From the moment you agreed to marry me. This is your domain." He dropped his shoulders and raised a hand to rub the back of his neck while he looked around them. "This is the drawing room. When I was growing up, it was where the family always sat together before and after mealtimes."

"It's lovely." He watched as Ellen took it in, looking from one side of the room to the other. "Though very lavender."

"I believe it is my mother's favorite color."

Her lips quirked upward at that. "Mine is blue."

"Then we will have it done over in blue."

If his quick statement surprised her, she didn't let it show. "The windows face west?"

"Yes." He glanced around and then came forward, waving to the hall. "Would you like to see the rest of the first floor? Then the ground floor, and the second floor after dinner?"

"Yes, please." She stepped through the door into the passage and looked both directions. "How many bedrooms are there?"

"Four, on this floor, then two smaller rooms adjoining the nursery upstairs." Her cheeks flushed and it took him a moment to realize why. Then he felt heat creeping up the back of his neck. He cleared his throat and stepped into the hall. "But they are all modest rooms. There is one dressing room, between your bedchamber and mine."

He showed her each of the public rooms and she looked about with interest, asking the occasional question about portraits or what the views from the windows were like. The sun had set shortly after their arrival, preventing him from showing her the grounds. He took her to the ground floor, showing her his study adjacent their small but comfortable library. Marcus could tell his wife would've lingered in that room for the rest of the evening, but he showed her a larger sitting room, the dining room, and the conservatory.

Though tempted more than once to take her hand, as that would be a natural way to guide her through the halls, Marcus was careful not to touch his wife. Her reaction to his kiss on the back of her hand, when all he'd meant to do was show how pleased he was she liked the house, stayed with him. She had not seemed to care for the familiarity of his touch.

The butler, Matthews, found them in the hall staring at a painting of a mountain neither could guess the location of.

"How could you not know where this is meant to be?" Ellen asked, hands clasped behind her as she studied the rocky ridges.

"I only spent a few weeks here every year," he said in his defense. "Mostly as a boy. Why would a boy ask about a painting when there are trees to climb and streams to play in?"

"I shall write to your mother and inform her of your complete lack of knowledge. Shameful." The pronouncement was made with a grave tone, but when she looked over her shoulder, Ellen's eyes held a teasing glint.

"Mr. Calvert, Mrs. Calvert," Matthews said. "Dinner is served."

"Ah. Thank you. Shall we, Mrs. Calvert?" He offered his arm and she took it after bobbing a curtsy, completely unnecessary and amusing.

"I would be honored, Mr. Calvert." She threaded her arm through his and Marcus's heart gave an odd sort of twist that he nearly found pleasant. Maybe not all touches would be abhorrent to her. Maybe she was nervous, or shy.

He led Ellen to the dining room with greater confidence.

CHAPTER 13

Marcus went through the notes on the growth and harvest of his apple and pear trees, hardly understanding some of them. The accounts had been provided by the farmers he employed to care for his orchards. He owned three hundred acres of apple trees, one hundred acres of pears.

Having grown up playing in the trees and sampling the fruits, he knew the most basic facts of tending to them. His mother never had an interest in the plants, and his father passed on before he could train either of the brothers to take on Orchard Hill. This meant the task of caring for the land fell to his mother's steward, who never took initiative to try new things and allowed the orchard go on as always.

While he had spoken with each of the three men tasked with ensuring a good growing season, Marcus was lost. They knew their business, but they did not possess many ideas for improving upon it. Marcus must be his own tutor, as no other gentlemen in the area grew trees as he did.

This was a fine time for farming, from all he understood, as advancements in the last several decades had made men wealthy from what had been only fields of food to provide for a family.

A soft knock on the door, characteristic of his wife, interrupted him. "Come in, Ellen." Her company would be a welcome respite from his studies.

The door swung open and his wife of five days put her head around it. "Tea?"

"Yes, please. I'm sorry, I didn't realize the hour." He started to stand, but her head disappeared, and the door came fully open, revealing Ellen carried a full tea tray. Marcus hurried around his desk to help her, but she twisted her waist enough to move the tray from his grasp.

"I have come this far, you may as well let me finish the trip," she said, her narrowed eyes challenging him.

Since their arrival, Ellen had taken the whole house in hand as her own. While he could not say he noticed any radical changes in the running of the staff or other matters, he did see the change in his wife. Ellen remained quiet, her thoughtful nature made that a fixture of her personality, but she acted with a decisiveness he did not know she possessed.

Although he should've, given how swift her decision to marry him had been.

"Let's take tea in the library." He went ahead of her to the adjoining door and pushed it open, allowing her to pass through first.

The library had become Ellen's. Marcus knew she spent part of her morning reading before the fire in her bedchamber, but evenings he found her curled in a library chair.

She put the tray down on the table behind the sofa and prepared their cups. She didn't hum as she worked, nor speak, but moved with a graceful sort of efficiency that he enjoyed watching. He waited until she handed him his cup, then he sat down with his back to her and the tea things.

"How are you this afternoon?" she asked, the slight clink of spoon on cup indicating she still worked behind him. "I've not seen you since breakfast."

"I am well, thank you. What have you been doing this morning?"

"Working in the stillroom, rearranging the music room. Hardly anything worth mentioning. Then I saw the time and knew you would not remember to take any nourishment." She came around the sofa and sat next to him, a pastry in one hand and her cup in the other. "You are single-minded when you work."

A smile tugged at the corners of Marcus's mouth and he shook his head. "I become absorbed in tasks. My mother claims a house could fall down around my ears and I wouldn't notice."

Ellen laughed; the pleasant sound that brought out his grin. "I think I must agree with her. In the days since we've been here, I've had to send people to fetch you out of your study for every meal but breakfast."

"Really?" He chuckled and sat back in his seat, stretching his arm across the back of the sofa. His hand rested above Ellen's shoulder. "I didn't even realize it until now, but you're right. Every afternoon, a maid reminds me of tea, and every evening a footman or Matthews raps on the door to tell me dinner is within the hour. I'll try to do better, Ellen."

"Nonsense," she said, angling her body more towards his. "I admire the way you dedicate yourself to the task at hand and no one is put out by it. You are master here, after all." She raised her eyebrows and hid a smile behind the rim of her cup, but Marcus caught it and grinned back.

"And how are you enjoying being mistress of Orchard Hill?" he asked, drumming his fingers on the back of the sofa, taking in her appearance with appreciation. Ellen's self-possession, her satisfaction, were evident in the way she held herself. During the day, he saw her move with purpose through the house, directing the servants with kindness. She was nearly always smiling, too.

"It's wonderful," she admitted, her cheeks turning pink. Ellen's eyes lit up as she told him about the music room and how she had rearranged it to suit her tastes. That was something else he liked, that her practicality thus far had lent itself to making improvements in the rooms without asking for extra funds, though he had expected there to be a more immediate need for purchases.

"What of your improvements to the library?" he asked, looking around the room. "I don't see any changes."

"I haven't decided on any yet." She reached over the couch to put her cup down on the table behind them, her arm brushing across his. Marcus felt a tingling sensation run through him at the contact, brief though it was. He quickly pulled his arm back, running his hand through his hair to try and make the movement appear more natural.

Days into this marriage and I'm as disconcerted as a schoolboy at his first ball. Marcus avoided her eyes, concerned she might see his thoughts within them. He'd managed not to have more physical contact thus far but being careful had necessitated becoming extremely aware of her nearness. That had to be the reason for the sensation her brief touch had caused.

"It isn't a very large library," he said, his eyes taking in the shelves built into the walls. "But we could add to it. If you like." He glanced at her from the corner of his eye and was rewarded with her expression of obvious pleasure.

"I would, very much. I made a list of titles from my father's library I would dearly love to have. But every time I come in here to catalog your collection, I get distracted and end up reading."

"That will not do," Marcus said, narrowing his eyes and shaking his head in as disapproving a manner as he could manage. "First, you must never call it *my* collection again. It is *ours.*" She lowered her head but he caught her lips turning upward. "Second, a proper catalog is essential to a well-maintained library. Come, I will help you make a start of it. Where are you recording your finds?"

Ellen's head came up and her eyes widened, their warm brown depths full of surprise. "But you are so busy," she said. "I do not wish to bother you with it."

"Nonsense. I could actually use the distraction this afternoon." He stood and went to one corner of the shelves. "Where did you start and how far have you gotten?"

Ellen rose more slowly, with the self-possessed grace he

admired, and went to the mantel where a slim leather notebook rested. She opened it and he saw a pencil inside. "It is nothing very extravagant. I thought to first catalog things then organize a system for recording and shelving the books."

"A good way to start." He held out his hand to receive the notebook from her and their bare fingertips grazed each other. Marcus ignored the spark that jumped from her hand to his and instead looked down at the page. "Ellen," he said, his eyebrows shooting up. He chuckled and showed it to her. "You've written down five titles?"

The blush flared in her cheeks again and she tucked her hands behind her back, shrugging. "I told you, I became distracted."

He let his shoulders slump dramatically and shook his head, affecting a disappointed frown. "Ellen, Ellen. What you need is some of my single-mindedness to complete this task."

"Very obviously," she answered, matching him look-for-look and dipping her head in a sage nod. "Shall I read the titles and you record them?"

"I think it best you move far from the shelves and record as I read them. Else you may distract us both by reading aloud from their pages."

She laughed, and he joined her, pleased she'd accepted his teasing for once. His wife, lovely and sensible as she was, did not laugh nearly as much as she ought.

Ellen gestured to the shelves with one hand and held the other out for the notebook. "Shall we begin?"

He handed it back to her, careful to hold the edge, avoiding another accidental brush of fingers.

They had been at it for ten minutes when Ellen interrupted him. "I think you should read that one, Marcus."

He paused and looked at the title again, having read it rather absently. "*Treatise on the Culture of the Apple and Pear.*" He pulled the book from the shelves. "Is it as thrilling as it sounds?"

She ignored his flippant remark. "I have read some of the author's other work from the Royal Society journals. He's a horticulturalist and I know he's written other things about orchards and farms."

"Sir Thomas Knight," Marcus read from the inside page. "Interesting. He's with the Royal Society?" It would be more than a dull memoir of a gentleman farmer, he realized.

"Yes. He must be something of an expert in the field. That is one of the books which distracted me yesterday. It was printed in 1801. I imagine there will be good advice inside." She stood and came to his side, turning the pages while he still held the book in his hands. She smelled of honey and the apple pastry from tea. It was a sweet scent, suiting her perfectly, and reminding him of spring.

"Here," she said, pointing down to a page and bringing him out of his embarrassing thoughts. Did other men stand around thinking such things of their wives?

Ellen was explaining the page to him. "You see where he explains his experiment? Can you imagine, ten thousand acres of farmland?"

"Intriguing." Marcus could hardly manage more, distracted by his wife's proximity. He looked closer at the page, ignoring Ellen as best he could, but as he began to read his eyes narrowed. "Most intriguing. You said he publishes in the science journals?"

"Yes."

Marcus looked up at his wife with a new perspective, taking in her earnest expression and the way her eyes shone. It was not so much emotion that made her glow the way she did as it was the intelligence she held, lighting her from within. He knew she enjoyed reading, and she admitted that she did not limit her literary choices to artistic works. Ellen's mind was more than practical, it was sharp and an instrument she employed regularly.

Closing the book, Marcus held it with one arm to his chest and bowed in his most courtly manner. "Mrs. Calvert, I owe you an apology."

Her mouth dropped open. "Whatever for?" she asked, her eyebrows drawing together.

"I did not at all appreciate your affinity for gathering knowledge from your reading until this moment. It is more than reading for entertainment. You read for your education. Enlightenment."

Her cheeks colored. Though Marcus hadn't meant to unsettle her, he could see the protests rising to her tongue before she spoke them. "I pass the time pleasantly with books. That's all."

"Ellen." He spoke her name with sincerity, but when she did not look up he reached out, tentatively, and touched her chin. He carefully guided it up until their eyes met again. The touch was necessary. He had to make certain she understood him.

"Do not belittle this. Reading means something to you. This book will be helpful, I am certain, but your advice and abilities will be much more necessary to me. Will you study the subject with me? I will send to London at once for a subscription to the Royal Society's journal and ask specifically for older issues with articles by Knight, if you think they will be useful."

A myriad of emotions shone from her eyes, many he could not name, but he saw hope chase disbelief away. When she released a long-held breath he felt the warmth of it on his hand. He smiled and very nearly raised his thumb to stroke her cheek, thinking to reassure her, but remembered himself in time to drop his hand safely to his side.

"Thank you," she said, her words softly whispered. "I will help in whatever way you wish."

Her modest acceptance of his request touched his heart. Had anyone attempted to understand his wife's love of reading before? It went beyond books and straight to her heart, of that he was certain, and he knew learning this had given him a greater insight to her than he had ever hoped to possess before.

CHAPTER 14

Ellen sat at the lady's desk she'd moved to the drawing room, Mrs. Burk seated next to her, going over a list of seasonal duties.

I wish we were not leaving for London, Ellen thought, shuffling the pages of her notes. *There is so much to do here.* And she would much rather be occupied in her own home than be a guest of Lord Calvert, Earl of Annesbury, in London. There would be naught for her to do there except attend the events her mother-in-law scheduled for her.

"What would you like done with the apple butter from last harvest, ma'am?" Mrs. Burk asked, flipping a page in her notebook. "It was not a very sweet harvest. The farmers informed us it rained too much last year and that deprived us of the richer tastes we are accustomed to."

Had Marcus heard that theory? Did it agree with Sir Thomas's articles? She would need to check. The memory of Marcus's compliments, the approval in his words and expression as he told her he *understood,* had taken up residence in her heart and mind. Though he may never love her, Ellen treasured the recognition and appreciation given her.

To be understood was almost, she told herself, as wonderful as being loved.

To rid herself of that distracting thought, she answered hastily. "Is it possible to use the apple butter in any of cook's recipes?"

"I will ask, ma'am."

"Thank you." Ellen made a note of that and was ready to end the meeting when a knock came at the door. "Enter," she called.

Matthews came in with a silver tray, holding the afternoon post.

"I will leave you to your correspondence, Mrs. Calvert," her housekeeper said after Ellen accepted two envelopes from the tray.

Ellen nodded her thanks, seeing the topmost letter bore Marianne's hand. The second piece of mail gave her pause. It was addressed formally. She broke the seal and unfolded the paper to reveal an invitation to a dinner party.

"Oh dear," she whispered to herself, reading over it carefully. It seemed the neighborhood had become aware of their presence at last.

She came to her feet and went in search of her husband, the invitation in hand.

But when she went out the door to begin her search, she nearly ran into him in the hall. She reached out, her hand brushing his arm to stop her forward momentum. "Marcus, pardon me."

He brought both his hands up to hold her forearms, steadying them both after the near collision. His deep chuckle made her heart's tempo increase.

"My fault, I thought I heard a step and didn't slow my own." He looked down at her, his brown eyes sparkling with excitement, and she tried not to admire the fading freckles across his cheeks. As much as they charmed her, she ought to avoid looking at them altogether.

"The weather is beautiful today. The sun has melted some of the snow and there aren't any clouds. Would you like to tour our property, Mrs. Calvert?"

Was that the cause of his eagerness? She knew he had seen the land in the weeks before their wedding, but the weather had turned the night of their arrival, which meant Marcus had been unable to show her the grounds yet.

"Yes, if you think it's a good day for it," she agreed, captured by his smile and the enthusiasm radiating from him. "I need to change."

"Excellent. We can meet downstairs in twenty minutes?"

"Yes, perfect."

His hands on her forearms gave a gentle squeeze, almost affectionate when coupled with his teasing grin. "Dress warmly." He released her and left, going to his own room to change.

Ellen belatedly remembered the invitation in her hand and sighed.

I really am too easily distracted. The problem was a thousand times more pronounced when Marcus was nearby.

It was the work of a quarter of an hour to summon her maid and dress. Ellen wore her riding habit of deep green, as well as a long red coat that would do well to keep her warm on horseback. Once her hat was pinned in place, she descended the stairs in search of her husband. He was waiting by the front door, hands clasped behind his back and rocking forward and back on his heels. He looked up as she set foot on the ground floor and his boyish grin appeared.

"You look ready to brave the cold."

"Indeed. And you look eager for it." She checked her gloves again and followed him out the front door. The horses waited, held by the young groom. A mounting block had been brought to the front of the house.

"Thank you, Banner," Marcus said. He shot a smile in her direction. "I thought the less trudging you had to do on foot, the better."

"I appreciate the thoughtfulness," she said, allowing the groom to hand her up into the saddle of a charming bay mare. "But I never trudge." What had made her say such a silly thing? Ellen blushed and opened her mouth, ready to explain away her frivolous words, but Marcus laughed before she could.

"No, of course you're right. You move with more grace than any woman I've ever met." As he moved his horse past her, he winked, then continued on as though nothing of consequence had been said. Which convinced her he meant it every bit as much as his considerate words from the day before.

They rode in silence around the house to the open field, covered in snow, that separated them from the apple orchards. She could see the bare branches from the upstairs windows, reaching up to the sky, unashamed to have lost their leaves.

As they crossed the field, their horses' breath puffing out in clouds of steam, Ellen took in the quiet landscape. Here and there she saw evidence of animals, where tracks of rabbits and birds dotted the ground, and she could hear a winter bird singing in the distance.

"It's beautiful, isn't it?" Marcus said, bringing her attention forward to where she saw him looking back at her. "Clean and bright. Not like London snow."

"Or Bath's," she said.

He pulled back on his reins and waited until their horses were even to continue forward.

"Did you like your seasons in Bath?" he asked, his eyes fixed ahead.

"When I had them, yes." Her eyes lingered on his profile. The angular line of his jaw would've looked stubborn on a more serious face, but on Marcus it added to his air of mischief. "I imagine there is more to do in London."

"Much more," he answered. "Though I would rather stay here and work, I hope we will enjoy our time there."

That he wanted to stay at Orchard Hill too gave her a measure of ease.

"I am certain we will." She looked down at her hands, shifting them on the reins. "We've had a dinner party invitation. A Mr. and Mrs. Harrison have requested our presence at their home tomorrow evening. I think the invitation was meant to arrive sooner, but the weather has been difficult."

Marcus nodded, his eyes on the horizon. "I met them before the wedding. I'm afraid I don't remember them very well from the years before my father's death. The rest of the neighborhood likely knew of the party for some time." He met her eyes. "Do you wish to attend?"

"I think we had better, given we have so short a time to make a good impression before leaving for London," she answered as evenly as she could. "Though meeting an entire party of strangers does not necessarily agree with me."

He chuckled. "I will be there to protect you, I promise."

Heat crept up her neck and into her cheeks. "Thank you, Mr. Calvert." She turned her eyes to the orchard and pointed. "Are all the apple trees the same?"

He launched into his understanding of how the trees were laid out and Ellen listened intently, trying to ignore the way his gestures and smiles played havoc with her heart. Loving him should have made their marriage easier, giving her leave to enjoy whatever relationship they had together. But instead, Ellen tried to ignore her feelings. Marcus had made it plain, from the beginning, he would never allow himself to love again.

But surely, her rebellious heart whispered to her head, *if he knew I loved him there could be no risk of his injury. I am not like Selene.*

Unbidden, the words he'd spoken to her in Collin's library returned to her mind. *I have no intention of entering into a romantic relationship again. I have risked my heart and lost it once. I will not promise you more in marriage than a fair partnership...*

"—So, if we attempt to breed these trees, we may find we have a sturdier variety without compromising the taste."

Ellen's attention came back to the present and she put on a mask of interest when Marcus looked to her, his hand gesturing to the trees around them. She had barely noticed they now rode beneath the snow-laden branches.

"That sounds ambitious," she said without pause. "But how many years would it be before you knew if you succeeded?"

"Several, I'm afraid. There is nothing quick about experimenting with fruit trees." His playful grin returned and he pointed further into the orchard. "The youngest trees producing fruit are this way. I'm told they're tart but are perfect for apple pies."

"Do you enjoy apple pie, Marcus?" she asked, her heart resisting as she attempted a more playful tone. Teasing him, accepting his banter, was not protecting her heart from damage.

"Very much. Especially Orchard Hill pies. I can remember requesting them every autumn." He launched into a story about stealing one from a cooling tray and eating himself sick, hiding beneath the hedgerow.

Ellen listened and laughed in the right places, but the shine had gone from the day. As soon as Marcus suggested returning to the house to warm up, she accepted the escape and barely spoke on the return trip.

She must learn how to love him without needing to be loved in return.

CHAPTER 15

E llen leaned forward in the carriage, peering out the window in search of the Harrisons' home. This would be her first event in the neighborhood and the first time she entered society as a wife. No longer would she sit to one side, allowing the evening to flow around her, wishing she were part of it. As a married woman, her place would be different, her role more important, the restraints less cumbersome.

Why then did her stomach roll and twist when she wanted to feel nothing more than happy anticipation?

Her husband chuckled and she turned to see him watching her, leaned up against the other side of the coach. Though it was dark, the lanterns on the outside of their equipage gave barely enough light for them to see each other.

He looked handsome in his dark blue coat and buff breeches. His cravat was elegantly tied, his silver stickpin in place, and a vest of deep blue peeked out above his coat buttons.

"Excited?" he asked her, a teasing smile on his face.

"Very." That was the correct answer, anyway. "I have had no visitors and I cannot contain my impatience in meeting the rest of the neighborhood. It will be good to have friends nearby."

A grin appeared on his face. "I am not enough company for you, am I?"

She tipped her chin up smugly and shook her head. "Of course not. Women require women. It is a fact. And as you have taken me far from my sisters, I am forced to find others to come drink our tea, eat our cakes, embroider cushions, and do all manner of feminine things with me."

He sat up straighter and fixed her with a mock-serious expression. "What about discussing books? You cannot take that from me. I enjoy our discussions."

Her heart skipped a beat at this admission. She enjoyed those moments, too, sitting before a fire in their library, book in hand. He always asked her opinion on what she read and of late they had taken turns reading aloud from a novel by Charles Maturin, an Irishman. They laughed and discussed some of the passages with real interest, as Mr. Maturin made a study of society through his fiction.

"If books are ever brought up in my company, I will pretend illiteracy," she promised him as seriously as she could. She earned a laugh for her teasing. The carriage slowed and stopped, causing her to turn back to the window. "Oh, you distracted me so I didn't get to see the prospect of the house."

He moved to whisper into her ear, causing a shiver of delight to run down her spine. "It was my wicked plan all along. I have deprived you of your window-peering."

A footman opened the door and Marcus stepped out before offering his hand to assist her. Once her slippered foot touched the gravel, he tucked her hand through his arm. "Step carefully. There is ice enough in hidden places."

Once inside, he removed her wrap and handed it to a waiting servant. They were shown to a conservatory, where other guests mingled. It was not an overly large party, but they did not immediately see the hosts. Marcus took it upon himself to begin making introductions.

"Ah, Mr. and Mrs. Yardly, allow me to present my wife to you.

Mrs. Calvert, Mr. and Mrs. Yardly reside on the west side of our village, with their children."

The older couple bowed and nodded. Ellen offered them a friendly smile. She noticed that while Mr. Yardly seemed all politeness, his wife's expression was less than welcoming.

"Is your charming daughter present tonight?" Marcus asked, his tone cheerful. "I should like to introduce Miss Yardly to my wife. They are near in age."

"Are they?" Mrs. Yardly asked, raising two gray eyebrows. "Dear me. I had not realized. I thought you were closer in age to your husband, Mrs. Calvert." Now her smile appeared, all coldness.

Ellen, surprised by the slight, recovered quickly. "Not quite, though I was in danger of spinsterhood when Mr. Calvert showed such generosity in saving me from that fate. Is your daughter very young?"

Marcus did not seem engaged in the conversation, peering around the room. Perhaps he had missed the veiled insult all together.

Mr. Yardly, after looking askance at his wife, answered her question. "She is about twenty-four."

"Then younger, but not by a great deal. I look forward to meeting her, since my husband finds her to be charming." She dipped a slight curtsy and gently pulled Marcus to the side. "We must first meet the hosts, I think."

"Quite right," Mr. Yardly answered.

"Ah, I see them." Marcus led her across the room. "Or Mrs. Harrison, anyway." He brought her straight to a woman dressed in green, with golden hair piled atop her head and a peacock fan in her hand. She looked a few years older than Ellen, which gave her reason to hope this woman would be friendlier than the last.

Marcus made the introductions to the hostess, who smiled politely. "We were all aflutter when we learned of your marriage, Mr. Calvert." She closed her fan and gave him a playful tap on the arm, her bright blue eyes alight with humor. "We have been waiting so long for you to take possession of Orchard Hill, but we hardly expected a wife to come with you. I think you have disappointed a great many of our young ladies."

Ellen's surprise at being so cut from the comments must have shown, for the lady of the house turned toward her. "I mean no offense, of course. I am sure you are lovely. But we have several young ladies who had anticipated Mr. Calvert's company. He is quite the favorite among them, you know."

"They will find new favorites soon enough," Marcus said, his usual amiable smile in place.

"Of course," Mrs. Harrison murmured, then glanced to one side. "Ah, here is Miss Emma Patterson. You must meet her, Mrs. Calvert." She beckoned to a doe-eyed young woman with raven black hair. "Miss Emma is a delightful musician. Maybe she will favor us with a piece later this evening."

"If the company wishes it," the young woman answered, then turned her attention to Ellen. "Do you play, Mrs. Calvert?"

"A little," she answered, her stomach tightening uneasily. She wouldn't be expected to play before so many strangers, surely. The program for the evening was likely set. "Mostly for my own amusement. Who is your favorite composer?"

The young lady waved her hand. "Oh, I haven't one really. So long as the music is lovely I am happy to play. But let us discuss something more interesting. How did you and our dear Mr. Calvert meet? I do not think I have seen you in London before, and my family attempts to go every year."

Marcus had turned aside to speak to a gentleman, Mr. Harrison, who had come to stand near them. They never discussed how to answer questions of this nature, but Ellen assumed the truth would not harm anything.

"We have known each other since childhood," she answered. "We met again but recently."

"I see." Miss Emma stepped nearer and lowered her voice. "Frankly, those of us who were in London two years ago were all surprised he married at all. It was no secret how much he cared for Lady Selene, or Lady Castleton is what we ought to call her now, I suppose. What a disappointed love affair that was." She sighed, lowering her eyelashes a touch. "But it is good to see he is healed from that. Especially given the rumors about Lady Castleton."

Ellen glanced aside to her husband, but he had stepped away several paces and appeared to be deep in conversation with several gentlemen. Putting her attention back on the young woman before her, Ellen forced a smile and shook her head. "I am afraid I am unfamiliar with any rumors you may speak of. Is the lady in good health?"

"Perfectly well in body." The younger woman hid a smile behind her fan, though she raised her eyebrows. "But not so well in marriage. Rumor has it her husband remains in the country while she resides in London, doing whatever it is she pleases, escorted about by any number of gentlemen. My mama says I should not worry my head over it, but I am rather anxious to get to town and find out for myself what is going on."

"Indeed." Ellen felt the bottom drop from her stomach and her shoulders tensed. "I am afraid, having never met her, I will not be a source of any interesting information."

A giggle made her turn to see a young woman standing near Marcus, gloved hand on his arm and a blush on her cheeks as she spoke to him. Ellen strained to hear, but Miss Emma was talking again.

"I am certain you will learn more as people discover your marriage. Any woman would want to be kept abreast of such things."

Ellen nodded absently. "Excuse me, won't you, Miss Emma?" She stepped away, toward her husband.

Marcus saw her coming and smiled warmly. "Ah, allow me to make the introductions. Miss Yardly, this is my wife, Mrs. Calvert." They made their curtsies. "Miss Yardly has been kind to me in London and allowed me to dance with her in many a crowded ballroom."

"Oh, it has always been a pleasure to stand up with you, Mr. Calvert." The young miss shot him a coy look from beneath her lashes and turned fully to Ellen. "Your husband is a very fine dancer. But I am sure you know that."

Ellen did not know that, and she realized how unlikely she would be to find out at any point soon. Married men rarely, if ever, danced with their wives.

As Miss Yardly looked like she expected a response, Ellen did her best. "Mr. Calvert is very adept at anything he puts his mind to."

Marcus looked down at her with an expression she could not entirely read, though his smile softened.

"You see? It is as I have been telling you gentlemen. My wife is a great compliment to me in life. I go about as I always have, and now she is here to attest to my brilliance in doing so."

A few gentlemen chuckled and Ellen tried to look pleased with the comment. Her handsome husband, who discussed books with great intelligence, who was insightful and compassionate with his tenants' needs, seemed a different person when in company.

He introduced her to the gentlemen standing near him and she stood at his side, mutely nodding in agreement from time to time with all he said. Though he had not been in residence at Orchard Hill for years, he knew everyone in the neighborhood either from London or visiting as a younger man. Gentlemen laughed at his jokes and ladies came near to receive a compliment or two before tittering and wandering away again.

With no desire to engage in private conversation, Ellen wondered why she ever thought being married would make events easier. When she was no longer a stranger, she would be able to enjoy herself more. At least, that's what she hoped.

It was nearly time to go in to dinner when a new face appeared near their circle and Marcus reached down to catch her hand, tugging her gently toward a tall gentleman. "Mr. Banner," he said, gaining the man's attention. "Please, allow me to introduce my wife to you."

Mr. Banner smiled brightly, the expression making his humble features friendly. "If I might introduce mine as well. One moment, please." He took a few steps to a gaggle of women, all conversing and flapping fans about with great animation, and gently took one by the arm. She returned with him, her lovely smile the friendliest Ellen had seen all night. "There now. I will go first. Darling Mrs. Banner, might I introduce my good friend, Mr. Calvert?"

Marcus bowed. "A pleasure, Mrs. Banner. I have heard a great deal about you, but I began to doubt you existed."

She laughed. "That is the fate of one who does not go to London. No one believes we are real." She turned to Ellen, her bright green eyes sparkling with good humor. "I understand you suffer the same fate, Mrs. Calvert. We are both in danger of vanishing all together if we do not spend more time in Society's clutches."

Ellen smiled hesitantly, not sure if she ought to trust this woman's tongue to remain kind. "It is true. I have never been to London."

"But we will remedy that soon," Marcus said firmly. "Will you come up as well, Mrs. Banner?"

"Perhaps," she answered. "For a few weeks. I must admit, it holds little interest for me, but my husband's business calls him there from time to time." Mrs. Banner gave her attention back to Ellen and reached out to touch her lightly on the arm. "Congratulations on your marriage, Mrs. Calvert. I am certain you must be a very special person and I look forward to knowing you better. Would you both come to dinner tomorrow, at my home? If you are going away to London, I must become your friend right away, lest you forget me while you are gone."

Ellen's outlook brightened. "That would be most welcome, Mrs. Banner."

"Excellent." Mrs. Banner slipped her arm through her husband's and nodded toward a set of doors. "I believe dinner is being served. I hope you will find me after. I want to tell you all about the neighborhood." The couple joined the small crowd going into the dining room.

Ellen looked up at her husband, some hope returning. "They seem kind."

"They are my favorite people in the county," he confided softly, bent to speak directly in her ear. "But don't tell anyone else. They would become jealous and I would lose my popularity. Then where would we be?"

"Home, reading a book," she muttered darkly, her mind on the previous conversations of the evening. But Marcus laughed out loud and then smothered the sound with his hand, earning several strange looks as people passed them to go to the dining room. She resisted the urge to smile and looked sidelong at him.

"I take it you would not mind that fate?" he asked, his humor restrained behind his eyes.

"Not very much," she admitted. "Let us go in and see how far apart they have put us." That was another of society's tricks. Marry a man and never dance with him in public or sit near him at dinner again. She sighed when she saw they were nearly at opposite ends of the table. She hoped her dinner partners would at least be reasonable people.

Her hopes on that account sunk rapidly. As a new bride, and with her husband's importance in the neighborhood, she was fairly close to the host. Two ladies outranked her, the wife of a viscount and the wife of a knight. She sat next to the viscountess.

"Mrs. Calvert, it is such a pleasure to meet the woman that Mr. Calvert finally chose to settle down with," the viscountess remarked in a tone which suggested it was anything but a pleasure. "I have been watching him with interest for years as he flitted about the finest balls and drawing rooms of London."

The viscountess could not be much older than Marcus; Ellen wondered at her unusual attentions to him. But the gentleman to her other side heard the conversation and broke in before she could respond.

"Yes, Mr. Calvert has always been a favorite with the ladies. I daresay, his brother the Earl is more popular, for all he is reticent in his duties to society."

"The Earl of Annesbury still mourns his late wife. I am afraid that makes him a more romantic figure than his brother," the viscountess agreed loftily. "Not to mention the title. Of course, with Mr. Calvert as his heir at present, I would have thought more young ladies would set their cap for him."

Ellen remained silent as they conversed freely about her husband's family, then chose another target in the company to aim their impolite conversation toward. She could hardly believe that people of such quality could be so rude as to discuss such private matters with each other. Ellen did not have much of an appetite, but she took what bites of the food she could.

The evening fast gave her a headache.

～

MARCUS TRIED to focus on the conversation of his dinner companions but found he could not stop glancing down the table at Ellen. She barely looked at her dinner companions, let alone spoke to them. Strange. He'd found the viscountess to be entertaining company in the past.

"Mr. Calvert," his hostess spoke, drawing his attention. "Would you tell us more of your bride? How did you meet Mrs. Calvert?"

He glanced to either side of him to find the other guests looked equally intrigued. "It is not a particularly intriguing tale. We have known each other since childhood. I have always enjoyed her company. I found it very natural to think of her when I turned my mind to finding a wife."

One of the female guests on his side of the table leaned forward to speak. "Very natural? What a way to speak of marriage. But why have we not seen her in your company before, in London?"

"Her family does not go to London. They enjoy a short season in Bath."

His hostess chuckled and dabbed at her lips with her napkin. "I cannot think of anyone I know who would prefer Bath to London. How extraordinary."

Marcus knew asking Ellen to wed would raise eyebrows, but he did not understand how much the questions along that vein would irritate him. What did it matter to anyone else who he chose as his bride? Once married, society recognized she was part of him and his prestige. Her family did not matter so much as her current place in his.

Casting a quick look down the table to check on his bride, he wondered if that was why Ellen appeared solemn and silent at her end of the table. Were people asking her the same intrusive questions?

Changing the topic felt like the most tolerable option. "Mrs. Harrison, you have exquisite culinary taste. This dinner is absolutely perfect."

She demurred gracefully.

In another moment, he praised a young woman down the table from him on her lovely voice, then spoke in general about the wintry weather and expectations for the season. Expertly, he turned the conversation from himself. Deftly, he laid out compliments and flattered one person after another. Before long, the dinner was complete, and the lady of the house stood to signal for the other ladies to accompany her from the room while the gentlemen enjoyed stronger libations than readily available in the card room.

Peter Banner came to his side of the table and sat, crossing his arms and leaning back. "For your first event as a married man, you are doing supremely well."

"It's hardly any different than it was when I was single," Marcus said, his voice low enough that his comments remained between the two of them. "Except that I'm no longer fending off single women."

Banner chuckled and then turned to converse with the man on his other side.

Marcus hadn't told his friend the entire truth. While he might carry himself as he always had, speak as he always did, he was worrying for Ellen. She had been nervous to come and being apart from her when she might be uncomfortable made him anxious. If nothing else, the *ton* had taught him to mask his feelings, and he did that now for her sake.

Ellen might not appreciate a hovering husband, he told himself.

He carried on through the after-dinner port as though nothing weighed on his mind, speaking of their plans to go to London.

When the host finally stood, it was time to rejoin the ladies.

Marcus sprung up faster than he intended to. He made up for it by allowing other gentlemen to precede him as they shuffled out.

He entered the parlor and surveyed the room, looking for Ellen in her beautiful mint green gown. He found her, sitting on a covered bench near the window, deep in conversation with Mrs. Banner.

"They will be thick as thieves in no time," Banner said, appearing beside him.

Marcus barely held in a sigh. "I hope so. Ellen needs friends here."

"She will have them. In time." Banner clapped him on the shoulder and went forward, making straight for his wife, and Marcus followed a step behind.

CHAPTER 16

A footman answered the door at the Banner home. He showed them inside and took their things, the only servant in evidence. Their home was not so large as Orchard Hill. Yet it felt warm and welcoming. The floors were polished oak, the walls covered in a simple dark green paper, with watercolors decorating the hall between doorways.

The footman led them to a parlor where a fire burned in the hearth. Mr. and Mrs. Banner stood as Ellen and Marcus entered, both of them with friendly expressions. Bows and curtsies were made, but then Mrs. Banner came forward with her hands outstretched to take Ellen's.

"Oh, I am glad you accepted our invitation. I know you must be in great demand, new to the neighborhood as you are."

Ellen glanced askance at Marcus, who likely knew how few invitations had actually arrived at their home for her. "Thank you for thinking to ask us."

"Please, come and sit. We usually enjoy each other's company before dinner is ready." Mrs. Banner moved to the comfortable looking maroon couch and gave the cushion next to her a pat.

Ellen accepted and sat, glancing around with interest. The walls were covered in a cream-colored paper with miniature portraits and larger paintings of landscapes. Dried flowers hung in a few corners, their colors muted but a lovely contrast to the walls. The furniture looked to be made less for decor and more for use, with sturdy lines and dark colors.

"How are you settling in as mistress of Orchard Hill?" Mrs. Banner asked.

"I think I am more used to the idea in my mind if not in practice." Ellen smoothed a wrinkle in her skirt and folded her hands tightly in her lap.

Mrs. Banner's laugh was low and soft, her expression merry. "I remember what it was like. You have ideas of how to do things, your mother's advice ringing in your ears, but you doubt yourself every time you change something the housekeeper has put into place."

"Oh, that's it precisely." Ellen could allow herself to laugh too. "I have to pretend I know what I'm about. But Mrs. Burk is rather wonderful. She listens to what I have to say and is always willing to try my ideas. Thus far."

"I rather like Mrs. Burk. She is the aunt of my cook, Mrs. Lawless. They occasionally have tea in my kitchen and let me pop in now and again to join them." Mrs. Banner wrinkled her nose and leaned in close to Ellen. "But you mustn't tell anyone about that. It would be scandalous that an employer takes tea with her cook and visiting servants."

Ellen could not repress her grin and she raised a hand to her heart. "I will not say a word to anyone."

"What's this?" Mr. Banner asked, coming closer to the women. He and Marcus had stood near the doorway, chatting quietly while their wives reacquainted themselves. "They are not in our house above five minutes and you already have Mrs. Calvert swearing fealty to you? You are devious, darling."

Mrs. Banner shook her head, pursing her lips at him. "Not at all. We are merely sharing secrets with one another. I only demand fealty from you, Peter."

"Secrets? Do I get to know any of them?" Marcus asked, settling in a chair a pace from where Ellen sat. "I am convinced my wife has any number of secrets, but I have yet to learn many of them."

Ellen blushed. "I don't have any secrets at all. Besides the one Mrs. Banner shared with me, and I am not at liberty to share that one with you."

"But you are so quiet most of the time. You must have many interesting thoughts you keep to yourself." He turned to Mr. Banner and spoke with near pride. "My wife is one of the most intelligent people I have ever met, for all she says few words."

"That is the mark of intelligent people, or hadn't you heard?" Mr. Banner chuckled and leaned back in his chair as much as his formal wear would allow. He steepled his fingers before him and raised his chin in a lofty manner. "Which is how you know, Mrs. Calvert, that your husband is not such a person. The fellow could talk the ears off a mule."

Ellen darted a glance at Marcus and saw he regarded the comment with amusement, which gave her the confidence to smile. "I am not certain that's true, Mr. Banner. If you will permit me to say so, I believe that people of great intelligence, or even good thoughts, tend to disguise the fact that they have such. Some with silence. Others by spouting nonsense."

"I'm not certain whether you paid me a compliment or not," Marcus protested through a chuckle.

"I was not speaking of you, but of Mr. Banner," Ellen quickly corrected, raising her eyebrows at her host and trying not to smile too broadly.

Mrs. and Mr. Banner laughed, the one daintily and the other with a roar. "Oh, you will do well here, Mrs. Calvert. You have brought us a kindred spirit, Calvert."

She felt heat creeping into her cheeks but pushed aside the desire to duck her chin when she saw Marcus's eyes glittering at her. "Indeed, I have. I grow more pleased with my choice in wife every day."

He did?

Ellen's cheeks must have gone red by now, but she turned her attention to her hostess, willing the blush away. That he would say such a thing in company gave her heart a lift she had not known she needed. "I understand you have children, Mrs. Banner. I am accustomed to being surrounded by toddling nieces and nephews and I confess I have missed the darlings. Will you tell me about your little ones?"

"Careful, Calvert." Mr. Banner's tone became cautious and his face a mask of seriousness. "This bodes ill for you."

"Oh, stop." His wife leaned forward enough to tap him on the wrist, narrowing her eyes at him. "Do not listen to a word he says, Mrs. Calvert. My husband adores our children. He has a level of affection one does not normally see fathers convey."

"It's true." He sighed and his shoulders slumped. "I am at their beck and call. The nursery bell has but to ring and I am there, ready to slay dragons."

"For our son, Arthur. He is three, but I think he has already decided he wishes to build a round table and go on a quest to find Camelot," Mrs. Banner confided with motherly pride. "And Peter encourages him."

"We have a daughter, too. She is but one year and a quarter." His chest swelled as he spoke of her. "But already walking about as if she owned the world."

"Every little girl ought to be confident," Ellen said, lips twitching at his obvious pride. Would Marcus feel that way about fatherhood? They had barely spoken of the idea of children. She knew he wanted an heir, at least, to carry on his name and inherit the estate.

Mrs. Banner's eyes glowed, gazing into her husband's similarly soft countenance. "They are the center of our world."

The footman reappeared and bowed, announcing dinner.

"We will not stand on ceremony," Mr. Banner said as he held his hand out to his wife. "We have kept the table small so we might all converse at ease, and I intend to take my wife in." He bent and brushed a kiss on her gloved hand.

Marcus stood and held a hand out to Ellen for her to take as she rose from the couch. They followed the Banners into the hall. Marcus bent down, bringing his lips near her ear, and spoke softly enough that their hosts would not hear. "You miss your family? Ought I to worry?"

Ellen looked out of the corner of her eye at him, tilting her head to one side. "Not yet. You are marvelous company, Marcus."

"That is something of a relief," he murmured, his eyes skimming her profile in a way that made her wish to duck her head. Instead, she tilted her chin up and did her best to exude confidence. It was easier to feel it here, among the Banners, than it had been at the party the night before.

～

AFTER DINNER, Marcus and his host remained at the table while the ladies retired to the parlor.

"We won't linger too long," Banner promised, leaning back and crossing his arms. "But I think the ladies might appreciate a few moments alone."

"I agree. In all honesty, your invitation came as a relief. Ellen is not comfortable in the neighborhood yet. I think a few of the matrons have intimidated her." Marcus knew he could trust Peter Banner to keep his confidences. The two had known each other many years and were of a similar temperament.

"Spiteful old cats." Banner rolled his eyes heavenward. "You have thwarted all their schemes for you, marrying a gentle person like her, and they will take out their ire on your wife."

"I am not certain it is as bad as all that." Marcus took a sip of the amber liquid in his glass. "But there have been very few invitations. Not that we have a great deal of time before we must go to London. But it would be good for Ellen to make friends."

Banner looked askance at him, his brow furrowed deeply. "I am afraid you're wrong, Calvert. My wife has heard the gossip and it isn't kind. Your wife is seen as an interloper. A nobody who has inexplicably risen in society. You know as well as I, if it is one thing people full of pomp and self-importance hate, it is a newcomer to the game."

Marcus stilled and he slowly shook his head. "She is the

daughter of a gentleman. Her education cannot be discounted. Ellen has grace and dignity, perfect manners. How could anyone perceive her as not belonging?"

"My dear fellow." Banner sat forward, forearms on the table, hands clasped as he spoke with earnestness. "Mrs. Calvert may be all you say, but there is no one who knows it. She has never been seen in illustrious company before. No one in this neighborhood knows her. Until she has proven herself equal in some manner, she will have a hard time of it."

"I should expect that as my wife she should receive the same courtesies shown to me. She bears my name. My family's name." He truly did not foresee this as a problem. Though he knew Ellen would require many introductions into the right circles, how could people not recognize immediately the quality of her person?

"On the surface a woman may be given all the polite treatment her husband's name brings, but there is always another, deeper layer of the game. Bringing her here, as your bride, and introducing her about to the women who wished to have you for themselves or for their daughters, could not go well." Banner picked up his glass at last, giving the liquid a brief glance before putting the glass down again. "They are jealous they did not claim you and they are offended that someone outside their circle of importance did."

Marcus scoffed and pushed his glass away, no longer in the mood to indulge himself. "I have never encountered such problems before."

"That is not entirely true, Calvert. You have told me many times how your connection to your family has made your life difficult."

"Because people sought connection to my family. Not to distance themselves from me." Marcus groaned and pressed a hand over his eyes. "Ellen has not said a word about any of this. Do you think she is aware of the hostility towards her?"

"Undoubtedly. Louisa is certain your wife has been given a few minor tongue-lashings already." The look Banner gave him was full of sympathy. "As much as she may fit the requirements of a gentlewoman in society, she is new to all of this. As a married woman, she must navigate on her own."

"No. She has me." Marcus pushed himself away from the table and stood, walking a path down the dining room, ten steps one way and then ten steps back. "How can I help her?"

"You might begin small." Banner's suggestion was accompanied by a bemused look. "Praise her in company the way you praised her here, tonight. That compliment you paid her made Mrs. Calvert bold."

Marcus slowed in his pacing and thought, frowning at the carpet, of all the times he offered his wife compliments. She usually dismissed his words as flattery or flirting, so he did not often say those things lest she continue to count them cheaply. That did not stop him from admiring her intelligence or her loveliness. But that silent admiration at home meant he said little of her before others.

"Ellen has always kept to herself. She has never been bold. Except with me. In private. She says the most interesting things."

"Is she shy?"

"Possibly there is more to it than that." Marcus took in a breath and released it slowly. "I don't know."

Banner stood and pushed his chair in. "I think we best rejoin the ladies. And I think you ought to have a conversation with your wife on these matters."

Marcus inwardly agreed.

CHAPTER 17

Tucked up in her favorite chair by the library fire, Ellen turned the page in an interesting volume on the subject of astronomy. The discoveries being made about the stars and nearby planets were astonishing. Though her grasp of mathematics was above what most considered proper for a woman, she still found a great deal of the book was beyond her reach in understanding. She determined to make a further study of the subject.

Ellen reached for her commonplace book, to write down the names of other authors the book suggested be read, when her husband came into the library. Even now, after weeks of marriage, Ellen's heart picked up its speed the moment he stepped through a door. Tonight, he looked to be deep in thought, a line appearing between his brows. He walked straight into the room and towards his favorite chair, across from hers, and slumped down into it.

"I thought understanding orchards would be a simple matter." He sighed and reached up to rub his eyes. "Ellen, I cannot thank you enough for Knight's book. I have been taking a mad number of notes and I've sent to London for more written by him. I am thinking of writing the gentleman a letter to see if there is anything else he would suggest I read." His lips quirked upward at the last and he cast his eyes down to her book. "What is it you study?"

"The stars in the heavens," she answered cheerily, placing a ribbon in the book to mark her place. "But if you would rather pick up our story about the Irish girl, I will not complain."

"You never do complain. About anything." But rather than smile at what she thought would be a praiseworthy trait, his frown reappeared. He placed both hands on the arms of the chair and heaved himself into a more upright position. "Which reminds me of a thing I have wished to discuss with you. Have you the time for a conversation of a serious nature?"

Ellen put the book aside and straightened her spine. "I do. I am always at your disposal, Marcus."

"Ah. Thank you." He stared into her eyes and she could see, behind the light brown irises, his gathering thoughts.

"We haven't received many invitations and you haven't had many callers."

"Both statements are correct," Ellen said, tilting her head to one side. "But it is a difficult time of year, with the weather, to be out visiting or entertaining."

Marcus shook his head. "I think you and I both know that isn't the case here."

Ellen's chest tightened and she looked away from him, to the fireplace. "You're right, of course. A new bride in the neighborhood ought to be of more interest than I have been." She sighed and put her hands in her lap, trying to remain relaxed. "I'm sorry, Marcus, if this reflects badly on you. But I don't think your neighbors have a wish to know me."

"Badly on me?" he repeated, sounding shocked. She glanced up to see his eyebrows high on his forehead and his mouth hanging slightly open. "I am not the least worried about myself, Ellen. I am concerned for how my neighbors' behavior has made you feel. I have reason to believe you are being slighted, and I cannot allow that. You are my wife. Under my protection."

Despite the uncomfortable nature of the topic, Ellen smiled.

"It's nothing, Marcus. I'm a stranger, and not a very interesting one. People will get used to me in time."

He repeated her again, much to her amusement. "Used to you?" Marcus continued to gape at her.

"Yes. In time." Ellen shrugged, doing her best to convey that this didn't bother her. Not much, anyway. "When we have more in common."

Marcus moved to the end of his chair, his elbows on his knees as his hands took up hers. "Ellen." The softness with which he spoke her name nearly made her sigh. But his eyes were boring into hers again, with a gentle intensity. "You have a great deal in common with the ladies here."

Ellen squeezed his hands and shook her head. "Not really. I don't move in their circles, so I don't understand their gossip. I have no idea of the history existing between them, of who likes who and who only tolerates another. And what do I know of the events they speak of? They talk of balls, concerts, and the theater of London. My experiences in Bath are inferior. I am newly married, so I cannot speak much about that life. I have no children, which eliminates another topic of conversation. And I hardly think anyone of your acquaintance would care to hear about my interest in botany, literature, or the sciences."

"I find those things interesting," he said. "I see no reason why others would find such topics of conversation lacking."

"Marcus. I am sorry if it pains you to have an unpopular wife, but..." She shrugged and looked down at her lap, not wanting to see the disappointment on his face. "I have always been quiet and I am used to keeping my own company. I don't mind. One grows accustomed to such things. Why else would I have never received an offer of marriage?"

Marcus's hands brought hers together, holding them safely in his warm grasp. She reveled in his touch, even though she knew she ought to withdraw.

"Ellen." He took in a deep breath and sighed, which made her curious enough to peek up at him, trying to ascertain his level of upset. It surprised her to see not disappointment but concern etched into his face. "I haven't any idea why Bath is full of imbeciles, but I am wholly grateful no other man was intelligent enough to see what a wonderful wife you would make. If I am pained by what is going on in my neighborhood, it's because I don't wish to see you disappointed. And I know you are, even with your denials."

Ellen's eyes prickled as tears formed behind them, but she determined to smile. "How would you know that, Marcus?"

He retained her hands in his left, but reached out to tuck a strand of hair behind her ear, his gaze never faltering. Her breath stilled.

"I can see it in your eyes. I've heard it in your voice. As happy as we are in each other's company, I know you wish for friendship. It's my fault, not yours, that they are standoffish."

Ellen did not realize she had been holding her breath until her lungs began to ache. She bit her lip and looked away, her thoughts muddled.

Marcus stood and went to the fire, clasping his hands behind him. "We will make this season a grand one for you, Ellen. We will attend balls, concerts, the theater, and walk the park in the fashionable hours. I will introduce you to everyone I know of importance. By the end of the season, the jealous pea hens will be falling all over themselves to claim you as an acquaintance." He looked over his shoulder at her, his teasing grin back in place. "And you might even enjoy yourself."

She managed a smile, though she felt some uncertainty over the plan. "I thought your intentions were to stay in town for a short while. To come back here and see to the estate."

He shook his head dismissively, turning to face her. "I can return from time to time and receive reports from our steward." He squared his shoulders and raised his brow in a lofty manner. "I made you a promise, Ellen. I promised I would be a good husband to you. This is one of the ways I am doing that. I will see to your happiness."

Ellen appreciated the thought, but in her heart, she knew it could not make her happy, to pull him from the work which meant so much to him. For what? The sake of her feelings over the spiteful behavior of a few women? Ellen could get along without them very well. Her letters to Marianne helped and she felt certain Mrs. Banner would be a good friend before long.

"I have been invited to visit Mrs. Banner tomorrow afternoon. Would that suit your plans?"

"Of course, weather permitting. I have had a few farmers tell me they expect a storm any day now. How they know, I cannot understand, but I trust their judgment." He came back to his seat and fell into it. "I'm glad you and Mrs. Banner like each other."

She offered a brief nod and then took up the book they had been reading together. "One chapter before we retire?" she asked.

He nodded and closed his eyes, relaxing in his chair. "Yes. Let's continue with the Irish."

Ellen found her place and began to read in her best voice, her tones rising and lowering as the emotion of the story called for, and before long Marcus was sitting forward, as engrossed in the story as she.

～

SARAH MADE certain Ellen's cloak was warm, fussing over her well-being enough to make Ellen feel coddled. But her husband did not emerge from his study to bid her farewell, nor did she know if she ought to interrupt him to take her leave of the house.

Ellen asked Sarah to be sure to inform the master of the house of where she had gone, in case he forgot about it in his business of the day.

Keeping to herself during the day did not usually prove difficult for Ellen. She had several things to occupy her, such as meeting with the cook and the housekeeper to go over meal preparations and house business, respectively. She would hold discussions with Sarah about her wardrobe, what should be mended and what put away. Then she would walk through the gardens in their winter slumber, enjoying the cool air and exercise.

If only people would call on her, so she might return the courtesy. But, as she told Marcus, she hardly expected anyone to go out into the weather. Despite the mild snowfall, it remained cold.

Visiting today, by specific invitation, lifted her spirits. Though they would be in London in another week, the time between now and then stretched into an eternity.

It did not help matters that Marcus made her aware of his determination to see her accepted and popular in society. If anything, the very idea made her nervous.

"I suppose I ought to be grateful he wishes to help," she murmured to herself in the carriage, watching out the window for the Banners' driveway. "But all I can think is that he must be disappointed he did not know then what he does now about my personality."

They turned off the country lane and she heard the crunch of gravel. When the carriage stopped, the footman helped her down and she made her own way up the steps. The door was thrown open by her hostess.

"Oh, Mrs. Calvert, good afternoon. I hope the drive over was pleasant?"

"Very, thank you." Ellen handed her things to a maid, with the exception of the small basket she brought with her, filled with embroidery materials in case busyness would be the order of the day.

"Would you come up to the nursery with me, Mrs. Calvert?" The woman of the house asked immediately, without even stepping into the parlor. "I usually take tea with the children before I enjoy my own. If you've missed the company of your nieces and nephews, I thought you might not object."

Ellen's heart warmed even more toward this kind woman. "Please. I'd like to meet them."

They went up the flight of stairs in the hall, but rather than climb to the level of an attic, Mrs. Banner took Ellen a few doors down the hallway. "I know it isn't generally done, but our children live on the same level as we do. It saves their small legs the stairs and I like having them near." She opened the nursery door and Ellen stepped into a room full of light and laughter.

"Mama has come for tea," Mrs. Banner announced from the doorway, then immediately knelt as a small figure hurtled towards her.

The boy looked a great deal like his mother, with dark hair and eyes. He wrapped his arms about her neck in an embrace. Then a smaller child in a long white dress, no leading strings, toddled over from the arms of the smiling nurse. The little girl's hair was fairer and her eyes a grayish blue. She babbled happily at her mother in the language of babies.

Arthur was talking, and while some adults might not understand, Ellen could tell his mother took in every word. Then the boy caught sight of the guest and fell silent, taking a step back from his mother to get a better look at the intruder.

"Arthur, this is Mrs. Calvert. She is Mama's friend and has come to take tea with us. Can you say hello?"

"Hello," the boy repeated obediently, still staring upward.

Ellen remembered her manners and knelt down as low as she could, offering a kind smile. "Hello, Arthur. Your mother tells me you like to slay dragons."

It was exactly the right thing to say; Arthur's face brightened and he began talking excitedly. "I'm a knight!" He turned and ran away from her to snatch up a picture book and bring it back, showing it to her with a pleased face.

Ellen took the book with reverence and read the cover. "*Saint George and the Dragon.* A very good book, indeed."

"But I wouldn't kill the dragon," the boy told her with great solemnity. "I would keep it."

Mrs. Banner laughed, hugging her daughter to her. "And a fearsome pet it would be, but I am not certain it could remain in the house, and I doubt the barn would do for such a beast either."

Arthur did not seem impressed by this but took the book back and handed it to his nurse. "Nurse knows where t'keep dragons."

The woman, in her late thirties, nodded sagely. "I have told him that a dragon would do very well living in the garden, frightening off the rabbits that eat Cook's vegetables."

"Nurse Hardy is very wise." Mrs. Banner kissed her daughter's head and gestured for Ellen to sit at the table near one of the large windows. Two windows filled most of the outside wall, with curtains pulled away, allowing the winter sunlight to flood the room. Warm carpets covered the floor and a fire burned cheerily behind a grate. The walls were decorated with water colors of animals, both domestic and wild. A basket sat in one corner, filled with wooden toys, and a small bookshelf was the repository of a handful of books.

"This room is absolutely perfect," Ellen said in a breathless sigh. An open doorway led to another room where she could see a crib and a small bed.

"Thank you." Mrs. Banner settled her daughter on her lap and waited patiently for her son to take his seat. Then Nurse Hardy brought over a tray that had been waiting on a taller shelf, covered to keep in some of the warmth.

"Would you like me to pour out, Mrs. Banner?" the nurse asked.

"Please, Nurse Hardy. Thank you."

Arthur received steamed milk in his cup and two biscuits on his plate. Little Esther took a biscuit from her mother and proceeded to break it into pieces before shoving bits in her mouth. Though crumbs rained into Mrs. Banner's lap, she didn't seem to notice or care. She was at complete ease in the nursery.

A longing began in Ellen's heart as she watched the sweet inter-play between mother and children. Nurse Hardy seemed completely accustomed to the tradition and helped mind Arthur's milk while she told Mrs. Banner what the children had accomplished since luncheon. Ellen nibbled a biscuit, content to sit and listen.

The children's tea did not take long and afterward Mrs. Banner excused herself to put the baby down for a nap. Arthur insisted he did not need one, but Nurse Hardy convinced him to at least rest his head while she read a story.

"He will be asleep in a trice," Mrs. Banner whispered as she led Ellen back out the way they had come. But as they neared the stairs, Mr. Banner appeared. "Peter, you may not go in. You have missed tea and it's nap time." Mrs. Banner spoke with a slight scold in her tone, though her expression remained affectionate.

Peter Banner allowed his shoulders to droop and lowered his head comically. "Forgive me. I didn't mean to miss tea."

"You take tea with the children too?" Ellen could not help her surprise.

"As often as I can," Mr. Banner answered firmly, standing upright again. "Tell me, Mrs. Calvert, in your unbiased opinion, are they not magnificent?"

"They very much are." Ellen watched the proud parents exchange amused glances.

Mr. Banner offered his arm to his wife. "Might I escort you both back down to the morning room? I believe there will be a more sumptuous tea there."

"And you are hoping for an invitation." His wife shook her head and sighed. "Such manners."

"I hardly think Mrs. Calvert would turn me out into the cold, forcing me to take tea all alone in my study." He cast his eyes back to Ellen as they descended the stairs. "Would you be so cruel, Mrs. Calvert?"

"I would not," she answered sweetly. "But I'm not the queen of this country. We must both bow to the wishes of Mrs. Banner."

"Please, call me Louisa. I feel we are going to be dear friends."

"Thank you, you are very kind. You may call me Ellen."

The tea passed with polite conversation, Mr. Banner teasing Louisa a great deal, but she never blushed. She teased him back. Ellen watched the exchange with a measure of envy. After a quarter hour, Mr. Banner took leave of his wife, kissing her cheek before he withdrew. Louisa watched him leave, a sparkle in her eye.

"You love him very much," Ellen said when the door had shut behind him.

Louisa nodded. "He is my whole world. He and the children. We've known each other many years, and loved each other nearly as long." She sat primly in her chair and looked expectantly at Ellen. "I understand you've known Mr. Calvert since childhood. I haven't had the chance to ask how you came to marry."

"We have known each other for many years. I was still a nursery child when we met. I saw Marcus every summer. Then we met again this autumn, at my cousin's home."

Louisa sighed and leaned back in an elegant repose. "It sounds like a beautiful love story, to be reunited with a childhood friend in such a way."

Ellen could not think how to answer that, as their story did not contain any love, except for that which she kept locked securely in her heart. "We care for one another a great deal. And we are good friends," she stated firmly, her eyes drifting down to her lap where she clutched her hands together. "I don't think I would've married, had Marcus not asked me."

Louisa made a sound of understanding. "Your feelings for him must be very deep."

Ellen felt the tears prickling at the back of her eyes but raised her head with a smile. "Yes. Well. Please, tell me more about your growing up here. It is such a lovely place and the country round about so pleasant."

For a moment her friend looked confused, but then obliged Ellen and spoke of the village, their neighbors, and offered insight into the local history Ellen had not yet received. Relaxing into this comfortable atmosphere, Ellen was not aware of the time passing. A clock on the mantel ticked quietly but did not chime.

Not until the room grew dark did Ellen look up. "Oh dear. I didn't mean to stay this long. I hope I have not caused your schedule any harm."

Louisa laughed and shook her head. "Not at all! These have been pleasant hours. I'm surprised we haven't been interrupted by the children." Louisa looked toward the window and frowned. "When did it begin snowing?"

Ellen rose and went over, looking at the small drifts upon the walk. She looked up at the gray sky. "I had better send for the coach."

"That won't be necessary," a male voice said from the door, drawing her attention to Mr. Banner. "Your coachman and I have been speaking. I am afraid none of us were giving the attention we ought to the weather. If you look out the windows at the front of the house, you'll see a sky nearly black with clouds. A storm is rising quickly. With snow already on the road, I didn't think it advisable for you to attempt a return home. Your coachman agrees."

Louisa came to her feet and went to her friend, putting her hand on Ellen's arm. "I'm terribly sorry, Ellen. If I'd paid more attention to the time, we might have sent you home, or sent someone on horseback to apprise Mr. Calvert of the situation. But we cannot risk that now." She looked to her husband who nodded in confirmation. "Mr. Calvert will be terribly worried."

"Likely not," Ellen responded, absently as she stared out the window. "He will trust you and our coachman, Mr. Henry, to keep me safe." She swallowed and forced a smile. It could very well be that her husband wouldn't notice her missing until the dinner hour.

Their routine would be interrupted.

"As soon as the weather clears, we'll send word to Calvert," Mr. Banner promised.

"Thank you, Mr. Banner."

"You can call me Banner, if you wish, as your husband does. All will be well. We'll feed you a good dinner and provide what you need for the evening."

"I am grateful for your kindness."

"If you will excuse us a moment, I think I'll go look in on the children." Louisa followed her husband from the room, skirts swishing behind her.

Lowering herself to the window seat, Ellen leaned forward to rest her forehead on the cold glass.

What would Marcus think when he found her gone? They saw each other when they took breakfast together. The meal had been interrupted by the morning post, which had letters from London acquaintances he seemed eager to read. He didn't stay in the room long after it arrived. Marcus didn't even mention her visit, possibly forgetting about it overnight.

He would trust the Banners to keep her safe, when he realized where she was. But would he miss her? Would he find the evening meal lonely or the house too quiet?

Granted, she didn't make much sound or fill much physical space, but she hoped he found her company pleasant when he took the time to share in it.

Louisa returned, a maid accompanying her, by which time Ellen had gathered her thoughts in a tidy manner.

"The children will come down to play before their dinner." She handed the tea tray to the maid. "And Susan will prepare the guest room for your use tonight. I'll make certain you have something warm to sleep in as well."

"You are so kind, Louisa. Thank you, Susan."

The maid bobbed a curtsy and left the room, steps quick and efficient.

"I do hope you will forgive me for being thoughtless of the time and weather." Louisa retook her seat, her concern evident in the lines above her brows. "That was neglectful of me. Do you suppose Mr. Calvert will forgive us for keeping you overlong?"

Ellen came back to her warm chair, rubbing her forearms. She'd grown cold sitting by the window. "There is nothing to forgive. Marcus will not suffer much concern, knowing where I am. The staff will make him comfortable and I'll go home as soon as the roads are clear."

Louisa blinked at Ellen and her lips parted as though she would speak, but she hesitated. "I can imagine Peter's worry if something similar were to happen to me. Even knowing I was safe, I doubt he would be able to sleep."

This would be the true test of Louisa's friendship, Ellen thought. To see what she made of the circumstances surrounding their marriage. "If you will not betray my confidence," Ellen said softly, "I'll tell you why I think as I do."

Louisa nodded and leaned forward. "Of course, Ellen. Nothing you say to me as your friend will be repeated to others."

"Good." Ellen nodded and took a deep breath before launching into a quiet, though thorough, explanation of her marriage to Marcus. As she spoke, Louisa's face betrayed a myriad of emotions, from surprise, to humor, to something resembling sadness.

"You see, Marcus won't worry for me any more than he would

for another member of the household. Ours is not a love match. He will view the situation practically." She meant to finish the statement strongly, but her voice faltered at the end and she had to look down to regain her composure.

"You wish it wasn't so," Louisa said, leaning forward to put a hand on Ellen's arm. "I am sorry, my dear friend. When you spoke of growing up together, I assumed your story would be similar to Peter's and mine."

Ellen took in a shaky breath and guessed her smile did not look so confident as she wished. "There is nothing to be sorry about. Many couples marry for reasons similar to ours. I feel grateful that the choice was left up to me, not made by my parents, and that Marcus and I get along. Our marriage is one of comfortable companionship."

Louisa didn't get the chance to respond. The door opened to admit the nurse and Arthur, with baby Esther on her caretaker's hip. Arthur charged into the room and climbed into his mother's lap, already talking rapidly about Nurse's stories and her promise of cake if he ate his meal.

Welcoming the interruption, Ellen asked to hold Esther and enjoyed playing a clapping game with the toddler, who didn't mind strangers very much so long as they kept her entertained. Playing with children came easily to Ellen and she hoped she would have her own one day, to share her heart with. Marcus would continue to receive her love, though he didn't know it, but it would be heavenly to have a little one to reciprocate tenderness and affection.

Much later that evening, as she stood in the guestroom provided by her new friend, Ellen looked out into the dark night outside her window. The snow continued to fall in sheets.

Determined to feel gratitude at being warm and safe, Ellen turned to her bed and slid between the sheets with a sigh. A warming pan had been applied moments before, yet her feet felt frigid.

Ellen curled onto her side and closed her eyes.

Despite her assertions on Marcus's feelings about her absence, her heart hoped he worried for her, at least a little.

CHAPTER 18

The sound of the front door closing echoed through the hall. Marcus stepped out of his study, a pamphlet from the Royal Society in his hand. He glanced to the entryway and saw the maid moving from the door.

"Sarah?" he called. She turned and scurried towards him, her round face smiling brightly. "Was that Mrs. Calvert leaving?"

"Yes, sir. She is on her way to see Mrs. Banner." The maid bobbed her curtsy as she spoke. "She said to be sure to tell you, sir."

"Oh." Blast. Marcus hoped to see her off. He wondered for a moment why she didn't say goodbye. Ellen didn't like to trouble anyone.

But he wished she would have known, would trust, that he valued her person and her time. She would be gone for a few hours, and told him of her going the night before, which left him no reason to worry. Yet he felt strangely bereft knowing she would not be about the house.

Sarah rocked back on her heels slightly, bringing him abruptly from his thoughts. "I apologize, Sarah. There is nothing further. You may go."

She dropped another curtsy and went on her way, humming softly.

Marcus looked down at the papers in his hand and sighed. He would've liked to discuss the information he learned with Ellen, but it could wait. There were some very interesting ideas on the proper nourishment for plum trees and he wondered if they might be beneficial to their apple orchards as well. He glanced toward the front door once more before taking himself back to his office to finish his reading.

He planned to write a letter to the Agricultural Society in London to inquire about visiting. Would Ellen enjoy going with him? Her mind absorbed information like a sea sponge absorbed water and she retained a great deal more than he thought he ever could.

He lifted another book Ellen had given him from his desk. A commonplace book. He had never used one before. But thus far, it had been a useful tool. He sometimes jotted down the name of a book and page number he would wish to refer to later, but he had copied down a few paragraphs in full. There was also a page in which he recorded questions to ask men more learned than he in the matters of caring for apple trees.

He took up his pencil and began to write what he had discovered from the pamphlet, but after a time he glanced at the clock, feeling it must be near tea time.

Barely half an hour had passed.

He frowned at the clock on his shelves and turned his attention to the estate account books.

The afternoon passed slowly, interrupted for tea, before he shook himself of the need to wonder when his wife would be home.

At some point, a footman came in and began to light more candles for Marcus to work. It was then he looked at the time and realized Ellen should return soon. He stood and stretched. Then he took up another book, deciding to sit in the front parlor where he would hear the carriage return.

There were a few things he ought to discuss with Ellen and he didn't see why he must wait until their usual conversations after dinner. And she might want to discuss her visit with Mrs. Banner. She'd been gone nearly the whole of the afternoon, which was encouraging. Louisa Banner was the perfect friend for Ellen. The woman was kind and intelligent; close in age to Ellen and mature in character.

Really, he ought to be pleased Ellen stayed out visiting late. But the sky grew darker and the time later. He finally rang for the housekeeper.

Mrs. Burk entered the parlor, her customary tranquility doing nothing to calm his concern. "Yes, Mr. Calvert?"

"Mrs. Burk, did my wife happen to say when she expected to be home?"

"I believe she planned on returning by dinner, sir." Mrs. Burk's mannerisms did not alter. "But perchance she saw the turn in the weather and decided to stay put. It appears as though a storm is beginning."

Marcus's head turned quickly toward the window. "A storm?"

"Yes, sir. I stepped outside a moment ago. I think the coachman would likely advise remaining where they are at present, given his cautious nature."

"You don't think he tried to bring her home ahead of the storm?" Marcus turned his back to her, walking all the way to the window, seeing the truth of her statement as a large fir tree near the drive rocked in the wind.

"They would already be here, were that the case. It's been snowing most of the afternoon."

He stared at the gravel path leading from the road to their door, realizing it was completely obscured by snow. Why hadn't he noticed? Why had no one informed him of the impending storm? Tension built in his shoulders as he considered the situation, knowing his wife was five miles away and likely stuck for the evening.

Ellen wouldn't be home for dinner or their conversation in the library.

She wouldn't sleep in the room adjoining his.

Nor would she be at breakfast.

Mrs. Burk didn't look concerned by these things and he wondered why.

"I ought to try to go for her," he said, turning to look at his housekeeper. "I could get there ahead of the storm and make certain she's safe." He took a step toward the door and opened his mouth to ask that his horse be readied.

His plain-speaking housekeeper's words stopped him in his tracks. "That would hardly be wise. You could do yourself or your horse an injury. Mr. Henry would've been here by now if they left ahead of the storm. The fact that she is not here means that Mrs. Calvert is safe and snug with the Banners."

Marcus knew her reasoning was sound, and more than likely correct, but he ought to do *something*. A man shouldn't sit at home in his library if his wife was stranded elsewhere in the middle of a snowstorm.

"You wouldn't make it very far before the storm rendered you blind, sir," Mrs. Burk said, her tone finally more sympathetic. "It's best you remain here, where you're safe, and go to fetch her back as soon as the storm clears. Tomorrow afternoon the roads may be better."

"Tomorrow afternoon?" He flexed his hands and began to pace the room, shaking his head from side to side. "That's a long time for Ellen to be trapped."

"Sir, she's with good company. The Banners will see to her every need and comfort."

But that was Marcus's job. He ought to be the one seeing to her. Why had the woman stayed gone so long? If she would've come home sooner, they could be readying for dinner even now, their routine uninterrupted, her safety assured. What could she have been thinking, to stay so long? It was hardly proper. Most visits to acquaintances lasted no more than half an hour. At most.

"It's a good thing for her, Mr. Calvert," his housekeeper, with an uncanny knack of reading his mind, stated. "This will be a fine way for her to grow close to Mrs. Banner and solidify their friendship. Even a small crisis can true friends make."

The woman was right. Her ability to view the situation for what it was, a small crisis, a passing concern, not at all an emergency, should have calmed Marcus. He did his best to dispel his doubts through a deep breath.

"Yes, Mrs. Burk. I see what you mean. Thank you."

"Shall I have a tray brought in for you, Mr. Calvert?" That was all. In Mrs. Burk's mind, the matter was settled, the conversation closed, and they must return to normalcy. "Or would you prefer to eat in the dining room?"

He stared at her, uncomprehending. Should he eat when he ought to be worrying about his wife? Marcus didn't feel equal to the task. But she stared at him, awaiting his response.

"A small tray, if you please. Thank you."

Marcus sat down again, looking at his books on the table. He supposed he ought to occupy himself, continue his studies, make notes for the things he wished to discuss with Ellen.

The dinner tray arrived after a short time and he put his things aside long enough to attempt nibbling at the meal. His eyes were drawn to the window, where the sky looked near black, despite the heavy white snow falling thickly. He put the meal aside and decided he would get nothing done in the parlor, staring down the drive.

He took his books to the library and sat in his usual chair.

But there, his eyes kept turning to the empty seat beside him.

"Stop," he muttered to himself. "She's perfectly safe with the Banners." He looked down at his book and realized he needed to turn to a fresh page before continuing his notes, but once the cream-colored blankness lay before him he stared at it for a time.

Perhaps it would be best if he sketched to pass the time until he went to bed. Such as a depiction of a new orchard he thought to plant, using the principles he was learning from his studies.

Marcus hesitated before telling himself, firmly, that he could sketch something as innocuous as a row of trees without becoming overly involved in the act.

He went to work quietly. Having avoided the practice since his unfortunate heart break at the hands of Selene, remembering well her mocking smile when he gave her the sketches he made of her likeness, Marcus hadn't wished to ever put another drawing on paper again.

But as part of his work, it made sense.

The page was too small.

Marcus glowered at it for a moment and looked at the pencil in his hand with the realization that it was an inferior instrument.

If he was going to draw, he would do it correctly.

Marcus went to his study where he had dropped the sketchbook and pencils purchased for him by his wife. He hadn't made use of them nor had he planned to. They were nestled in the bottom of his desk drawer, underneath a pile of old ledgers. He dug them out and opened the finely made book to the first page. He began to draw the apple trees and the rows in which he would plant them.

The exercise soothed him and occupied his mind more than his studies had. His mind on other things, he forgot, for a short time at least, that Ellen was not at home where she should be, sitting by the fire with him.

Soon his paper was filled with a well-ordered forest of apple trees neatly in a line. But something was missing from the drawing.

The trees are enough. This isn't an artistic exercise. Planning.

But his hands lingered over the page, pencil in hand, pointed tip touching the paper. Finally, giving in to temptation, he allowed his wrist to move first, then his fingers, and another image appeared among the trees.

Even though they had not been married long, Marcus knew what her silhouette looked like. He knew how she placed her hands on either side of her hips when she stood at her ease, he knew the tilt of her head when she was amused, and he knew the set of her shoulders when she relaxed.

Ellen's form appeared on his paper, standing beneath his trees, looking into the distance.

Marcus stared at the image of his wife, looking at work he had yet to do. Without meaning to, he drew her pleased by her surroundings and his labor. Would she like his plans? Did she care, one way or another, how he went about running their estate? He felt certain she must, given the amount of time and energy she spent in her conversations with him.

Something still bothered him about the drawing, but he couldn't put his finger on it. He didn't think it was the trees. He knew what apple trees looked like well enough. *Ellen* gave him the unsettled feeling.

He turned a page and tried to sketch her, alone, to make certain he could do the job properly. He drew her form again, in a similar pose, but larger, making her the focal point of the page instead of an extra detail.

He focused on the lines of her shoulders and neck, the slight curve of her hip, and then the sloping folds of her gown. Slippered feet peeked out below the hem of her skirt and it was then he began to see his difficulties.

He turned another page, determined to do her justice.

Marcus cleared his throat and sat back for a moment, scrubbing his eyes with his hands, attempting to rid himself of the ideas at the forefront of his mind.

"What is wrong with me?" he muttered into the quiet of the study. He stood and paced before the fire, trying to put his mind back where it had started. All he wanted to do, all he set out to do, was sketch his apple orchard.

Sketching, drawing, giving himself over to that artistic endeavor, had never caused him difficulties until Selene. At his most enamored of her, he spent hours putting her likeness on paper, agonizing over her form, the turn of her head, the shine on a single curl. Marcus slaved over those depictions of the woman he loved with a fever. He filled sheets and sheets with every detail of her face until he felt he memorized her perfectly.

The day he confessed his love to her and made his offer, he had first shown her his masterpiece. Drawn in ink, on a beautiful piece of parchment, he felt certain when she saw it she would realize the strength of his feelings. But she glanced at it with mild interest, pronounced it a pretty rendering, and laid the work upon a table filled with gifts from admirers. Selene gave him little of her time that day and acted with impatience when he confessed his love.

He'd never wanted to draw again.

Though he recognized the folly of his infatuation, at the time Marcus did not want to bestir the memory of Selene ever again. A part of him believed if he had possessed more skill she would have realized the depths of his devotion and considered him more seriously for her husband.

Marcus stopped his pacing beside his desk and looked down at the new page, blank before him, and wondered at himself. His skills with drawing would never earn him more than faint praise from society, and it would likely be with derision if any of his peers spoke of it, mocking time spent on a meaningless accomplishment. Most men left drawing behind, in the schoolroom, if it was not necessary to their future income.

But he enjoyed it.

And he meant to enjoy it again.

He sat down and took up his pencil, but his mind remained full of Ellen.

"I wonder," he murmured aloud. His previous attempt to draw his wife, while it left him discomfited, came to his mind. He did not, on the previous page, attempt to draw her face. Only her figure.

Ellen, his companion since coming to Orchard Hill, would be a fascinating subject to attempt. While pleasing to look at, his wife did not bear the features of someone classically beautiful.

But most people did not look very closely at the fine things right under their noses.

Marcus began to draw, starting with a basic outline of her face and shoulders, beginning a portrait.

The howling sounds of the storm outside began to fade, and beneath the graphite of his pencil, her image slowly appeared.

CHAPTER 19

D awn's light crept across the room until it slid over
Marcus's eyes, causing him to groan and sit up slowly. He
sat in his chair by the fire in the library, his sketchbook in
his lap. He left the study, late in the night, when he had the idea to
sketch his wife sitting in her chair, reading a book.

He tried to stretch his abused muscles and shook his head.
"Getting too old for this," he muttered, pushing himself up.

Marcus looked down at his rumpled clothing, his lack of coat
and cravat, and sighed. Drawing would always turn him half wild as
he chased his muse. He knew he must look frightful.

He took a staggering step towards the window to look out on
the bright morning scene, disheartened to see snow piled high
everywhere. His wife would not return to him early. Not in the
carriage, with all the world covered in thick, white blankets.

If he could go to her, assure himself of her safety, and bring
Ellen home, he would be more settled.

It took several moments of staring blankly at the landscape out
his windows before Marcus sucked in a breath, hit with an idea
which would satisfy his frustrations.

"Mrs. Burk," he shouted, tearing from the library and into the entry. "Mrs. Burk!"

Sounds from below stairs, a metal clash and a loud exclamation, turned him in the right direction. Marcus made it as far as the top of the stairs before his housekeeper appeared, looking up at him with wide eyes.

"Mr. Calvert? Is anything wrong?"

"Wrong?" He blinked down at her. "Not at all. But I want my horse readied at once. And send Cray up to me. I must dress quickly and be on my way."

"Your horse?" She came up the stairs, her eyes never leaving his. "Where are you going, Mr. Calvert?"

It surprised him she needed to ask. He opened his arms in a wide, obvious gesture. "To fetch back Ellen, of course." Then he turned and hurried away to climb the staircase to his room, determined not to waste another moment. If Cray didn't come quickly enough, he could see to himself.

But he had barely divested himself of his waistcoat when his valet came through the door which connected the dressing room to the bedroom. "Sir, I apologize, I didn't know you would need me so early." The valet looked to his master's bed and froze, eyebrows drawn together.

Marcus waved a hand toward the bed, not slept in. "Surely you noticed I never went to sleep last night."

The servant drew himself up as though his dignity had been challenged. "Mr. Calvert, you have given me leave to retire if you do not ring for me before a certain time. I thought last night was one of those evenings. If I failed you in some way—"

"Not at all, Cray. Unless you fail to have me ready to leave, braving the snow, in a timely manner." Marcus grinned when that got his manservant moving quickly, gathering up clothing and shaving equipment. "Don't worry about the shave. I am seeing no one who will be concerned. I want to get underway as soon as possible."

His valet froze and stared at him in absolute horror. "Go about unshaven? Mr. Calvert, I cannot allow that. You are to see Mrs.

Calvert, are you not? She might be concerned with your appearance."

Marcus had to concede to that point. If he must go rescue his wife, he ought not to look half wild. "Very well. But it must be quick."

"Yes, sir." The valet drew himself up and set to work.

In an impressively short quarter of an hour, Marcus's butler assisted him into his great coat, beaver hat, scarves, gloves, and informed him all was made ready.

Ellen's maid, Sarah, provided him with her mistress's riding habit.

Marcus thanked his valet, who still hovered nearby, the butler, a footman, his housekeeper, and then his groom as he climbed onto his horse. They all watched him, from inside and out of the house, but Marcus didn't care if they thought him mad.

In the night, drawing and redrawing his wife, Marcus came to a marvelous realization. Though his efforts did not reach the fever pitch of frenzy attained drawing Lady Selene, he recognized in his work a devotion to the subject of his sketches. Each line made, each stroke of his pencil, he made with great care and sincerity. He wanted to put Ellen onto the paper in such a way that she appeared to come off of it. He wanted her image to be real to any who looked on her.

Ellen's portrait must convey her intelligence, her love of learning, her kindness. He wanted more than her smile and freckles rendered; he wanted her humor and compassion on the page.

The more he worked, later and later into the night, the more his heart warmed towards his wife.

Marcus, to know her so well, in such a short time, drew her with a deep affection and dedication he could not remember ever feeling before. Waking at dawn, those feelings still nestled within his heart, he must discover what they meant, and quickly, lest the determination fade with time.

And so, he decided to go after Ellen. Immediately.

Even if it scandalized the servants.

~

ELLEN LOUNGED IN HER BED, staring up at the canopy, wondering what she would do in these early morning hours. When she awoke early before marriage, she made herself useful by attending to household matters. As a married woman, she had a tray brought to her with chocolate and she would read in her room, until she judged it near the time Marcus would be awake and seeking food downstairs. But here, in a household completely new to her, she did not know what would be best.

Ellen didn't like inconveniencing people.

She sat up and pulled the blankets to her chin, noting the room had grown chilly during the night and no one had come yet to stoke the fire in the guest chamber. She shivered and slid from the bed, picking up a shawl to wrap around her shoulders. The carpet felt cold against her feet, standing at the window, looking out on a world of white.

Her shoulders fell. What if the roads were completely covered?

Ellen wouldn't know until she consulted with the Banners and her coachman.

She decided to dress, then she could seek out the kitchen and something warm to drink. Making inquiries of the servants would be better than besetting the Banners with questions.

She slipped into the hallway after donning her dress from the day before. Mercifully, she could do up her own stays with an effort, so she was properly attired when she realized she was not alone in the hall.

"Good morning, Mrs. Calvert," a voice said, startling her.

Ellen looked down to see Arthur crouched beneath a hall table. "Arthur, you surprised me. Good morning. Are you supposed to be out of the nursery this early?"

The boy shook his head slowly. "Nurse is sleeping and so is Essie. But I'm awake." He crawled from beneath the table and gave her an earnest look. "And hungry."

"Oh dear." She reached her hand out to him. "We cannot have

that. Let's go downstairs. I will take charge of you for now, and I'll help you seek out some toast."

His eyes lit up. "With jam?"

"Yes. Lots of jam." Her heart warmed as he grinned and put his hand in hers. Children were a wonder, allowing such small things as toast and jam to light up their faces so brightly.

The servants were already awake and going about their duties, preparing food for the day, cleaning and polishing boots and flat-ware. There were eight of them in the kitchen, and Mr. Henry the coachman was one of them, eating a bowl of hot cereal.

"Good morning," Ellen sang into the room, trying to put on her most confident smile.

A chorus of good mornings met her ear as the servants hastily stood.

"Please, sit down and take no thought for me. I brought Master Arthur down to see about some toast and jam. He woke with a terrible hunger."

All eyes went to Arthur, who beamed at them without shame.

It became apparent, very quickly, just how much the staff loved the sweet child.

Mrs. Lawless, the cook, began preparing toast and sent the kitchen maid to fetch "Master Arthur's favorite strawberry jam" from the pantry. The single footman gave Arthur the seat of honor at the head of the table and pulled out a chair for Ellen almost as an afterthought. In their bustling about to attend to the child, Ellen could lean across the table to speak to her coachman.

"Good morning, Mr. Henry. I was wondering when you thought we might attempt to return to Orchard Hill. Are the roads passable?"

He shook his head over his bowl of oats and sighed. "Not at present. The sun may help our cause as the day goes on, and other people using the road for horses, but I've no hope as yet. I'll check again, after the noon hour, to see if progress has been made upon it."

Though the news disappointed her, Ellen smiled and nodded at the man. "Thank you, Mr. Henry." She turned her attention back to

Arthur as the cook placed a plate in front of her, piled with breakfast rolls, a rasher of bacon, and jam.

"Might as well feed both of you at once," Mrs. Lawless said with
a cheery smile. "Would you like some tea or chocolate, Mrs.
Calvert?"

"Chocolate, please." The dark, bitter drink was not highly
favored in society, but with a dollop of cream and sugar, Ellen quite
enjoyed it.

Soon enough, Arthur was licking the crumbs from his fingers,
and Ellen thought it would be best to take him back to the nursery.
She rose with that intention when a sharp knock sounded on the
kitchen door.

"Who could that be?" Mrs. Lawless asked. The footman went
and opened the door, revealing a man in a tall hat, thick coat, with
scarves wrapped about his throat. From his bearing and the clothes
he wore, anyone could tell he was a gentleman of means.

From the dancing brown eyes and the tilt of his head, Ellen
recognized her husband.

She forgot herself in her surprise and gasped out his name.
"Marcus."

He already looked at her, having spotted her before even setting
foot in the door. He came inside, amid bows and curtsies. Ellen felt
sorry for the servants, having their work interrupted by people who
had no right to be in their domain.

"What are you doing here?" she whispered, looking up from her
chair, too stunned to move. "How did you get through?"

Everyone in the room remained still, except the footman who
was wise enough to at least shut the kitchen door before enjoying
the spectacle before him.

"I rode my horse," he answered with a shrug, his voice muffled
by his scarf. He groaned and reached up to tug the woven cloth
down from his face, revealing a broad smile to match the twinkle in
his eyes. "I came to fetch you home."

The kitchen maid chose that moment to sigh in a manner that
Ellen wished she could allow herself, but that sound brought her
back to where she was and she hastily stood.

"We had better return Arthur to his nurse." She scooped up the boy and hurried from the room, not daring to look over her shoulder. Her cheeks felt as though they were on fire.

The maid sighed because she thought Marcus's actions dashing and romantic. But Ellen, who knew him better, could not understand his sudden rescue, even though she felt thankful for it.

The sound of his boots behind her did nothing to ease her rapid pulse. Did he intend to follow her all the way up to the nursery?

Ellen stopped and turned, Arthur on her hip. "You ought to wait in the parlor. I will be there directly." Her eyes took him in, his grin still in place, the freckles across his cheeks lending to his charm.

Marcus nodded, but remained standing there, looking down at her. "Whatever you wish, Ellen."

Her heart skipped a beat. His manner of speaking her name sounded tender, though she must have imagined it. Ellen swallowed, gave him one sharp nod, and hurried to the staircase. Arthur didn't protest being returned to the nursery, especially since he had a small breakfast to tide him over. Ellen shut the door behind him and stood in the dark hall, trying to catch her breath.

Why would Marcus go to so much trouble for her? Had he missed her?

Ellen's heart beat at a rhythm she was not accustomed to and it made her feel light-headed.

A door opened down the hallway and Louisa stepped out, tying her robe around her waist. Her hair was still in a braid, her smile sleepy. "Ellen. I heard someone out here. I thought it was Arthur. He rises early."

"It was the two of us," Ellen answered, staring at her friend, wondering what she ought to say but feeling as though she needed to ask advice. "We had toast and jam in the kitchen. I've returned him to the nursery."

Louisa chuckled and shook her head, coming further down the hall. "He's a scamp. Thank you for seeing to him. I hope he didn't wake you."

Ellen shook her head. "No. Not at all. I found him when I awoke."

"Why are you up so early?" Louisa covered a yawn with a delicate hand, raising her eyebrows in question.

Ellen shook her head. "I wanted to check on the roads. They are still impassable. But—" She bit her lip, fighting a strange desire to laugh. "But Marcus is here."

Louisa's mouth formed an "o" and she pulled her robe tighter, looking behind Ellen toward the stairs. "He is? But, how?"

"He rode his horse. To come for me." Ellen couldn't quite keep the awe from her voice and hurried to speak, trying to cover it. "I don't know what he's thinking. I left him in the parlor."

"And now you're standing up here talking to me, like a ninny." Louisa put both hands on Ellen's shoulders and turned her about too quickly for Ellen to protest. "Go straight back to the parlor, Mrs. Calvert, and speak with your husband. I will dress and be down shortly. A man on a rescue mission shouldn't be kept waiting."

Ellen allowed a laugh to slip, permitting herself to feel happy and flattered by his attention, and she hurried on her way, tossing a grin over her shoulder at her friend. Her husband cared enough for her to come across the snow-covered landscape to bring her home with him. It might be out of a sense of duty, or even some sort of lark for him, but she would appreciate the gesture for its thoughtfulness, whatever the reason.

When she entered the parlor, Marcus knelt near the fire, tending to it himself. He rose when she entered and turned to her, that grin a little smaller now but still present.

"I've caused a stir among the servants, I think."

Ellen raised a hand to her stomach in a vain attempt to still the fluttering she felt inside. "I believe you have. We'd said the roads would be impossible, and there you appeared, as though summoned."

Marcus pulled off his scarf and then began to unbutton his coat. His hat, she noticed, rested atop the mantle. He really must've surprised the servants. Nothing else explained why no one had seen to his comfort yet.

"Let me help." Ellen came forward, her warm fingers making quick work of the buttons. He turned around and she caught the heavy coat after it slid from his shoulders. She looked about for a moment and decided, since it was dry, she could lay it over the back of the couch. "Your gloves?" She held her hands out and he quickly stripped himself of the leather and put them in her hands. His bare fingers brushed hers and Ellen realized how cold he truly was, though the shiver that went through her body had nothing to do with the chill.

"Please, go back to the fire. You're frozen through." She put her hand on his arm, gently nudging him in that direction, her eyes meeting his fully for the first time since entering the room.

His expression softened and he half-bowed to her. "As my lady wishes." He took a step back before he turned and held his hands toward the cheery blaze. "But we shouldn't stay long. The horse is being walked by the stable boy. If you will gather your things, we might be on our way. I brought your riding habit." He nodded to a bundle on the sofa she hadn't noticed before. "To make it easier."

"Oh." Ellen took the bundle up in her arms. "Marcus," she said, looking up into his handsome face. His wide grin faded, turning into a gentle smile. "Thank you."

He bowed deeply, keeping his eyes on hers. "You are always most welcome, Ellen."

She dropped a curtsy and then whirled to hurry from the room. She went back to her guest quarters and began to undress down to her under garments. A light rap on the door gave her pause, but a maid had arrived to help her into her riding habit.

With her day clothing bundled up and her warm riding habit upon her person, Ellen hurried back down to the parlor. Marcus stood where she had left him, speaking in low tones with the Banners. They all looked up when she entered, each smiling.

"This is quite the rescue for you, Mrs. Calvert," Banner said in a teasing tone. "If I wasn't aware of Calvert's impatient nature, I'd be offended. It's not as though we are brigands holding you captive, after all."

Ellen's eyes turned to her husband and her heart lightened. "No, but as he's saved me from many a brigand, dragon, and wicked king, I'm afraid all he knows is how to rescue me."

Marcus's eyes brightened, and she knew he was remembering their time as children, too. Tucked up in attics, under hedges, in trees, while she played the fair maiden in need of rescue.

"It was all excellent practice for this moment," he said, with more sincerity in his voice than she expected. "Are you ready? If we hurry, we could be back in time for breakfast."

"And there's the Marcus Calvert I know. Always looking out for his next meal." Banner clapped Marcus on the shoulder.

"I'm glad you could come, Ellen." Louisa came forward and embraced Ellen as warmly as any of her sisters ever had. Then she said, in a voice meant only for Ellen to hear, "He cares for you more than you think, my friend."

Ellen returned the embrace but said nothing.

"Thank you for keeping her safe," Marcus said, bowing to their hosts.

In minutes, they were at the back of the house and Marcus brought Ellen to his horse. With no mounting block in sight, Marcus put his hands on her waist and lifted Ellen into the saddle. She blushed and quickly adjusted her seat so he could swing up behind her.

The coachman had been instructed to wait until the road was passable. This meant that once Ellen and Marcus turned out of the Banners' lane, they were alone in a world of white.

Ellen reveled in the feeling of his arms around her, even if it was just to keep control of the horse. He had never held her before. Never embraced her. To be so near him that should she wish it she could turn and press a kiss to his cheek—

She swiftly pulled that thought back and stiffened in the saddle. Realizing she had let her thoughts carry her into a realm of fantasy, when she needed to stay firmly in reality, dimmed her enjoyment of the situation considerably.

Marcus must've noticed the shift in her body, if not in her mood. "I hope I didn't ruin things for you, coming as I did." He spoke in a tone that matched their surroundings, his words calm and soft.

She matched his manner of speaking, not wanting to disturb the silence around them. "No, it's a relief to be going home. The Banners are wonderful hosts, but I'd far rather be in front of my own hearth at night."

Did she imagine it, or did he lean closer to her?

"I missed our reading together last night."

The admission made her heart stutter and stumble as it picked up speed. Had he really? His next words caused still greater confusion within her.

"And I worried after you for some time."

Ellen felt his warm breath on the back of her neck when he spoke. His arms around her shifted, the one at her back adjusting to hold her closer to his chest. She bit her lip and turned to see his expression.

Marcus saw her look and smiled. He winked at her. "Uphill here."

Oh. He was making certain she was secure as they tilted back, the horse climbing a small embankment to leave the road for an open, snow-covered field. When they evened out again, she leaned away, determined to put the distance between them before he could. If she initiated the move it would be less painful than him withdrawing.

For a long time, they were both silent, but when she caught sight of a line of apple trees she recognized, Ellen relaxed.

"Nearly there," he said, as though he'd read her mind. Then he added, with hesitation, "After you have rested we might read what we missed last evening?"

Ellen closed her eyes, imagining she heard the same hope in his voice she felt in her heart. All she wanted, all she needed to be happy, was to be near him. Even though it hurt, at times, to know he would never care for her as she cared for him.

"That would be lovely," she answered at last.

They said nothing more until they arrived home at Orchard Hill.

CHAPTER 20

T he days continued on as they had before, except Ellen saw more of Marcus than previously. He joined her for tea without being reminded, or he appeared at her elbow if she entered the library, and he came into the music room while she practiced the pianoforte. He remained attentive when in her company. Their dinners together continued as usual and his enjoyment of their time reading together lifted her heart.

They finished *The Wild Irish Girl* and turned to reading Shakespeare, taking turns with the parts of *The Taming of the Shrew*. But Marcus insisted on reading for Kate, making Ellen laugh heartily every time he pitched his voice as high as it would go. He asked her to read Petruchio with equally humorous results.

The roads eventually cleared, and the news came from London that passage would be safe, at least until the next storm. Their things were packed in a hurry. They must go to London for at least part of the Season to show support to his brother.

"And allow Mother to throw us a wedding ball. She enjoys her parties," Marcus informed her.

Ellen winced at the thought of being the center of attention, but she knew it to be her duty to appear when the family desired.

Besides, having never been to London for the Season, she thought standing up at a ball would be a small price to pay to enjoy the other spectacles of society.

"As long as I can also attend a few plays, maybe see the museums?" Though she meant to make it a condition of her attendance at their ball, it came out sounding a great deal like a request.

Marcus grinned at her over the portmanteau he held. He had brought it down from the attic for her use. "I would have thought you would be interested in the libraries and booksellers. I thought we could go together to find new volumes for our humble library."

"Together?" Her excitement made her bounce on her toes. "Yes, please. I would like that very much."

He bowed. "Make certain all is ready; we leave in the morning." Without another word, he disappeared down the hall.

The journey would take four days, if they stopped when they had no sun to travel further.

"It would be wonderful," she murmured when they were both in the carriage after several hours, "to make a journey of this distance in but a day."

"Can you imagine the speed you would have to move at?" Marcus responded, humoring her as he normally did instead of dismissing her fanciful thoughts. "Or if we could make the journey continuous, not stopping to even change horses. This puts me in mind of the steam boat we were reading of the other day."

"Oh, the American improvements on Lord Dundas's invention, yes." Ellen sat forward with interest. "Though water is most certainly more easily traversed than land, it is a marvel he could travel 150 miles in but thirty-two hours. What an incredible ride that would be."

"If only we could find a way to use steam travel over land, instead of horses." Marcus pursed his lips in thought. "But the engines required for such a thing would need a constant source of fuel."

They postulated for a long stretch of time how such things could be done, even speaking of the iron rails used by coal mining companies to move large quantities of their product with pulling horses.

Marcus made such discussions lively. He always listened to what she shared with him, whether it had a practical application in the moment or not, and often shared his own thoughts on the subject at hand.

They arrived in London exhausted, but in good spirits. The roads remained traversable, with it staying cold enough to keep the dirt paths from turning into mud. When the carriage stopped for the last time, before the Earl of Annesbury's townhouse, Ellen breathed a sigh of relief. "I'm grateful we will not be making the journey in the opposite direction for some time."

Marcus put a hand to his heart, widening his eyes comically. "Madam, you wound me. I thought you enjoyed my company, my completely undivided attention, these four days past." He stepped from the carriage and held his gloved hand out for hers. "Was I not entertaining enough?"

Ellen, amused by his teasing, stepped down and quickly tucked her hand back in her muff. "I liked our conversations, of course, but it will be nice to sit upon a seat that does not move, bounce, or jostle about."

He chuckled and nodded. "I will confess, I look forward to that as well. Come, let's get inside quickly, and we can get to our rooms before Mother discovers we are here."

Ellen giggled and hurried with him, up the steps and into the house. She felt happier and lighter than she had in many years. She was less worried about her time in London. The carriage ride with Marcus, as exhausting as the travel had been, made her grateful for the time spent with him.

They avoided the earl and his mother and were shown to adjoining rooms in the family wing. The house was large, by town standards, but not near the size of the more prestigious ducal homes they'd passed in the neighborhood. Bidding each other a quick farewell, Ellen and Marcus parted in the hallway.

Ellen entered her room and found Sarah already there, hands

folded primly before her and eyes as wide as saucers. "Sarah, how was your journey?" she asked brightly.

"Oh, lovely, ma'am. We had a grand time in the carriage." The servants left earlier that morning, from the last inn, in order to prepare the way for their employers. "And I've unpacked and put some things in the clothes press for dinner tonight. I asked 'round to see if it warranted anything special." She began to help Ellen out of her traveling costume. "There's to be a few guests to welcome Mr. Calvert and yourself to town."

That gave Ellen pause. "Oh? Any idea who?"

"Friends of the earl and a few ladies." Sarah shrugged, quickly wrapping a dressing gown around her mistress's shoulders. "If you'll sit, I'll take out your hair so you can relax a bit before dinner."

"Thank you. A nap might be just the thing." Ellen allowed her maid's ministrations and listened with half an ear as Sarah told her all about the household, the staff, and her impression of the city she had never thought she would visit.

Sarah had finished tying a ribbon at the end of Ellen's braid when a soft rap came from the door separating her bedroom from her husband's. Sarah and Ellen both turned to the door and stared at it in silence for a long moment.

"Ought I to get it, ma'am?" Sarah asked, eyebrows raised at the door. "I'm not sure what propriety dictates."

"Take these things to be cleaned, Sarah, if you will." Ellen waved vaguely at the clothing she had cast off and stood, tightening the sash around her wrap. "I'm sure it's nothing." She walked to the adjoining door but waited until Sarah had gone before she leaned close. "Who is it?"

What a ridiculous thing to say. As if anyone would knock at that door other than her husband.

A little thrill shot through her at the thought.

"Might I have a word, Ellen?"

Ellen took a deep breath before opening the door a crack. How silly, for a wife to hesitate in opening a door to her husband.

"Yes, Marcus?" She tried to look more at ease than she felt.

He stood on the other side of the door, head cocked to one side as he peered in at her. He appeared half-dressed, without a coat or neckcloth, and lacking shoes. When she noticed his stocking feet, Ellen quickly pulled her gaze back up to his face, hoping her blush was not overly visible.

Marcus half-grinned at her. "I've been informed there is to be a dinner party tonight. I think your abigail is aware. But I wondered if you are up to attending, given we have been on the road for several days. It would be an easy thing for you to be ill or exhausted from travel."

"Only me? Do you plan to attend, either way?" she asked, curious.

"Yes. It would appease Mother if one of us is at dinner."

"Then I will attend as well. I think after a short nap I will be equal to the task."

"Excellent." He leaned his shoulder against the doorway, seeming in no hurry to end their conversation, for all it resembled border guards discussing the weather. "Is your room to your liking?"

She glanced over her shoulder at the beautiful furnishings and the sumptuous bed. Her body positively ached. "Yes, very much. Especially that beautiful bed. I want nothing more than to crawl beneath its covers."

She turned her attention back to him and his grin had returned, in a most crooked manner. When she realized what she said, and how it must sound, and how they both were lacking in proper attire, her face went up in a blaze of embarrassment.

"I must retire now. Excuse me. Good afternoon," Ellen stammered before she shut the door abruptly, feeling it clip his shoulder as the handle snipped into place.

Standing perfectly still, Ellen heard him chuckle, and then his soft footfalls on the polished floors padded away. She turned and walked dazedly toward her bed and sank into the mattress, pulling the blankets over her head.

"He must think me a complete simpleton," she muttered.

But he had been the one to break their unspoken arrangement, their adherence to complete privacy.

Of course, four days on the road together, in the same carriage, meant a great deal of that privacy from home had evaporated. But she assumed once their travels came to an end they would pick up their usual habits. For Marcus to so blatantly change the rules unnerved her.

Or, she thought with a frown, after those days together in the carriage, during which time he touched her to hand her in and out of the conveyance, he no longer thought they need worry over those barriers.

Rolling over, Ellen gave her pillow a harsh thump. "You knew what you were getting into, marrying him," she muttered to herself.

Ellen forced herself to close her eyes, tried to make her body relax, and had achieved some measure of peace when her eyes flew open and she sat up, staring at the doorway between their rooms.

There was no lock on her side of the door. Nothing. No keyhole. No bolt. Just an intricately curved handle.

She fell back into the pillows and shook her head. While she doubted her husband would breach the doorway, the fact that he could, the fact that he was expected to by whomever arranged their rooms, made her stomach clench and her mind whirl.

Her plan for a nap before dinner was thoroughly ruined.

~

MARCUS MADE his way downstairs early, ready for dinner but searching out his brother. He had not had word from Lucas since the wedding and was curious what was happening in Parliament. He made his way to Lucas's study, hardly noticing the familiar sights of the family townhome. The floors were tiled with black and white marble, paintings and family portraits hung along the walls, and vases of flowers were on every table.

He knocked on the dark oak paneled door.

"Enter," his brother called and Marcus stepped inside. "Marcus, there you are. You avoided us rather neatly this afternoon." Lucas came from around his desk, extending his hand to Marcus, who accepted the firm handshake. Lucas clapped him on the arm as he stepped away. "And how is Mrs. Calvert?"

"She is well, though perhaps uncertain about her first season in London."

"Abigail was nervous the first year we married," Lucas said with an understanding nod. "Would you like a drink?"

"No, thank you." Marcus followed his brother to the desk where they each took a chair on the same side. "Did you worry after Abigail that year?" He could not imagine his brother's late wife had been too uncomfortable. Not like Ellen. Abigail had been the eldest daughter of an earl and had been born to the lifestyle of the *ton's* elite.

"For a time, I didn't leave her side," Lucas admitted, his eyes taking on a faraway look. "There are a different set of rules for the married women of the *ton*. After a few weeks, she found her footing."

Marcus tried to imagine what his brother's life might be like. He knew Lucas and Abigail had a love match, adoring each other from nearly the first moment they met. What would it be like to find that connection to another person and then lose them?

"I hope Ellen can find her place. She'll not have a title to lift her in society, only connections to you and the Falkhams."

"And to you." Lucas raised his blond eyebrows high. "You are her most important connection. I hope you'll not forget that."

Marcus nodded. "I will do all I can to see to her comfort."

"You are getting on with her?" Lucas asked, tilting his head to one side. "I have wondered, given the nature of your marriage, if you'd find a practical wife suitable after the passage of some time."

"More so than ever," Marcus answered. "Ellen is a godsend. She took the reins of the household and everything runs smoothly. It's a marvel, and all the servants respect her. She's been helping me with my education in tree-farming as well. Truly, her advice and perspective have been invaluable to me." The pride he felt in his wife and her abilities must've shown on his face, and he let slip more in his expression than he meant to.

"Marcus." Lucas leaned forward and clasped his hands together beneath his chin, a speculative gleam in his eyes. "Do you have feelings beyond your obvious gratitude for your wife?"

"I admire her a great deal," Marcus said slowly.

"I see." Lucas raised his eyebrows higher. "And?"

The two of them had always been close. Marcus trusted his brother with his life but trusting him with the secrets of his heart was more difficult. He wanted to run his hands through his hair, to tug at his too-stiff collar, to stand and pace like a caged lion at the Tower menagerie. But Lucas's earnest expression, and Marcus's uncertainty, finally won out.

"I think I'm falling in love with Ellen."

Lucas sat back, his eyes going wide. "That's *wonderful* news, isn't it? You don't look like you think it's wonderful news."

"I don't know that it is." Marcus stood, unsettled, and gave in to the desire to pace. If he touched his hair or collar, after all, both his mother and his valet would have his hide. "I have no knowledge of her feelings for me, and love has done neither you nor I any favors."

"It has caused a great deal of pain," Lucas said, his voice somber. Marcus paused, seeing the shadows from the fire deepening the lines of sorrow in his brother's face. "But only because it was taken from me and not returned to you. I think you should tell Ellen."

"I think I should wait."

Lucas shook his head and leaned back. "You know best. But what have you to lose if she doesn't return your feelings? You are still married. You have your whole life to woo her."

"If she doesn't return them, she could be disgusted completely by them." Marcus dropped back into his chair with a grimace. "She could be put off by me. Become uncomfortable in my presence. Any number of awful things could happen should I speak before she is ready to hear."

"Then you had better get her ready to hear." Lucas shook his head and pointed at the glass cabinet on the wall. "Would you like that drink now? You look like you could use it."

Marcus groaned and dropped his face into his hands. "I told her I didn't hope for romance. Told her I couldn't allow that into our relationship. Ever."

"Then you lied, didn't you?" Lucas asked, a faint trace of humor in his tone. "But she'll likely forgive you, if you ask politely enough."

Marcus shot an irritated look at this brother. "Don't say anything about this, Luc."

"Not a word, Marc." He stood and bowed. "But you can't blame me if I enjoy watching the dance between you."

"I suppose not."

Lucas went to the cabinet and began to prepare their drinks, his back to Marcus. "Did you hear that Selene is in London?"

Marcus's shoulders dropped and he closed his eyes tightly. "Of course she is." He would rather not think about her at all, especially given the situation he found himself in with his wife. Lady Castleton could take herself off back to the Continent, as far as he was concerned, as he had enough trouble at hand without whatever cloud of gossip trailed behind her. "I hope no one speaks of it to Ellen."

"It's the *ton*, Marcus. Everyone will positively rush to tell her."

Marcus hated that his brother was right.

CHAPTER 21

Ellen slipped into the impressive library of her brother-in-law's home and stood near the fire, leaning against the mantle-piece. She closed her eyes and rested her head against the marble, soothing her headache by pressing against the cool stone. She could hear the rest of the family and guests in the entryway, saying farewell and goodnight.

At least she did not have to become overly accustomed to these events, she told herself. She was not the countess, only the wife of a second son.

Watching Marcus converse with and flatter the other ladies in the party all evening surprised her, but she supposed she ought not to have expected his behavior to be different. No one else thought it strange for him to behave as he always had before.

The voices in the hall grew more faint, with fewer participants speaking, and then she heard the click of boots moving toward the stairs. The family must be alone in the house at last. Ellen relaxed and sighed. She might finally obtain some rest. Supposing Marcus felt no need to rap on the door adjoining their rooms again.

The door to the library opened and Ellen hurriedly stood

straight and away from the wall, attempting to appear properly composed.

"It's me, Ellen." She turned and Marcus stood there, closing the door behind him. "I knew you'd be here, if you hadn't already gone to bed." He looked about the room, at the roaring fire and the shelves of books. "How do you like the library?"

Ellen stared at him and offered a shrug. "It's very fine."

"Very fine?" he repeated, coming forward. "That will never do. Not from you. You've not taken the time to appreciate it fully." He held his hand out to her and she slipped hers in without a thought. Marcus tugged her gently towards one of the well-cushioned sofas in the room and motioned for her to sit.

"I will appreciate it more from this vantage point?" She settled on the couch and then looked towards the shelves. "I'm afraid it looks the same, but that isn't a bad thing. It is a *very* fine library, Marcus."

He settled next to her and looked around again. "I always liked it. I spent many afternoons here reading while my mother entertained callers."

"As a boy?"

His expression turned inward, though he remained facing the fireplace. "Mm. And as a young man. And an adult. Conceivably as a married man, too, while you both wait upon the finest ladies of London society."

Unable to help it, Ellen shuddered at the very thought. "Your mother, is she in great demand still? Even as a dowager countess?"

He nodded slowly. "Yes. She is a great favorite to many. I think it's because she isn't a toad eater. Mother is always honest in her words and relationships. That's rare in society, especially when a person is able to be that way and remain kind."

Although she didn't speak, Ellen wished to ask why he would spread flattery around so liberally with the example of his mother's finer behavior before him. Instead she leaned into the back cushion more, allowing her eyes to linger on her husband.

"I have always liked your mother. I cannot be surprised others find her as I do."

Marcus stretched his arm over the back of the sofa, his forearm resting above her shoulders. He leaned back and sighed.

"They will like you, too, Ellen. You are kind, intelligent, and have a good heart. People will see that. The cats in society will hate it, poke their fun, and then leave you alone when you don't rise to meet their behavior. But the truly noble women, and men, will admire you."

Though her heart warmed at his words, she reminded herself this was but the latest in a long list of compliments bestowed by him tonight. The words sounded sincere, but she couldn't allow herself to be overly moved by them.

She forced a smile. "I have no need for admiration. I'm content if I have a few friends and if I do the family credit when I am out in society. That is enough for me."

He turned to her, his eyes meeting hers, filled with an emotion she could not place. Admiration? No, it must be fondness. He lowered his hand from the furniture and placed his arm around her in a way he never had before. The gesture made her stomach flip.

"You are a wonder, Ellen. I am forever grateful we met at your cousin's. I am glad of it, and glad to have you for a companion."

She sighed and lowered her hands to her lap. They were both being too serious, and she must dispel the air of such talk quickly, lest things become uncomfortable for either of them. He spoke of her as a companion, as one might speak of any chum or even a favored hound.

"You're glad of it because I don't make frivolous demands of you. Perhaps I ought to. I ought to demand that you take me to the park tomorrow, during the fashionable hour, and parade me about to all of London." He blinked at her in surprise, though his lips twitched slightly.

She continued her list with enthusiasm. "Or I could insist on visiting the Palace gardens, as I hear they are lovely even in the depths of winter. Or we could attend the saloons I have heard so much of or go to Gunter's to see and be seen." His smile grew with each idea, his eyes twinkling at her. "Let us go to the zoo and look at the tiger. Or to the university to tour the grounds and sit in lectures. I might even persuade you to take me to a surgical theater."

His words finally burst out. "Surgical theater? I cannot think of another woman of my acquaintance who would suggest such a thing, even in jest."

He started laughing and drew nearer her, his leg brushing against hers and his arm tightening around her shoulders. Her stomach performed that strange flip again and her head felt light, as it did when she imbibed one glass of wine too many at her sister's wedding. She laughed too, more out of nerves than anything. Her husband sobered after a moment, looking down at her, the last vestiges of humor still glittering in his eyes.

"Ellen, you must know, I would take you wherever you wished to go."

Ellen could not hide her surprise. "Would you? Even to the surgery? Or to university lectures?"

"Yes. Anything, anywhere. I have seen and done all that I can in London. It would be diverting, and an honor, to squire my wife about town and allow you to see everything you wish." He leaned his head back, closing his eyes. "There are many things to see in London."

Although tired, Ellen could not bear to leave an opportunity to learn more about her husband. "Which are your favorite places? Where have you been?"

"I enjoyed the Pall Mall Picture Galleries."

Ellen tilted her head up, meeting his look with surprise. "You did? The art museum?"

"Of course. And there is the Royal Museum, as we spoke of before. I think you'll enjoy it."

She was still trying to picture him walking around an art gallery and commenting upon the English masters hanging there. "What else?"

"Most places in London are made for people to go and be seen. But there are quiet corners here and there. Private galleries, parks that see little use when everyone is busy parading down Rotten Row. Shops hidden at the ends of streets."

"And you seek such quiet places out?" she asked, her voice growing soft. Ellen liked picturing him on his own, in solitary rambles throughout the city. "We may have more in common than I thought."

Marcus looked down at her and she detected surprise in his expression. But the hour grew late and her eyes heavy. She closed them and rested her head on his shoulder, resisting the voice in her head that said she ought to go to bed. She did not want their conversation to end, knowing how busy the days to come would be, and realizing that when they shared their time with others he would not be this attentive.

She *had* fallen asleep against his shoulder once, in the carriage, and he had not seemed to mind. Surely he wouldn't mind her leaning upon him this once. She would rest her eyes for a moment.

When he spoke, he matched her tone. "I believe we do have a great deal in common. I suppose that is why we have always been comfortable around each other."

Ellen wished he were not quite so comfortable. She wished, most ardently, that he found her interesting and invigorating. *Comfortable* was not the word she would use to describe her feelings for him, after all.

He shifted, bringing her closer to him in a cozier manner, and she felt his cheek press down into her hair. Ellen hoped her hair pins were out of the way.

She sighed and murmured, "You must show me all those places, Marcus. I want to see them."

His voice when he spoke remained soft, less amused and sincerer. "If you wish it." Ellen imagined he dropped a kiss on her forehead and she could not help but smile and sigh. "Dear Ellen." She heard no more, as she slipped at last to sleep.

～

A WARM, soft body snuggled against his chest, smelling of apple blossoms and summertime. Marcus smiled and adjusted his arms, settling more closely to the delightful apparition in his arms. She sighed and shifted.

His eyes blinked open.

He saw rows and rows of books. Marcus looked down, at the top of a coronet of black braids and curls. His breath caught and his heart thudded to a painful stop before resuming a faster rhythm.

Ellen lay asleep in his embrace. He was fully reclined on the library sofa and his wife rested half atop him, her hands tucked up beneath her and the skirt of her gown covering both their legs. The room was bathed in the blue-gray light of dawn, slipping through the curtains enough for him to see the curve of his wife's cheek.

Marcus closed his eyes, his mind searching for an explanation of the situation, and how he might wake Ellen without causing embarrassment on her part. But then she made the slightest sound in her sleep, a quiet hum, that made a tremor run through his body and convinced him not to move. He wanted to enjoy holding his wife, providing her warmth and comfort. At least for a few minutes longer.

One of his arms rested about her shoulders, the other around her waist. Her slow, even breathing soothed him and he found his breaths were in unison with hers.

Marcus hadn't realized how much he ached to hold her until that moment, when having her nestled against his heart filled all the empty places in his soul. Whatever he had thought of love before, however he had imagined it in the past, was nothing compared to the peaceful joy suffusing him in the quiet of the library.

It could not last.

Servants would be awake soon, if they were not already, going through the house to prepare it for another day. Ellen wouldn't want to be awoken by a servant's entry to the room. It fell to him to break the spell, though he would've remained entrapped by it all the day long if he had the choice.

"Ellen," he whispered, the hand at her waist coming up to stroke her cheek. "Ellen, darling. It's morning."

She made a noise halfway between a moan and a protest, then

snuggled closer to his chest. He couldn't help but chuckle, and at the sound her body stiffened.

Ah, now she's awake.

Marcus held his breath and waited, wondering what her reaction to their situation would be. Did Ellen long for more between them, as he did? Would it please her to find him near upon waking?

Ellen's hand moved from between them up to his shoulder, then she spread her other palm flat against his chest, carefully pushing herself upright. Their eyes met, hers wide and disbelieving, and Marcus tried to remain relaxed. The cold air rushed to fill the space between them.

"Good morning," he said in a near-whisper. "How did you sleep?"

Her cheeks blazed red, but her body remained hovering there, semi-reclined. "Well. I think." She took in a deep breath and lowered her eyes to his chest. "I can't move." For a moment, his heart warmed towards this admission, but her eyes darted up to his again and he saw in them a measure of distress. "I think you're on my skirts."

"Oh." He ignored his disappointment and instead swung his legs down from the sofa, careful not to snag his shoes on the hem of her gown. He sat up, his arm around her shoulders to help steady her as she did the same. Ellen sat stiffly beneath his arm, holding herself away from him. Marcus's heart plummeted somewhere below his stomach and he released her, running his hand through his hair.

"I'm terribly sorry," she said, her voice a whisper. "I cannot think how this happened."

"Quite all right." Marcus looked to the slit between the curtains, noting the blue-gray was starting to grow more yellow. Morning was upon them. But no one would expect either of them to be up so early, after the late night. "If we go quietly, we can likely return to our chambers without anyone being the wiser."

Her fair skin brightened again with a blush and her eyes met his, worry straining her features. "Do you think anyone noticed?"

Marcus stared at her, trying to decide why it would distress her so. Was it maidenly modesty? Or was she upset at anyone perceiving their connection being more than friendly? He could not be sure, but he knew what he hoped.

"If anyone happened upon us last night, I doubt they would think a thing of it. We were both tired and it isn't as if we need a chaperone."

Her eyebrows drew together and she nodded. "That's true. I suppose we might be excused. I would hate to be the subject of gossip, though."

Deciding he would accept that as his answer, Marcus sighed and pushed himself up from the sofa. He held his hand out to assist Ellen to her feet as well. "The Annesbury servants are loyal. I doubt anyone outside of this house would ever hear of it."

She stood and tucked her arm through his. "That's good, I suppose." Her uncertainty with the situation did not give him any ease of thought.

"If we hurry, no one but our personal servants will ever know we didn't sleep in our own beds last night." He had to force his smile and he wondered when it had become so hard to pretend a lighter mood than he felt. After years of negotiating the *ton*, wearing a mask of solicitude and amiability, he could now hardly summon the energy to convince his wife the whole situation was something to be laughed about.

Marcus didn't want to laugh. He wanted to curl back up on the sofa with Ellen, holding her in his arms, and find the peace he'd felt upon waking to find her there.

Instead, he led Ellen from the room and through the halls. Her evening slippers made no noise on the marble floor or grand staircase, and he treaded lightly enough that his own steps were nearly silent. They saw no one as they went down the halls to the family quarters, where he stopped before her bedroom door.

"No one will expect you up for hours yet," he told her, looking down through the hall's shadows into her beautiful eyes. It was harder to see her here than it had been in the library, so he may have imagined her blush. "You can take a nap if you wish."

She nodded and tipped her head to one side, regarding him with curiosity. "What of you? Will you go back to sleep?"

Marcus traced the delicate lines of her jaw with his eyes, then took in the dark ringlets framing her face and the locks of hair that had escaped her elaborate coiffure in the night. Her loveliness, her soft features, drew him to stand closer. He longed to kiss her but fought not to stare at the curve of her soft pink lips. Instead, Marcus took her hands up in both of his.

Ellen's breath caught and he wondered if his nearness alarmed or excited her. Would he ever have the courage to find out? If she could not love him, her rejection would wound him more deeply than a woman like Selene ever could.

"I doubt I will be able to sleep, even if I tried, with the same peace and comfort I enjoyed before waking this morning." Let her make of that what she would. The admission drained most of his energy and Marcus could not bear to lay any more of his heart open to her yet. He did not meet her eyes as he dropped a kiss upon her forehead, then he turned and walked the several paces to his door.

The sound of her door opening and closing again with a soft click was all he heard, then he ducked into his bedroom and closed the door, leaning against it heavily.

Despite his weariness of spirit, Marcus knew he would not sleep. His eyes darted to the door connecting his bedchamber to his wife's and he shook his head. He went to the wardrobe and dug through it until he found his riding clothes. Without calling his valet, something he knew he would have to explain to Cray later, Marcus undressed and dressed himself with haste.

A bruising ride through the park was exactly what he needed to face the world at large and, as his wife had once told him, to clear the cobwebs from his mind.

CHAPTER 22

Accompanying his wife through the town lifted Marcus's spirits considerably. Ellen's curiosity of nearly everything to do with London had him remembering lessons in history, deportment, and geography. Though Ellen expressed her desire to take everything in as quickly as possible, their tour was confined to the shops on his mother's orders. Ellen was to find a suitable ballgown for that very evening and commission another one with haste.

"She cannot appear in ballgowns from last season. From *Bath's* last season," his mother had proclaimed in horror upon seeing Ellen's wardrobe.

Marcus visited several seamstresses with his wife, until they found a woman whose French accent was better than the others' and who took one look at Ellen and announced she already had the perfect dress.

"It will take a little altering. Another client commissioned it, of course, but now finds she cannot be seen in blue. Imagine, giving up a dress so exquisite on a whim." The seamstress sniffed disdainfully and raised her shoulders in a way that nearly convinced Marcus she had come from France.

"Come with me, Mrs. Calvert." She took Ellen by the hand and led her into a back room for a fitting, and when Ellen looked back at him with a helpless smile he shrugged and waved.

Marcus sauntered around the front of the shop, looking at some of the fashion plates left on tables to tempt customers, but then his eyes strayed up to the window and he looked out on the street.

Lady Selene, now Lady Castleton, stood on the walk and stared up at him. She tipped her head to the side, a slow, feline smile changing her features from lovely to exquisite. No one in England knew how to play up their features to such perfection as she did.

He waited to feel pain at the sight of her, for his heart to leap, or any of the old reactions to come. Instead, his relief washed over him.

She held no power over him any longer.

With that knowledge to fortify him, Marcus went out the door and directly to her.

"My, my. Marcus Calvert," she said, holding her hand out to him in greeting. He took it and bowed, in as slight a manner as he could without giving offense.

"Lady Castleton."

"Oh, dear man, we are old friends. Surely you will still call me Selene?" She lowered her lashes, falsely demure.

Marcus smirked, realizing she was trying to play the game with him. But he had already won. "That was years ago, my lady, and I feel I do not know you so well as I thought. But it's of no consequence. We will not be seeing each other again. I wished to say goodbye."

She blinked up at him, confusion momentarily clouding her crystal blue eyes, but she pushed her bottom lip forward in a pout he had once found adorable. What had been wrong with him? The juvenile behavior did nothing to recommend her anymore.

"But, Mr. Calvert. Marcus. How could you say that? We are both in London. It is the season. And I wished to invite you to the theater with me this week."

"That will be impossible," he said firmly. "I intend to go to the theater next week, with my wife, but we already have a full schedule until then." He couldn't help grinning when she narrowed her eyes at him.

"I have missed you," she stated, the look in her eyes bolder. "Surely you know what you meant to me. My marriage is without warmth of feeling or kindness of spirit. I merely thought you, someone who cared for me, might offer some comfort."

Her meaning hit him squarely between the eyes and he took a step back. "My lady, you are most mistaken in the nature of our relationship in past or the present. I must also say that there will be no future conversation between us. Good bye." He tipped his hat to her, then turned and fled back into the dress shop.

Ellen stood at the front of the shop when he entered, her brows furrowed in a deep frown. "Who was that?" she asked, glancing back to the window where he saw Selene's figure marching rapidly down the street. "You made her upset."

Marcus shook his head. "It's no one of consequence. Someone I used to know." He looked around the shop, not seeing its keeper anywhere. "What of the dress? Will it suit you?"

"I believe so. They will make a few small alterations and deliver it this afternoon," she answered slowly, regarding him with a quizzical frown. "Are you well, Marcus?"

"Yes. Very." He smiled and offered his arm to her. "Would you like to go home by way of the book shops?"

Her eyes brightened and Marcus knew he had hit upon the right topic to inspire a change of subject. He had no need to speak of or to Lady Castleton ever again. Whatever the spell she had placed him under, it had been successfully broken by the woman at his side. Ellen's was the only smile that would ever have power over him again.

CHAPTER 23

Ellen stood next to Lady Annesbury, her eyes taking in the crowded ballroom. "This is the most people I have ever seen in a room together," Ellen said, barely loud enough for her mother-in-law to hear.

Lady Annesbury, who insisted Ellen call her Mother, chuckled and waved her fan in a languid manner. "Dear child, you have seen nothing yet. This ball had a very select guest list. Never you fear. In time you will be at ease in these circumstances."

Though Ellen appreciated her mother-in-law's advice, she did not see it coming to fruition any time soon. They had arrived at this, her first ball in London, half an hour previous and still Ellen couldn't bring herself to make eye contact with anyone. She'd been introduced to several lords and ladies by Lady Annesbury, but she doubted she would remember their names.

Bath society, which had once seemed more than adequate to her, she saw as a pale shadow compared to what London could offer.

She also missed Marcus's company. Lucas had taken him off to speak to a lord-something-or-other about the French war. Ellen would much rather have gone with them and listened in on the political conversation than attempt to make an impact on the social circle of Lady Annesbury.

As if her morose thoughts had summoned him, Lucas appeared at her side. "If it isn't my new sister. How goes it, Ellen?" he asked, bending to speak directly in her ear.

Ellen narrowed her eyes at him. "Do not even attempt banter with me, *brother*. You took my husband away with you and have yet to return him." She had found herself comfortable with her brother-in-law nearly at once. He had come and spent weeks at her cousin's home in their childhood, after all, and had teased her mercilessly back then.

"I do apologize for borrowing him for so long," he said. His eyebrows lowering, Lucas assumed an expression of contrition. "It could not be helped. I needed a second opinion and I trust his."

"And did you lose him?" she asked, making a show of looking about them. "You ought not to be so careless with your brother. Especially now that you have me to answer to."

Lucas chuckled and then offered her half a bow. "I apologize, Mrs. Calvert. My brother was snatched out of my care by a very insistent baron who wished to have a word with him. Lord Falkham."

"The Falkhams are here?" Ellen asked, her eyes widening with excitement. "Why didn't you say so straight away? Where are they?"

"On the other side of the room."

"Ellen," her mother-in-law said, "you may go and greet them, but I do have others I wish to introduce you to." She gentled the command with a smile, but a command it remained. Ellen nodded her understanding.

"Mother," Lucas said, straightening to his full height. "Come now. It's Ellen's first London ball. It's a time for dancing, not introductions to all our stuffy friends." Lady Annesbury huffed, but Ellen saw a twinkle of humor in her eye.

"Very well, very well. Go see your friends, dear."

"Thank you, Mother," Ellen said, trying to keep from smiling. She dropped a curtsy before taking Lucas's arm. But rather than lead her around the crowded dance floor, he walked directly to it.

"Will you dance with me, Ellen?" He tilted his head to one side and offered her the barest smile. "You haven't danced yet. I would like to be the first."

"Very well." Ellen sighed as though put out. "But you cannot distract me after that."

He nodded, pursing his lips most seriously, and took her out on the floor to join the next set, a reel. Ellen relaxed, especially when she realized she and her brother-in-law would start the set by merely standing and staring at one another until their turn to move came.

"How are you enjoying London?" he asked from his side of the line.

"It's big and loud, and terribly crowded," she answered, lifting her eyebrows. "But besides all of that, I like it tolerably well."

Lucas seemed to bite the insides of his cheek at that and it took him a moment to answer. "Your head is not turned by the dazzling dresses or sparkling wealth?"

Ellen shook her head, lowering it slightly as she did. "Does that disappoint you?"

"Not at all. I think it's perfect, for you and Marcus. He doesn't enjoy society either, you know."

That comment took her by surprise. "But he does so well here."

"He wears a very fine mask," Lucas answered, but then said no more as their turn came to join hands in the reel. The movement of the dance separated them for a short time, but when they came together again, at rest while another couple promenaded, Ellen took up the subject once more.

"What makes you think Marcus doesn't enjoy the season?" Although she had caught Marcus out in preferring the quiet places of London, he had never said that he disliked the whirl of society.

"He's told me," Lucas answered simply, shrugging very slightly to keep a proper dancing form. "I have known him all my life and he is happiest when he is not on display. I'm afraid being the second son of an earl, and now the younger brother of one, does not give much pleasure."

The dance caught them up again, Ellen joining hands with another man and stepping as lightly as she could, given the new thoughts in her head.

Marcus doesn't like it any better than I do. Ellen wanted to laugh. It made perfect sense, putting together all the pieces of his personality she understood. When she had first heard rumors of his flirtatious behavior, years ago, she had at first been surprised. He had always been quietly playful, the summers she spent time with him. Ready to tease and laugh, but never one to put himself forward. She thought he must've changed. But he hadn't.

Marcus wore the mask and played a part, as he had told her before they wed. He knew what society expected and wanted from him and that is what he gave it. He protected his brother, he did nothing to sully his family's reputation, and he did his mother's bidding. None of this was wrong, of course, but Ellen realized it was not necessarily a life he wanted to live.

At Orchard Hill, at *home*, he spoke with sincerity and without flattery. Here in London it seemed every word that slipped from him was cloaked in a double meaning, or else meant to stroke the vanity of his listeners. He understood society well enough to play the role it had given him, but that did not mean he liked it.

Then what are we doing here? she asked herself, looking down the row of dancers.

Lucas returned to stand before her and when their eyes met, she watched his expression change from cheerful to curious. "Something has changed since I saw you last, sister, and that was but moments ago."

Ellen forced a smile and put her thoughts away. She would examine them more closely at another time. "I missed you, brother," she said, then tried his trick of dropping a quick wink.

The earl's lips twitched upward, the closest thing to a smile she'd seen on his face. "Very good, Ellen. You will learn to play the game too."

She nodded at what he must've intended to be a compliment, but Ellen didn't think this was a game she'd ever enjoy playing.

When the dance ended, Lucas took her arm again and led her through the crowds. Ellen caught sight of Marcus's coppery hair first, sadly devoid of its curls since he'd had it cut again, and then saw Collin's taller head.

"Marianne," she exclaimed when they were steps apart. "I'm so glad you've come." She released Lucas's arm and went to embrace her friend, despite being in a crowded ballroom of onlookers.

"And I'm glad to see *you* here, my dear. Looking so elegant, too." Marianne laughed and set Ellen at arm's length, looking her up and down. "It seems that marriage suits you, as I knew it would." The twinkle in her eye, playful as it was, caused Ellen to blush without knowing why.

"Thank you." She leaned closer and whispered in Marianne's ear. "How are you feeling?"

Marianne colored slightly. "Very well, at present. Collin takes good care of me."

Marcus met Ellen's eyes at that moment, his smile warmer and more genuine than she'd seen since their first night in town, in the privacy of the library. The memory of that night, and waking the next morning in his arms, still flooded her with a pleasurable warmth she tried not to dwell upon. Did he think of it too?

Her husband moved to her side while Lucas and Collin began a conversation on Parliament. Marcus stood close enough to lean down and speak in her ear. "Did you enjoy your dance with Lucas?"

"Very much. He is a delightful brother." She tipped her head to the side enough to meet his eyes. "Have you danced yet?"

"The only woman I wish to dance with was occupied, first with my mother and then my brother." He bent even closer, his lips almost against her ear. "And for some reason, society frowns upon a man dancing with his wife."

A shiver played up and down Ellen's spine, though it had nothing to do with the room temperature. Her husband's nearness would continue to affect her, it would seem. She smiled and lowered her eyes.

"Must you always do what society wishes you to do, Marcus?" she asked, her voice low. She wasn't sure she dared look at him, or why she had made such a brazen suggestion.

But she felt his hand at her elbow, then it slid down her arm to her wrist, and his fingers caught hers in their warm grasp. "I think, in this case, I must not," he said, his tone warm and firm.

Ellen looked up at him, her lips parting in surprise.

"Dance with me, Mrs. Calvert?" he asked, his eyes on hers, taking up her whole world.

"Yes."

And she became aware enough of the world around them to see Lucas over his brother's shoulder, his eyebrows raised, and Marianne to one side looking pink with pleasure.

But Marcus didn't look back at them. He pulled her hand gently to the crook of his arm and led the way to the dance floor. Ellen's ears picked up, as if from far away, the faint strains of a waltz.

A waltz.

Though the dancing forms called for them to occasionally be paired with others, Marcus would be her primary partner, spending most of the time holding her in his arms.

They came to the floor, bowing and curtsying to those opposite them, and then began.

Ellen lost count of the number of times her hands clasped his. She went through the steps but could have missed nearly every one without knowing it. Marcus's eyes remained on hers, regardless of which lady he partnered, guiding Ellen through the movements with no more than a smile in her direction.

They stood still at last, facing one another, waiting for their turn to step forward once more.

"Is that the new Calvert woman?" someone said from behind her, loud enough that she couldn't help but hear.

"It is, but I've never seen her about before. Odd sort of creature, isn't she?" another voice answered.

Ellen's face caught fire.

Marcus's expression changed to a frown and she wondered if he hadn't been able to hear. He was farther from the speakers than she.

"I heard she was a spinster. No one wanted her. Wonder why Calvert picked her up?"

It didn't matter who stood behind her. Ellen knew no one in town. How did they know her? How did they know the bitter truths of her story?

Marcus moved forward and she realized, a half-step too late, that she should do the same. He caught her hand up anyway and drew her closer to him than the dance called for, his deep brown eyes pulling her in.

"Ellen, don't listen to them," he whispered.

They stepped apart again and her mortification was complete. Marcus *had* heard. She looked down at the floor, uncertainty replacing her earlier enjoyment of the dance.

"You are a Calvert now," he whispered when they stepped together once more, and he gently squeezed her hand. "More importantly, you are *my* wife."

Her eyes filled with tears, but she tipped her chin up. Ellen would not disappoint him. As a Calvert, and his wife, she was meant to uphold the family pride and position. But when her eyes met his again, Marcus's gaze was filled with tenderness. Not pride, or even reassurance.

Marcus looked as though he wished to hold her, protect her, and Ellen's heart responded in a quick, fluttering moment.

Together, they moved down the line, holding each other's hands. Marcus did not take his eyes from her and she did not look away again.

"We are in this together, Ellen. Forever." And then he smiled, as though being joined to her was the greatest possible fate. They stood apart again, and as the waltz ended he bowed, his eyes never leaving hers.

Lady Annesbury appeared the moment Marcus and Ellen stepped away from the floor, her smile perfectly in place as she embraced Ellen and kissed her on the cheek. Ellen, confused by the gesture, tried not to show it.

When her mother-in-law spoke, loudly enough for several nearby to hear, Ellen realized what Lady Annesbury was doing.

"My darling children, I had hoped your first dance would be at your wedding ball. But seeing the two of you together, it positively made my heart burst for happiness. You are truly meant for each other." She released Ellen to put her arm through Marcus's.

"I couldn't help it, Mother," her husband said, also loud enough for those nearest to hear. "It's cruel to keep husbands and wives apart when they prefer one another's company to all else." He took Ellen's hand and she saw the flash of defiance in his eye.

The family was sending a message, which meant the comments Ellen overheard could not be all that was said that night. Not if Lady Annesbury had come forward to publicly approve of their dancing together.

Lucas appeared next, Collin and Marianne with him, forming a tight circle around Ellen.

Ellen's immediate gratitude for her family, for their obvious support and defense, nearly made up for her disappointment. If something so simple as dancing with her husband could cause a need for this show of strength, and if the gossiping cats of the *ton* already knew their story, how could she ever fit here?

Bath society had not been so strict, though it had its rules. She had never been important enough to be of any notice. She had no wish to be important now. Ellen wanted to do her new family credit, uphold their image, and make them proud.

Instead, they were coming forward to save her.

"Now, you gentlemen had best be off," Lady Annesbury said. "Go dance with a few young ladies to smooth ruffled feathers. We will look after Ellen."

Ellen's heart fell. At least before marriage she had not been a burden. It was one thing to be ignored and another to have to be *looked after*.

Marcus's hand slid into hers once more, offering a gentle squeeze. She forced a smile onto her face and darted a glance at him. Then his brother pulled him away and the men disappeared.

Marianne stepped closer and put her arm around Ellen's waist. "Your gown is lovely. I didn't have the chance to ask before, where did you acquire it?"

Minutes of meaningless conversation passed, and then Lady Annesbury was moving them across the floor again, introducing Ellen to a list of people she had no hope of remembering. Marianne stayed with them, at Ellen's right hand.

"How do you do it?" Ellen asked when her mother-in-law was preoccupied with speaking to a friend. "Marianne, how do you enjoy being on display? Being talked of?"

Marianne kept her polite smile upon her face, lowering her head as she answered. "This is how it has always been, Ellen. I was born to this. With a duke for a grandfather, I've been trained since I was in leading strings." She adjusted a glove, a small frown appearing on her face. "How are you managing?"

Ellen hid her grimace as she answered. "Terribly."

"If you will excuse me for a moment, my dears," Lady Annesbury said. "I see someone I need to have a word with."

"Of course, Mother," Ellen answered, her dutiful smile in place again.

Lady Annesbury sailed away from them, more graceful than any *debutante* Ellen had seen that evening.

"Let's walk near the windows," Marianne said, gesturing to the other side of the room. "We can get some fresh air."

Together, they walked arm in arm. As they neared the windows, Marianne veered slightly to a potted fern of an enormous size. "Stand here, Ellen, and take a few deep breaths." Marianne's instructions came with a friendly smile. "No one can see you tucked behind the plant."

Ellen chuckled and raised a hand to her brow. "If I lose my smile now, I may never get it back. This is not at all the way I thought it would be, Marianne. I'm not meant for London."

"Nonsense. Anyone who wishes to belong can. Especially as connected as you are." Marianne offered an encouraging pat on Ellen's arm. "And I'm here now. I will see you through it."

"That's the thing," Ellen murmured, feeling her eyes begin to prickle. "I'm not sure I want to see it through."

Marianne opened her mouth to argue, but another voice reached them first, from just beyond the fern.

"Is that Lady Castleton?"

A second female voice answered. "Dear me, it is. I had heard she was back from Spain, but I hadn't thought to see her."

"Is that her husband with her?"

"No, no. The count didn't come," said a third voice, a man's.

"Then who—?"

"That's the brother of the Earl of Annesbury."

Ellen could not hear more. She looked up to Marianne, entreating her friend with her eyes to *do* something.

Marianne said a very unladylike word beneath her breath, startling Ellen, but she followed Marianne away from the false safety of the plant. They walked along the wall of the ballroom. Marianne kept darting gazes toward the center of the room, but Ellen stubbornly trained her eyes on her friend's back. She had no wish to look and see what Marcus was doing or who he was with.

"It's her," Marianne said, bringing them to a halt behind a column and looking over Ellen's shoulder. "But Marcus isn't anywhere near her. Not anymore."

"Can I plead a headache and return home?" Ellen asked, smiling weakly and half joking.

"Not so soon after Lady Castleton's arrival. That would cause gossip." Marianne bit her bottom lip and moved from behind the column. "Ah. There's Collin. He's coming our way."

Less than a minute later, Collin stood near them. "Little cousin, there you are." He held his hand out to her. "Would you do me the honor of joining me for the supper dance?"

Ellen's eyes widened. "Is it as late as that?"

"Indeed." Collin's smile widened and he sighed. "Aren't you dreadfully tired? I always am by supper."

"Then he gets his energies restored to him." Marianne laughed, a light and polite sound Ellen didn't think she could possibly replicate.

Marcus came around the column next, appearing less cheerful in countenance than his friend. "Ah. Here they are. Lady Falkham, would you do me the honor of joining me for the supper dance?"

"I see." Marianne looked between them and then at Ellen, relief in her eyes. "They mean to take us into supper together."

"It was Marcus's idea," Collin said. Then his eyes focused on Ellen's and his smile vanished. "Cousin Ellen, what's wrong?"

Ellen didn't know when she had stopped trying to appear pleasant, as though all was well with the world. Perhaps when Marcus arrived and would not meet her eyes. He looked up when Collin spoke, though, the concern apparent on his handsome face.

"Ellen?" He moved to block the view of anyone behind them who might glance their way. "Ellen, are you well?"

It was all she could do to keep from begging to leave, to go home to the quiet of a house where she would not be on display. London was not what she had hoped for. In the days since their arrival, they had not been able to go to any of the places Marcus told her about. They had managed shopping for her dresses and a stop at a bookseller. Otherwise, she had been with her mother-in-law, attending teas and visiting with people she didn't care to know.

Just as she had done before she married.

"I am well enough," she answered. Ellen forced the corners of her mouth upward and straightened her posture. "I'm going to dance with Collin, after all." She turned from her husband and held her hand out to her cousin, who took it with a firm nod.

"That's the spirit, Ellen," her cousin said. As he led her away, she cast one look over her shoulder to find Marcus and Marianne trailing behind them. Marianne's lips were moving rapidly, though she smiled, and Marcus's brows were pinched together as he listened.

"Selene was here," Ellen said, turning to look at Collin. "Did you see her?"

A grimace passed over his face and was gone so speedily she could barely be sure she saw it. "I did. I also saw your husband nearly give her the cut direct, which would've been disastrous for you both considering he is untitled and she is a countess."

Ellen's heart gave a happy thrum at that news. "Marcus no longer admires her?"

Collin's expression changed to one of obvious surprise. "Ellen." They took their positions on the floor. "How could he, when he has you?"

The music began and Ellen did not have opportunity to answer that question, for her cousin or for herself.

CHAPTER 24

M arcus made his way to breakfast later than usual, but that was to be expected after an evening at a ball. He dreaded knowing in two days' time he and Ellen would be made spectacles of at the ball his mother threw in their honor. It wasn't for himself he worried, but for Ellen. By supper the night before, she'd been wilting and hardly said two words to him, though he and Collin managed to make certain she was seated between them.

And in the carriage home, she had leaned against her side of the conveyance and claimed a headache when he asked after her. Why had she not leaned on him? He would've happily held her against the bumps and jolts of the road.

London was too much for her. Marcus had to admit it was often too much for him, and he was more used to it than she.

"Good morning, Marcus." Lucas sat at the breakfast table looking through a stack of handwritten notes.

"Good morning." Marcus looked at the table and then to the sideboard. "Has Ellen been down yet?"

"She sent for a tray." Lucas turned a page over and continued reading. "As did Mother."

Mother always sent for a tray, but Ellen never had. Not in all the time they'd been married, at Orchard Hill or in town. Had her headache grown worse? Ought he to check on her?

"Are we going to talk about what happened at the ball?" Lucas asked. Marcus's eyes darted back to his brother, but Lucas still wasn't looking at him.

"What happened at the ball that is worth speaking of?" he asked, folding his arms. "It was a ball."

Lucas sighed in a long-suffering manner. It was the same sigh that accompanied most of his brotherly lectures. Marcus usually didn't mind them, but today the sound of that sigh made his eye twitch.

"Sit down, Marc. We need to talk."

Marcus obliged, but chose a seat several chairs from Lucas. "Very well. What are we talking about? The perfectly ordinary ball?"

"That is as good as place as any to start." Lucas reached up to massage his temples. "I had my doubts about your marriage. Not because of Ellen. I must make that clear. I've always liked her; even as a child she showed more intelligence than most. But the way you entered your marriage with her left me disappointed."

Marcus folded his arms across his chest and leaned back in the chair. "I entered it in a church."

"You know that isn't what I mean." Lucas shook his head and tapped the table to emphasize his point. "I mean the haste you used, Marcus. You rushed headlong into this. You gave Ellen no time to consider what she was doing. Then you told me, the very day on which you were wed, that you'd informed her of your feelings. Or lack of feelings."

Marcus's heart sank. It was true. He'd told Lucas everything, and felt the truth of such sentiments at the time. But things had changed since then.

"Ellen married you anyway. Bless her for that. But seeing you here in town, watching the two of you, I think you've made an incredible mess of things." Lucas's drumming fingers moved more rapidly as he spoke and his brows were drawn down in an impressive scowl.

"A mess of things?" Marcus sat straighter, affronted. "I may be in love with her. I'm trying to do things the correct way. I'm being a good husband—"

Lucas interrupted impatiently. "After making it clear to her, excessively so, that you would *not* love her as a man ought to love his wife. And the ball last night proved you haven't any idea in your head as to what you're doing to her."

Marcus's shoulders tightened and he sat straighter. "Excuse me?"

"You danced with her, for all the world to see, in effect baring your soul to everyone." Lucas shook his head. "You're enamored with your wife. Mother is beside herself you decided to make such a display of your feelings, but I think it was well done. Especially given the gossip I'd heard snatches of."

"I heard it too," Marcus answered, his temper flaring at the remembrance. "But I thought to correct the assumptions, and—"

Lucas cut him off with a dry chuckle. "Did you not see Ellen's expression while you danced? I did. The whole of it. The poor woman's heart was in her eyes."

Marcus looked away. "I wanted to dance with her, Luc. Not to stop tongues wagging, but to *dance* with my wife."

"I understand. I truly do. You never had a courtship with her, and now that you're married, and in love with your wife, you should get one."

Starting at his brother's boldness, Marcus opened his mouth to protest. Lucas, in his typical fashion, did not allow it.

"Marcus, not half an hour later you were seen with Lady Castleton. For the second time this week, I might add."

"How did you—?"

"You were on the street with her, in front of a popular *modiste*. People saw you." Lucas shrugged and ran his hand through his short blond hair, a frown pulling his mouth down. "Falkham told me you nearly gave her the cut direct at the ball. Your marriage, new and talked about as it is, doesn't need more gossip attached to it."

Marcus slumped over, elbows on the table and face in his hands. "I hate London."

"Your wife does too."

His eyes came up at that. "How would you know? She's always wanted to come, to see the museums and galleries, the libraries."

"I'm sure she has. But she dislikes society. I can't say that I blame her. I feel it too, especially with the absurdities of our Parliament this session. We're fighting a war with Napoleon and the Americans are in a snit over the trade embargos and impressments." Lucas shook his head. "It's a room full of fools at times, and the few of us with sense are shouted down. But we're not talking of that. Forgive me. We're talking of you and Ellen."

"Last night, at the ball. What would you have done in my place?" Marcus kept his voice low, trying to sound reasonable. "If it had been Abigail—"

Lucas groaned and sat back. "Abigail and Ellen are not the same. Not at all. Abigail was born to this—"

"Ellen can learn," Marcus argued. He raised a hand and waved it around the room. "She can learn all of it. You said it yourself, she's intelligent."

"I'm trying to tell you," Lucas said, enunciating each word carefully, "that she doesn't have to learn it if she doesn't want to. We both know you don't like it here either."

"I like London well enough."

"You think you have to like it," Lucas said, obviously unimpressed with Marcus's protest. "You find things about London to enjoy, but you would rather be a country gentleman than a member of the *ton*."

Marcus sat back, his hands staying outstretched on the table. "You need me here."

"I have enjoyed having your support," Lucas said, meeting his brother's eyes. He leaned forward, his blue eyes glowing with intensity. "But I do not need you here, Marcus. I can see to myself, and it's time you do the same. Find out what your wife needs, and if it's to stay in London you must stay. If Ellen feels as you do, if she would rather return to your home, take her back to the country and be happy."

Lucas's expression changed, becoming almost pained. "But please, Marcus. Please, stop wasting time. It's a precious thing. Do what you must to make your wife your primary concern. Court her, cherish her, and tell her how you feel. You never know when it might be too late."

Marcus's heart ached for his brother. "Will you take your own advice and find happiness again, Luc?"

The mask of the earl fell back into place and Lucas returned to his letters. "My happiness is not your concern. Ellen's happiness is."

With that the conversation ended. Marcus, no longer hungry, took his leave.

ELLEN PACED THE LIBRARY FLOOR, going from one end of the shelves to the other, her mind a tangle of unpleasant thoughts.

The letter in her hand protested when her hand tightened around it. Ellen frowned down at it, her name written in Teresa's hand across the front. Her sister's news was simple and happy, full of excitement for her impending confinement and new baby. The letter was also full of questions about London and Marcus. Questions Ellen didn't wish to answer.

She tucked the letter in the band about her waist and continued her pacing.

In two days' time, their wedding ball would be held in the family's townhouse, and the guest list was a yard long. When looking through it, she'd recognized a handful of names. What was she to say to a group of strangers come to celebrate her marriage to one of their own?

Marcus was well liked by many, that was easy enough to see. Everywhere he went, people greeted him by name. He knew what to say and how to act, even if he didn't find pleasure in it, and fit with these people well. Ellen, on the other hand, stuck out. No one knew her or her family. They'd never heard of her until they learned of Marcus's marriage. So far, people had either seemed mildly curious, completely indifferent, or openly hostile upon meeting her.

There was no time, either, to get to know anyone. After being introduced to someone at tea, they left a quarter of an hour later. Meeting a lady at a ball meant a minute and a half of conversation. How did anyone make friends in London if this was forever the way of things?

"You will get used to it," her mother-in-law had told her when she ventured to speak of her concerns. "The more you are about in society, the more familiar faces will become. You will carve a niche for yourself in due course."

Longing to do more than socialize, Ellen had asked about the possibility of venturing out to the menagerie, or the lending libraries, or art galleries. But each time she had mentioned the possibility, Lady Annesbury had declared it impossible. She had engaged them for various teas, morning calls, or else declared it to be their at home day. Marcus had bowed to his mother's wishes when he was present.

Her husband had barely spoken to her for the last several days, though he was often in the same room. Marcus sat brooding, and sometimes she caught him watching her with a speculative look in his eyes.

Was he beginning to see what a terrible choice in wife she had been? Seeing her in the light of London's spectacles could not have been less flattering.

Ellen paused in her steps and raised a hand to her forehead, attempting to hold back her painful thoughts. It was no use, she knew, to deny what he had seen. She was too quiet, too withdrawn, and too unused to society's ways. She might make a very fine country wife, and indeed Kettering looked far less daunting now that she had London to compare it to, but how could she ever be like the ladies of the *ton*?

Especially when all she wanted to do was curl up in a chair with a good book or escape the madness of morning calls to attend a gallery, or the Royal Society's building. Anything would be better than sitting and listening to women discussing the same gossip she had heard three times already.

Ellen paused and put one hand out to touch the spines of the books nearest her. Pulling one out at random, she went to sit on the couch. The moment her eyes fell onto that piece of furniture, however, all she could think on was the night she and Marcus had spent resting upon it, in each other's arms.

Heat crept into her cheeks and she hugged the book to her chest, staring at the spot where his head had lain. Here she stood, a married woman, and that moment when she woke in his arms had been the happiest of her life. They had never spoken of it again.

She turned away and went to one of the chairs instead, opening the volume hastily. She sat in the chair and frowned down at the page, trying to make sense of what she saw. It appeared as though she'd chosen a volume of poetry. She flipped the book closed and read the spine. *Reliques of Robert Burnes.*

"When I upon thy bosom lean/And fondly clasp thee a' my ain, I glory in the sacred ties/That made us ane, wha ance were twain." Ellen scowled down at the book and slammed its covers closed again.

"Not to your liking?"

Her head snapped up and Ellen saw her husband standing in the doorway, watching her with that strange, curious look again. It was as if he'd never seen her before and tried to puzzle her out. But he had known her so well at Orchard Hill.

"I am not in the mood for poetry, I'm afraid," she whispered, then cleared her throat. She stood and turned her back to him, going to the shelves to restore the book to its proper place.

"That's a shame." He came further into the room, his manner casual. "What would you like to do, Ellen?"

Ellen closed her eyes and spoke before thinking. "I would like to go home to Orchard Hill."

Silence, long and heavy, filled the space between them. But she would not turn to look at him, would not look to see his reaction to her words. He had asked and she answered.

"Is London so terrible?" When he broke the silence his voice was softer but resigned.

Ellen shook her head and placed a hand on the shelves in front of her, gripping it for strength. "No, but I find I'm not made for it."

His step came nearer. "That isn't true, Ellen. It will take some getting used to, but—"

Ellen let out a laugh and whirled around, her gaze colliding with his. "I know. And I have not given London a fair chance. But you asked what I wanted and I gave you an honest answer, which is more than what I can say for nearly everyone I've met since coming here. How do you live like this, Marcus?"

He stared at her. "It's how my life has always been."

"I know." She raised a hand to her head again, a headache coming on. "But it isn't easy for me. I'm trapped by the invitations given and received. I'm happy to make friends, but no one here seems capable of real feeling. Everyone wishes to outdo each other. There is no genuine behavior or emotions."

"Ellen," he said, coming another step closer. He raised a hand as if to reach for her and then lowered it. "Ellen, would you like to come with me today? Would you like to go for a ride in the park or visit Gunter's? Maybe we could visit the Tower."

Though that was precisely what she wanted, Ellen shook her head. "I have a fitting for my gown. The seamstress is coming here, at your mother's insistence."

"I see." His hands at his side opened and closed. He looked away. "Tomorrow?"

"Ball preparations," she answered, her tone apologetic. "And the day after that is the ball."

"I will at least see you there," he said, a note of levity in his voice. "And we may dance without comment, as it is held in our honor." Marcus raised his gaze to her, a charmingly crooked grin on his face.

Ellen wrapped her arms around her waist, holding herself together. How could he look at her like that and not know what it did to her heart? Would he ever know her feelings as well as he seemed to know her habits?

"That is something to look forward to," she said, forcing a

smile. "Will it be as much of a crush as the last ball we attended, do you think?"

He shrugged and moved closer again, bringing them to stand a foot apart. "Likely, since it is the Earl of Annesbury and his lady mother hosting. Between his title and her popularity, all of London will wish to attend." His smile was almost apologetic. Did he know how much she dreaded being on display?

He reached out, holding his hand palm up to her. Ellen hesitated, then put her hand in his. "You look lovely today, Ellen." He said it simply, but with the expression she'd seen him wear dozens of times when he paid compliments to others.

"Thank you." Her words sounded tired to her own ears.

Marcus's brows drew down. "What is it? Is something wrong?"

What could she say to that? She withdrew her hand, folding it under her other arm again. "Not really."

"Please, Ellen. Remember, I said no secrets between us." Marcus's hand curled into a fist and he dropped it to his side. He attempted a teasing smile. "That should also mean no half-truths."

Yet how many of those had she told? And how many times had he spoken a kind word to her that could as easily have been said to a stranger? Ellen knew she was keeping plenty of secrets, locked up in her heart. Perhaps it was time to let one slip.

"Very well. There is something that bothers me, but I know addressing it will hardly do more than cause divisiveness between us." Ellen looked down at the carpet, thinking her words through carefully.

"Tell me," he said, and she watched his hand rise again, as if to reach out to her. At the last moment he withdrew it to run through his hair again. He chuckled. "I think I'm due for another haircut."

Ellen sighed and turned away, finding it easier to collect her thoughts when she did not stand so near him. "I'm afraid you will think me the worst sort of person or accuse me of jealousy or—I don't know. But since we have been engaged, and every time we have come in contact with others in our marriage, I've heard you offer lists of compliments to people, some half-meant. You said it's part of what people expect from you, who you are. But the lack of sincerity, the ease with which flattery falls from your lips, is difficult for me to hear."

There was a pause before he answered. "You don't like that I'm kind to others?"

"I love that you're kind to others," Ellen said, then bit her lip when she realized she had used the word *love* in his presence. She was more tired than she realized. "It's a fine quality. What I struggle with is the easy flattery. When you say such things to me, how can I believe you mean them?"

Marcus stepped nearer her but she kept her back to him, lifting her gaze to look out the window onto the busy street before the house.

"Ellen, I've never said a word to you without sincerity. In fact, there is more I would say—"

She closed her eyes, unwilling to hear compliments she could not trust. "Please, don't. You are too used to the part you have assigned yourself. I have no doubt you mean well, but I'd rather not have the same words you say to every woman you encounter." She pleaded with him, her vulnerability more apparent in her words than ever. "I have so long been *just* Ellen and I am unused to flattery."

"It isn't flattery," he argued, stepping around her, between her and the window.

Her eyes opened, and she could feel the sting of tears building.

Marcus's expression changed from one of entreaty to shock. "Don't cry," he said, reaching out to take her shoulders in his hands. "Ellen, I never meant to hurt you." He pulled her gently forward, wrapping his arms about her.

She buried her face in his shoulder, her heart aching. He'd never embraced her like this and it undid her. Ellen's tears could not be held back and she cried into his shoulder.

"Has it been so terrible?" he whispered into her hair, one hand stroking her back while the other supported her. "London? Me? Ellen, darling, what can I do?"

Ellen shook her head. "Nothing. I'm tired." She gripped the front of his coat, allowing herself to stand within his arms a moment more before she pushed herself away. "Excuse me. I ought to rest." Turning, Ellen made it a few steps before he spoke again.

"What can I do, Ellen?" he repeated. "Please, tell me. I don't want to see you like this, hurting."

She considered the question, glancing over her shoulder at the pained look in his eyes. Was he in earnest? What could she possibly say to him?

The truth would be best, though Ellen knew she couldn't expect to receive it in return. Not yet.

"Someday, I would like to know what is in your heart, Marcus. I would like to understand how you truly feel, about me, about the life you live, without having to guess at your sincerity. But I know that is asking a great deal from one who protects himself as fiercely as you do." Ellen watched his shoulders fall. "But in the meantime, perhaps you would grant your wife one small request."

"Anything," he said, opening his arms in an expansive gesture, his tone eager. "Anything you ask."

"Don't always be in such a hurry to cut your hair," she said, her lips lifting in a weak smile. "I rather like it when it curls." She turned and left, unable to stay a moment more. It was unwise to reveal too much of herself when he took pains to hide so much of his heart.

She put her hand to her waist where her sister's letter pressed against her and an idea which would bring relief to her exhausted spirit came into her head.

As ill-suited to London as she was, it would be best if she took herself away from all of it. At least until she had better possession of her emotions.

It was something to think on, at least.

CHAPTER 25

Marcus waited beneath the staircase for Ellen to descend. Guests would arrive soon and they were expected to stand in the entry to greet them for the first half hour of the evening. His mother already stood next to Lucas, the two of them resplendent in their formal attire.

"You didn't cut your hair before the party," his mother said, tapping her fan lightly on his arm. "I thought you said you would take care of that today?"

He reached up, his gloved hand finding one curl near his forehead. "I thought I might try something different. Cray attempted a more windblown look. Does it suit me?"

"More than the Caesar," Lucas said, glancing at the style with interest. "I keep thinking my own is terribly short. Why bother having hair at all?"

Marcus chuckled. His mother took Lucas's arm and moved closer to the door. "I hear carriages, I think," she said. "Marcus, you had better see if your wife is having trouble?"

Ever the obedient son, Marcus nodded and turned to the stairs, taking three steps before he looked up—and froze. Ellen, his beautiful bride, stood hesitating on the top stair.

Ellen wore a gown of lavender, with an overlay of glittering ivory lace. The effect made it appear as though she wore a dress made of summer sky, filling with stars before the sun set. Her midnight-black hair was piled upon her head elegantly, small dark twists escaping, artfully brushing the bare skin of her neck. The only jewelry she wore was a simple silver necklace.

Her cheeks turned pink under his gaze and she lowered her eyes, descending the stairs slowly, her ivory satin slippers peeping from beneath her gown with each step.

Marcus watched her, his heart full to bursting, and he knew he could no longer deny his feelings. He loved her, with everything in him, and he wanted her to know. Even if she couldn't return his feelings, if she admired him as a friend, he must tell her. He must try to win her love, whatever it took.

"Ellen," he said when he reached his hand out to take hers. "You are stunning tonight."

She hardly reacted to his words, nodding her thanks and sliding her fingers into his. The warmth of her touch, even through their gloves, moved slowly through him until every limb was affected.

"Hurry, dears," his mother called.

Marcus helped his wife down the last several steps, then kept her hand clasped in his as they walked to form the reception line.

Lucas glanced their way and grinned when he saw Ellen. "Ah, there's my new sister. You look lovely, Mrs. Calvert. You will be the queen of the ball."

Marcus watched his wife's cheeks go a brighter pink and a genuine smile curl her lips upward. "Thank you, brother."

Why couldn't Marcus solicit a response like that from her?

Because she cannot trust my compliments, he remembered. *They are given too freely.*

He would remedy that this very night, he promised himself.

The first guests arrived, and Marcus squared his shoulders. He would present his bride to everyone this evening with the pride and admiration he felt for her, and Ellen would see what was in his heart.

"Have you met my wife, Mrs. Ellen Calvert? She is the most intelligent woman I know."

"This is my wife, Mrs. Ellen Calvert. Isn't she stunning this evening?"

"My bride, Ellen Calvert. Easily the most beautiful woman of my acquaintance."

At first, his compliments made her blush, which he counted as a victory. But after a dozen introductions had been made, Ellen stopped reacting. During a lull in the line, she leaned towards him.

"Marcus, what are you doing?" she whispered.

"Making sure everyone understands how special you are to me." He grinned down at her, but the feeling of victory faded when he realized she appeared distressed.

"Please, stop." Ellen's hand on his arm gripped him tighter as she spoke. "Everyone will think it strange. I don't need such praise."

"What do you need, Ellen?" he asked, raising a hand to cover hers, but she withdrew at his touch and stood instead with her hands clasped before her.

"More guests," she said, nodding to the doors.

Marcus couldn't care less about the new arrivals. Taking her hand and dragging her back to the library for honest conversation would be more in harmony with his wishes. But he knew his duty. He fixed a smile upon his face and gave his attention to the new arrivals.

He heard his wife sigh, deeply, and it made his heart ache. Ellen wasn't happy. She wasn't pleased with him, with society, with London. What was he to do?

At last his mother turned to them both. "I think it's time to go in and begin the dancing. Enough guests have arrived. But I expect Marcus to introduce you to as many people as possible, Ellen."

Ellen nodded once, then moved as if to enter the ballroom on her own.

Marcus caught her elbow and she started, her surprised eyes meeting his.

"We go in together, darling," he reminded her, wondering where her attention had gone.

"Of course." She put her hand through his arm. Lucas escorted his mother inside. It would fall to Ellen to lead the first dance, and Marcus would partner her. But before they made it entirely to the dance floor, she paused and looked up at him.

"I'm leaving tomorrow," she said, her voice nearly lost in the sounds of the ballroom. "I have arranged to borrow a carriage from Lucas so you will have use of ours."

"What?" He couldn't have heard correctly. Marcus's heart pounded painfully against his ribs and he shook his head, not understanding. "But—"

"I'm going to my sister, Teresa. She is expecting her child's arrival soon and I am at last a fit companion for her." She smiled, but the warmth of the expression did not make it into her eyes. "After, I will return to Orchard Hill for a time, but it will be good to be with family." Ellen tugged on his arm and moved him toward the floor, where people were forming the lines for the first dance.

Marcus wanted to shout in frustration that he didn't understand, that they needed to discuss the matter, but instead he had to put on a mask of contentment as he joined his bride for a Scottish reel.

Leaving? Without warning? Without consulting me? And Lucas—

His eyes searched the crowd for his brother, whom he saw watching him. Marcus narrowed his eyes and frowned, which made Lucas raise his eyebrows and tip his head forward as if to say, *I warned you and you didn't act quickly enough.*

"Marcus," his wife whispered, stepping forward to clasp his hand. "Dance."

He obeyed. Up and down the line they went, clasping hands with others, and all the while he could not quite meet his wife's eyes.

Why hadn't she mentioned leaving before now? True, they had barely seen each other for more than a few minutes since their last conversation in the library. Ellen had stayed busy with his mother and preparations for the ball, and he had been out more than usual with Lucas. But there must have been some opportunity before now to tell him, to speak to him? Especially if she managed to arrange things with Lucas.

The traitor, Marcus thought. The young woman currently holding his hand blanched and he realized he had been scowling down at her. He quickly resumed his pleasant demeanor.

The dance ended, he bowed to his wife, and an instant later another gentleman asked for her hand. Ellen danced away from him.

A hand landed on his shoulder and Marcus turned to Collin Falkham.

"Good evening, Marcus. Sorry we missed the first dance."

Marianne stood at his side. He looked between them both. "I need to speak with the two of you, if you please." Without another word, he turned and walked to the corner of the room. When he reached his desired location, a place no one yet stood to gossip, he looked back and saw his friends hurrying to keep up. He folded his arms across his chest and waited.

"What is it, Marcus?" Marianne asked, raising a hand to her heart. "Is there trouble?"

"There's more than trouble," he said, his voice as low as he could make it and still be heard. "Ellen is leaving."

Collin turned to look at the dance floor. "She appears to be dancing with the Baron of Gattersby."

"I don't think he means at this moment, my dear," Marianne said, fixing Marcus with a curious stare. "When, Marcus? Where is she going?"

"She said to one of her sisters. Tomorrow." Marcus shook his head. "I didn't know until a moment ago. But—"

"How unexpected." Marianne bit her bottom lip and shared a frown with her husband. "Did she say why?"

"Some excuse about being a fit companion for her—Teresa, I think," he said, closing his eyes. "But after that visit she intends to go back to Orchard Hill." Marcus raised a hand and ran it through his hair, uncaring if he upset whatever it was his valet had done attempting to please Ellen. He dropped his hands at his sides helplessly. "I don't understand."

"Has something happened to upset her?" Marianne asked, reaching out to touch his arm.

"She hasn't seemed happy in some time," he admitted. "We've hardly seen each other. Mother has kept her busy and—" *And I miss her.*

Collin moved slightly, better blocking Marcus from anyone near the dancing that might look to their corner. "Do you want her to go?"

"Of course not. Not unless she takes me with her." As his mouth closed over the last word in that sentence, Marcus's heart cracked. He didn't want to be left behind. Wherever Ellen went, he wished to be at her side. Why hadn't he made certain they were together here, in London? They'd spent nearly every evening together, since their wedding, before coming here.

The last time they'd sat together, just the two of them, they'd fallen asleep on the couch the night of their arrival.

He'd promised himself after the snowstorm that he would stay nearer her, make certain she understood he enjoyed her company.

It's my fault she's leaving, he realized. But what could he do about it?

"Marcus?" Marianne's voice brought him out of his thoughts. "Ask me to dance, Marcus. We can fix this."

He gave her his arm. "Dance with me, Lady Falkham?"

She nodded, but when she took his arm she practically dragged him to the floor. "We need to discover what it is Ellen wants," she said. "I will ask, if you wish?"

Marcus shook his head. "I already know what she wants." He would not say more, despite Marianne's curious expression. They danced, all the while his heart and thoughts racing.

❧

ELLEN HAD NOT MEANT to startle Marcus with news of her departure, though she had asked Lucas to allow her to be the one to tell her husband. In truth, Teresa had no idea Ellen meant to come visit. The letter she'd received from her sister had extended an open invitation, for any time in future, but Ellen had clutched at it like a line in a storm. The post with Teresa's letter had come the same afternoon she spoke with Marcus in the library. It seemed like a Godsend, granting her the escape from London she longed for.

She'd gone almost immediately to Lucas, her plans half formed. Once she was gone from London, she could do as she wished. She would see her family, enjoy a brief time in their presence, and then return to Orchard Hill. There she would be happy, out from under the judgmental gaze of the *ton*.

After her third dance of the evening, an hour into the ball, Ellen slipped away from the ballroom floor in search of refreshment.

Marcus appeared at her side, as though he'd been waiting for her. She startled, then looped her hand through his arm as naturally as she could. "Marcus, I was going to get some punch."

"Excellent. I'll take you." His words were measured, his face a mask of politeness. Had he already accepted her plan? Would he not attempt to change her mind?

Her heart shrunk and she pressed her lips together.

"I'm coming with you tomorrow," he said, causing her step to falter.

"What?" Surely, he had not said—

"I will accompany you to your sister's home." He made eye contact with her, his jaw remaining set and his brows furrowed.

"No, thank you." Ellen stepped away from him, to the punch bowl, where she quickly went about serving herself. Why would he attempt such a thing? Was he acting out of a sense of duty? He certainly didn't look happy about the decision.

"Ellen," he said, stepping closer. "I wish to be with you."

She could not bear it. Not now. Ellen as much needed an escape from him, from the feelings continually pressing upon her heart, as she needed it from London.

"I will be well enough without you," she said, her words coming out more harshly than she intended. Ellen forced herself to meet his eyes. "A maid and groom will accompany me and all will be well." Her hand shook as she lifted her cup to her lips.

"But Ellen," he said, leaning closer. She couldn't help but see the expression in his eyes, a look of contrition, of gentleness. Pity? "Ellen, I have to tell you why—"

"For my protection, I know," she said quickly, desperately cutting him off. She couldn't bear more pretty words, more flattery. Her emotions were already in a delicate state.

Marcus reached for her free hand, taking it in both his own. "I care for you, Ellen. More than care. I—"

Her fingers slipped and the cup fell, but as they both hurried to catch it the liquid inside splashed out, soaking Ellen's gloves. Thankfully, it missed her dress entirely and the cup stayed in Marcus's hands.

Marcus's eyes widened and he hastily put the cup on the table. "Ellen, I'm sorry—"

Ellen shook her head, stepping back. "It's only my gloves. I'll go change them. Excuse me." She wished she could stay in her room the rest of the night. She'd no wish to come back, to listen to his words, his flattery, whatever it was he was attempting to do.

More than care?

She couldn't even think on it. His offer to attend her on her journey was a kind gesture, nothing more. Her husband was a good man; he wouldn't want her to leave London on her own.

Ellen didn't look back when she left the room, and she pasted a smile on her face. If anyone made eye contact with her, Ellen nodded politely and hurried on her way, leaving no room for anyone to speak to her.

The hall was filled with people conversing, likely trying to escape the heat of the ballroom, but she ignored them and went to the staircase. Lucas stood near, and when she met his eyes he opened his mouth as if to speak, but Ellen shook her head and hurried past.

Changing her gloves, she decided, would take the better part of half an hour as she attempted to collect herself.

Ellen's chambers remained dark except for what little glow came from the fire. No one expected her to be back in her room and Sarah was assisting with the ball below stairs. Knowing she would leave in the morning with barely any time to pack, Ellen had no wish to return to the ball.

Her mind needed settling and the best way to do that would be to focus on another task. Packing for a few minutes would perfectly fulfill that need.

Stripping off her damp gloves, Ellen laid them on the table. She moved to the mirror to adjust the pins in her hair but paused. In the reflection of the mirror, she saw the door adjoining her room to Marcus's stood ajar, a soft light pouring from within. Ellen looked through the doorway and realized someone must have left a lamp lit in his room.

Her task would be easier with light, she told herself. At the threshold of her husband's room she hesitated, looking inside a domain unknown to her, but then she stepped inside.

Marcus was downstairs and he would not begrudge her the light.

Going further in, Ellen soon found the source of the glow at a desk near the window. She went to it and reached for the lamp. She stopped when her eyes fell upon the very sketchbook, leather-bound and of the finest material, she had given to her husband as a wedding gift.

Without meaning to, she put her hand down upon it and remembered the day she'd made the purchase, full of hope and longing, wanting nothing more than to belong to Marcus, to care for him. He'd very nearly scoffed at her gift, she'd seen it in his eyes.

Why was it here? In London?

The ribbons meant to tie it closed were loose, and wrinkled, as though they'd been tied and untied many times. Had he used it? Though he claimed to no longer draw, had something inspired him to renew the habit? It came from Orchard Hill with him, which must mean something.

Ellen's hand stayed on the cover, sliding slowly to the corner, her fingers itching to open it and see what her husband had laid down on the blank pages. Was he as good an artist as she remembered?

She loved him. She wanted him to love her, truly, and not merely try to win her through his flirtations and practiced words. Ellen needed him to understand her, to value her as more than a companion. If only he would love her as a man ought to love his wife, as she ached to be loved.

It would be breaking his trust to look at his sketches, like reading a diary or a private letter. Ellen gave the cover one last stroke and reached for the lamp.

"You should look," Marcus's voice said through the darkness, sounding nearly breathless. Ellen turned, realizing she had not heard him enter the room because he stood in hers. He stayed there, hovering between their chambers, one hand against the door frame.

"Please, Ellen," he said, his eyes dark, his expression unreadable. "Look inside."

Her heart pounded a steady, firm rhythm in her chest. She swallowed and shook her head. "It isn't my business."

But he didn't move, or speak, his only entreaty was the change in his expression, bereft of hope but full of longing.

Longing?

Ellen shook her head and reached for the cover again. One sure way to dispel the tension would be to give him what he wished, to see why he carried what he had claimed was not important. In a hurried motion, Ellen took the corner of the book and flipped it open, laying bare a sketch several pages in. She drew in a quick breath and raised her hand to cover her mouth, lowering the lamp as she gazed upon the page on which her likeness resided.

It was her, yet not the way she saw herself. The face that looked up at her, the eyes were dark and mysterious, the smile barely present. A curl behind her ear looked as if it had just fallen free of its pins. She reached out and traced the curl with one finger, then took the page in hand and turned it, to see another sketch of her, less detailed, more fluid in depicting her walking on a garden path.

She turned back to the beginning to find an orchard as it would appear in spring, full of life and leaves, and her figure walking down the row of apple trees.

Ellen splayed her hand over the sheet and closed her eyes,

steadying herself. "What is this, Marcus?" she asked, her voice barely above a whisper.

She heard his step but did not turn. The warmth of him at her back met her and she leaned into him. One of his arms went around her waist, slowly, hesitantly, and the other hand went down to cover hers on the sketchbook.

"This is everything to me," he said, deep voice husky with emotion. "You are everything to me. These are not empty words, Ellen, but my vow to you. I love you. And if one day you might feel the same—" His voice broke on the last word and Ellen could stand still no longer.

His words were sincere. She could see the truth of them in his drawings, giving her leave to trust him as nothing else had.

Turning in his arms, she reached up to put her hands on either side of his handsome face. The light danced in his eyes as he stared down at her, his whole being bent on showing her his sincerity. *He loved her.* Years of adoring him, loving him, dreaming without a hope of ever having those feelings returned, were as nothing. The weeks of their marriage were more precious, and this moment marked a new start to her life.

"Marcus," she said, her heart leaping within her. "I have *always* loved you."

His expression changed slowly from one of earnestness to one of surprise. "You have?" There was wonder in his voice, and awe.

"Ever since I was a little girl," she admitted, her cheeks warming beneath his growing smile.

"Ellen," he whispered, her name a caress as he spoke it. "My wife." Then he dipped his head slowly, his arms coming up to hold her. Though she had never been kissed, Ellen knew instinctively what to do. Her hands slid behind his neck and she lifted her chin, closing her eyes and meeting his lips with her own.

The world around them shattered and put itself together again in that kiss, and others followed, each opening doors in her heart that only led her closer to him. One of his hands reached up to cradle her head, and she returned the touch, threading her fingers through his wonderful coppery curls.

How much time passed, Ellen couldn't say, nor did she care. Marcus held her, caressed her, his tender kisses growing warmer and more urgent until he pulled back at last and rested his forehead against hers.

"Ellen," he whispered.

"Hm?" She didn't possess enough coherent thought to form a better answer, though she opened her eyes at last and met his.

"Don't go tomorrow. Or take me with you. I cannot bear to be apart from you. Not now, not ever."

"I find I feel the same." She lifted her lips to his again, tentatively caressing his mouth with hers, and he responded at once, gathering her closer to him.

When they parted, she laid her head upon his shoulder, unable to even think of stepping away. The circle of his arms was where she belonged, had always belonged.

"When did it happen?" she asked, her eyes closed as she committed the feel of his arms around her to memory.

He gathered her closer and kissed the top of her head before speaking. "I cannot tell you. It came on gradually, I think. But the moment I finally understood what was happening, how much you meant to me, was when I started to draw you in the orchard."

Ellen tipped her head back enough to meet his eyes, reflecting the light and his love back at her. "And when did you draw that, Marcus?"

His cheeks darkened and his dimple appeared with his crooked smile. "The night of the snowstorm."

"I was so worried you wouldn't even care I was gone." The memory of that forlornness no longer pained her. "That wasn't very long ago."

Marcus nodded and moved his arms from around her back to settle his hands at her waist. "I loved you before, but I hadn't stopped to realize it. But that night, as I drew you over and over again, I worked onto the page what I hadn't been able to admit to myself. You are my whole world, Ellen. You are my friend, my partner, my dearest love." He bestowed another gentle kiss upon her. "And you've really cared for me, all along?"

She nodded.

"You must be the most patient woman in all of Christendom."

Ellen laughed and rose up to kiss him again, decidedly *impatient* with all their talk. She knew they ought to rejoin the ball, but nothing at all would persuade her to care. Finally, she was exactly where she wanted to be.

EPILOGUE

One week after his confession of love, Marcus and Ellen took leave of London. Lady Annesbury protested until Lucas spoke. "Mother, you can hardly expect newlyweds to want to be in society. I can think of nothing that would appeal less to me in their situation."

Lady Annesbury had pursed her lips and looked from a blushing Ellen to a grinning Marcus and thrown up her hands in submission. "Very well. Be gone with you both. But *next* season, you will stay for the whole of it."

"As much as Orchard Hill can spare us," Marcus answered. Strangely, his mother seemed pleased instead of miffed at his answer.

Not long after the carriage was made ready.

"You don't really mind, do you?" Marcus asked when she settled in against him. "All of those things you wanted to see in London—"

"As your mother said, there is always next season. There is work to be done at Orchard Hill." She snuggled in closer and when his arms wrapped around her she sighed in contentment. "Are you certain you can leave your brother to himself?"

"Lucas is an earl. I think he can handle London without me. At least this once." Marcus kissed the top of her head. "And there are many other better things for us to do at home. As you said."

"Yes, darling. Such as begin our family." Though her cheeks turned rosy as she spoke, Ellen laughed at his look of surprise.

Nothing in the world had ever sounded as sweet to him as her happiness. At Orchard Hill they would build their home and orchards, and a family, with joy and love.

~

IF YOU ENJOYED THESE STORIES, make certain to continue reading with *The Earl and His Lady* to find out how the Earl of Annesbury, Lucas, and Virginia fall in love.

TITLES BY SALLY BRITTON

THE BRANCHES OF LOVE SERIES:

Prequel Novella, *Martha's Patience*

Book #1, *The Social Tutor*
Book #2, *The Gentleman Physician*
Book #3, *His Bluestocking Bride*
Book #4, *The Earl and His Lady*
Book #5, *Miss Devon's Choice*
Book #6, *Courting the Vicar's Daughter*
Book #7, *Penny's Yuletide Wish*

INGLEWOOD ROMANCE SERIES:

Book #1, *Rescuing Lord Inglewood*
Book #2, *Discovering Grace*
Book #3, *Saving Miss Everly*
Book #4, *Engaging Sir Isaac*

FOREVER AFTER:
The Captain and Miss Winter

ENTANGLED INHERITANCES:
His Unexpected Heiress

TIMELESS ROMANCE:
An Evening at Almack's, Regency Collection 12

NOTE FROM THE AUTHOR

Ellen's story is very dear to me. It was the first I wrote in this series, though it made more sense to start publishing with *The Social Tutor* and *The Gentleman Physician*, which is the order in which these stories have been published. Ellen and Marcus's engagement and marriage take place at the same time as events in the other two novels, and all these love stories branching in different directions will one day connect. In the meantime, I hope you enjoy these characters and their romances as much as I have enjoyed writing them.

If you would like to be the first to know of new novels, please visit my website at AuthorSallyBritton.com and sign up for my newsletter. I also enjoy connecting with readers in my Sweet Romance Fans Facebook group.

Thank you for reading.

Sally Britton

Printed in Great Britain
by Amazon